HOLLYWOOD PSYCHO

BRYAN CASSIDAY

Bryan Cassiday
Los Angeles
Published in the United States of America
First Edition: August 5, 2025
ISBN 979-8988189558

The movie wasn't doing boffo at the box office, but it was doing OK. It ranked in the top ten movies last week. The filmmakers hoped word of mouth would help stimulate sales.

Grant wasn't expecting much. He had seen hundreds of horror movies and had written several horror novels which had disappeared without a trace. He doubted any new movie could scare him. He just went because he wanted to escape his train wreck of a life. Horror movies seemed to be the only things that were worse than his own reality and therefore could pull him out of his depressing thoughts about his miserable life.

The pervasive odor of buttered popcorn greeted his nostrils as he took his seat in the half-full theater. He took in a low-budget matinee because of his skimpy bank account.

He could lose himself in the dim lights of the theater. It was even better when the theater went full black, and the movie took the place of his life—if it was a good movie, anyway. A lousy movie did nothing for him. He hoped this movie was going to be good. The reviews he had read about it made it sound interesting.

As the lights dimmed, he had to watch five very loud previews of horror movies, none of which looked promising.

A waxed paper barrel of buttered popcorn in his hand, a rotund middle-aged guy with a grizzled beard sat down on Grant's left with an empty seat between them and proceeded to watch the screen and munch his popcorn.

Grant never ate snacks during a movie. He wanted to become immersed in the movie without the interruptions of taste-bud sensations to detract from it. Unfortunately, he couldn't escape the olfactory sensations stimulated by the buttered popcorn of his neighbor. It wasn't an odor he found pleasant. He found it cloying.

He liked popcorn, but popcorn smothered in butter wasn't his thing.

He could hear his bearded neighbor raucously slurping his jumbo tumbler of soda through a straw, making as much noise as a thirsty horse lapping water at a trough.

Shifting in his seat, Grant wished the movie would start.

He wanted to be scared stiff, so terrified he would forget about his mess of a life.

The theater went black. The feature began.

5

A worker at a crematorium feared she was either becoming possessed or going insane. She was hearing voices, one voice actually. It was telling her to kill people.

Grant could relate to the woman. He heard voices when he wrote his horror novels.

The obese man sitting near him slurped on his soda, distracting Grant's attention from the movie.

Kill that fathead. He's wrecking the movie. They shouldn't allow a sideshow of noisy pigs in here while the movie is running. Kill him.

Now Grant was hearing voices.

He leaned toward his neighbor. "Can you hold it down? I'm trying to watch the movie."

The guy shot a baleful look at him. "I'm trying to watch the movie too. Why are you interrupting?"

"I'm just asking you to hold it down," Grant said in a low voice so as not to disturb the audience.

"Hold what down? What are you talking about? The only one running his mouth is you."

"I'm trying to be polite. Hold it down, and everything will be fine. It's all good."

The guy munched a handful of popcorn. "I'm gonna have you removed from the theater if you keep making so much noise."

Kill the son of a bitch. You tried to be polite. See where it got you. Kill him. Assholes like him only understand one thing. Death. Kill him. You'll be doing the other theatergoers a favor.

The voice Grant was hearing was a case of life imitating art. How come he was hearing a voice like the heroine of the movie? How could a demon in a movie cross over from the movie into the real world? It couldn't happen.

Maybe watching the demon on screen had triggered an urge inside him to create another book. Grant could be hearing one of the characters in his head manifesting itself for a new horror thriller.

The voice wanted him to kill, though. He never imagined voices of characters that ordered him to commit murder.

"Hold down your noise and we'll be fine," Grant whispered to his neighbor.

6

"I'm not fine. You keep interrupting the movie. I'm not fine with that. Show some consideration for others in the audience."

The guy was ticking Grant off, trying to make him feel guilty when it was beer belly who had caused the disruption of the movie with his noisy slurping of his soda.

Kill the fat slob. Stab him in the eye so he can't watch the movie. Make him pay for wrecking the movie.

How could the demon voice from the movie be telling him what to do?

"You're the one making all the noise," said Grant, beside himself with anger.

Why was he talking to this guy, or *was* he talking to him? Could he be imagining the conversation? Normally he kept his opinions of other people to himself and didn't rile the water. True, he was under a lot of stress, but it wasn't like him to cause a disturbance by trying to pick a fight with someone.

As a writer he imagined dialog in his novels. He must be imagining this dialog with the slurping beer belly. He did, in fact, sometimes imagine dialog with people he didn't like.

He was having difficulty restraining himself from attacking the rude slob.

Grant always carried a hunting knife strapped to his ankle in case a mugger assaulted him on the mean streets of LA. He felt like reaching for the knife and burying its blade in beer belly's head.

Knife him in the eye. Kill him. The rude son of a bitch needs to be taught a lesson.

His eyes fixed on the movie screen, the guy slurped his jumbo soda through his plastic straw. He withdrew his cell phone from his trouser pocket and read an e-mail. The phone's light flashed in Grant's eyes, drawing his attention away from the movie.

Kill him. He's ruining the movie for you.

Grant couldn't get the voice out of his head.

He was finished talking politely in his imagination to the guy to persuade him to stop ruining the movie. Smoldering, he reached down his trouser leg for the knife secreted in a leather sheath strapped to his calf.

He slid the knife out of its sheath.

7

This wouldn't take long. All he had to do was reach over the empty seat and make an underhanded thrust at the target.

His heart beat a rataplan as he broke a sweat, anticipating what he was about to do.

The blade would make a satisfying squelch as it plunged through the guy's eyeball, through the vitreous- and aqueous humor, and into the brain.

Kill him. Stab him through the temple. He deserves to be killed for being an asshole.

The sloppy sucking on the straw would stop on a dime.

Chapter 2

Grant returned to his apartment, which sounded like a battleground thanks to the cacophony of banging, jackhammering, and buzz sawing of construction going on in the condo next door. Grimacing at the noise pollution, he couldn't hear himself think.

He felt his cell phone vibrate in his trouser pocket.

He took the call.

"Hi, I'm in New York," said Sherry, his ex-girlfriend. "How are you? Are you OK?"

Grant didn't want to talk to her. He knew what she wanted. What she always wanted.

"I'm OK," he said.

"Good. I need money."

Of course.

"I can't help you," he said.

"Don't you understand? I'm in New York. A modeling agency invited me here. They said they would pay me for a job I did for them. I went to their office. It was closed. The sign on their door said they went out of business."

"Yeah."

"Don't you understand? They're not gonna pay me. Ever. They're bankrupt."

"And so am I. Because of you."

"I'm all alone in New York. How can you do this to me?"

"Do what?"

"Leave me here. It's not safe for a young girl like me to be alone here. I'm scared."

"You already spent all my money."

She was always blaming him for everything bad that happened to her, as though it was his fault her modeling agency had gone belly up.

The hammering next door continued unabated. He could barely hear himself think, let alone hear Sherry.

"I'm all alone in New York. I think somebody's stalking me," she said, lowering her voice.

"You took my life savings," he cried above the deafening racket. "I sold my car to help you. It's time for you to start paying me back all the money you borrowed."

"What's that noise?"

"What?" said Grant, wincing thanks to the commotion.

"What's all that noise?" Sherry yelled.

"Construction."

"You're having construction done and you can't afford to send me money on Venmo?" she said in stunned disbelief.

"They're not working for me. They're working for the neighbors in the condo next door."

"This is urgent. Send me three thousand dollars on Venmo so I can rent a decent room here."

"I don't have any Venmo."

"All right. Use CashApp or PayPal. I need it today."

"I don't have it. Why are you demanding more money from me?"

"How can you do this to me?" she said, and began to cry.

"What am I doing to you? I didn't send you to New York. You went there on your own."

"But it's not safe here. I'm a young girl and I'm alone in the big city. It's scary."

"Maybe you can stay at the Y."

"You're making me stay at the Y?" she said, outraged.

"I'm not making you stay anywhere," he said, seething.

She continued crying. "How can you treat me like this? Don't you care if I'm assaulted here?"

"I have nothing to do with your being there. Why are you blaming it on me?"

"I can't believe you're doing this to me," she said through her tears.

Grant's head was throbbing on account of the raucous construction echoing through his apartment. He felt like screaming.

"At least send me two thousand dollars so I can fly back to LA," said Sherry. "You can use Zelle."

"I don't have it."

"Then use PayPal. PayPal is good."

10

"I don't have any money."

"I'm your girlfriend. How can you do this to me?"

"Not anymore." He was fed up with getting bombarded with her demands for more money.

"I'm scared. I'm alone in New York—"

"I can't help you."

"I'll pay you back."

"I've loaned you $700,000 so far. Everything I had. You haven't paid me back three cents."

"I can't pay you back yet, but I will. I promise."

"It's all gone," said Grant, exasperated. "You can't borrow more money if there's nothing left."

"How can you do this to me?" she cried. "I'm alone in New York—"

Grant terminated the call.

He couldn't deal with her shrieking combined with the nerve-racking construction slamming his ears. How many times did he have to tell her he was penniless for her to believe it? She couldn't get it through her head that the well had run dry. A high-maintenance girlfriend was the last thing he could afford. Nowadays he was lucky if he could afford to pay his rent and avoid eviction.

What really annoyed him about her was that she had promised to pay him back every time he loaned her thousands of dollars for her medical needs, probate lawyers, trips to Key West, or whatever. She had said she was inheriting two million bucks from her deceased uncle who had owned houses in Key Biscayne, Florida, and in Lansing, Michigan. According to Sherry, the houses were in probate and she couldn't sell either of them until probate concluded. The fact that the houses were in different states complicated matters, because each state had different probate laws.

Probate had been dragging on for over two years now. Grant didn't think it would ever end. Either that or Sherry didn't have a rich uncle who had bequeathed her two million bucks. The whole rich uncle thing could have been a scam from the get-go. Regardless, at this point he figured she would never pay him back the seven hundred thousand she owed him whether she inherited the two million or not.

His bankruptcy court trustee claimed she would sue Sherry to recover the funds that Grant owed to creditors. That suit had made no progress that Grant knew of, and Sherry kept demanding more money from him.

Well, she wouldn't get any more. He was done lending her money. He had no plans on going into debt again to satisfy her whims with the one credit card he had left. She had maxed out the rest of his cards. The providers of those cards were the creditors that would benefit from the suit the bankruptcy trustee lawyer would file against Sherry if he ever got around to it.

Fuck it. He didn't want to think any more about the mess she had made of his life. She was like a hurricane wreaking havoc on everything in her path of devastation, in the middle of which was him.

He heaved a loud sigh.

At least the horror movie had been good. It had made him forget Hurricane Sherry for two hours. He felt sure it was going to give him nightmares tonight. The demon that had possessed the movie heroine seemed utterly believable. He could've sworn he could hear it talking to him, trying to take over his life the way it had hers.

Kill. It had kept telling her to kill.

Except he was trying to remember something that had happened during the movie and he couldn't grasp it. Whatever it was lay just out of reach. It was on the tip of his tongue, but it eluded him.

He shrugged. If it was important, he would remember it eventually.

He kept hearing that movie demon's eldritch voice resonating through his mind. *Kill. Kill.* The voice was so real. It seemed to have taken up residence inside his head. Not a memory but actually inside his head. He could understand why moviegoers were saying *Necromaniac* was such a scary movie.

Maybe he should write a book about a writer who thought he was possessed and started killing . . . killing people.

Nah, nobody would buy it.

The movie *Necromaniac* really stuck with him. He didn't think he would ever forget it. The critics were wrong when they

12

said *Necromaniac* was nothing more than a trashy exploitation horror movie.

If you couldn't get a movie out of your head, it meant the movie must be good.

Chapter 3

When Grant awoke the next morning, he opened his apartment front door and retrieved the morning newspaper.

Through bleary eyes he read the headline.

"Filmgoer Murdered While Watching *Necromaniac*."

The movie had involved a series of murders. How ironic that a murder had been committed during it.

Grant read the article.

The victim was murdered while watching the movie, according to police, who were releasing few details, since it was an active investigation. The LAPD admitted to having no suspects at this time. The murder had taken place in the dark during the movie, and nobody in the audience had seen a thing. It was only at the end of the movie after everybody had filed out of the theater that one of the teenage ushers had noticed the motionless body slumped in its seat.

On the op-ed page an editor wondered if it was possible that the horror movie *Necromaniac* might have caused a filmgoer watching it to commit murder. The editor asked, was it possible that movies could cause viewers to kill? If so, the movie should be pulled from theaters. After all, Stanley Kubrick had pulled his movie *Clockwork Orange* from theaters in the United Kingdom because of the prevailing opinion that it was causing viewers to commit violence. Kubrick, who had been living in the United Kingdom at the time, denied that art motivated people to kill, but he pulled the movie.

Grant realized with a shock that he had attended the movie theater where the murder had taken place and he was there at the time of the murder. He could have been the audience member who had been murdered.

Which was why he always carried a knife strapped to his ankle.

He heaved a sigh of relief.

14

He lifted his trouser leg and eyed his knife. He froze. He could make out blood on the knife. How could blood have gotten on it?

He withdrew the knife from its sheath and inspected the blade, which did indeed have traces of coagulated blood on it. He didn't know how the blood had got there.

Had someone stolen his knife, used it, then put it back? Such a scenario seemed unlikely. But what other explanation was there? He hadn't used the knife recently. He inspected the blood. Was it animal or human? Only a lab would be able to tell.

He didn't like the idea that somebody had used his knife without permission. When did the sneak thief jack his knife? Grant had no idea that he had ever been without it. Of course, he only noticed the knife when he dressed and undressed. He could have been without it for many hours but not for more than one day. He would have noticed it missing from its sheath when he undressed at night to go to bed. Therefore, the knife could only have gone missing during a period of sixteen hours or less and then replaced.

But he had no idea when it had vanished.

He took the knife to the kitchen sink and washed the blood off the blade. He dried off the knife and returned it to the leather sheath strapped to his ankle.

He resumed reading the newspaper.

The newspaper movie critic called *Necromaniac* the scariest movie ever made. Grant had to admit it was good. The critic wasn't surprised that a filmgoer had been murdered while watching the movie. The critic felt like he too wanted to kill someone while he had viewed the movie. Could the demon jump from the silver screen into an audience member's body? Maybe the movie's plausibility was what made it so terrifying.

Grant wondered if more or fewer moviegoers would attend the film after a murder had taken place in a theater showing it.

Someone knocked on the door.

Grant answered it.

Chapter 4

A fortyish blonde wearing a black leather biker cap with a catenary silver chain draped above the bill stood in the hallway. Clad in a matching black leather outfit and gleaming black vinyl boots, she had curly locks that tumbled out from her hat.

Grant had never seen the woman before.

"Yeah, I thought it was you," she said.

"Do I know you?" said Grant, puzzled.

"No."

"Well, I'm busy now. You'll have to excuse me," said Grant, making to close the door.

"I wouldn't do that if I was you," said the woman, sticking her boot in the way of the door. "You'll want to hear me out."

"I doubt it. Will you get your foot out of my doorway?"

"I'm Mandy. I saw you at the theater yesterday. Understand?"

Grant stopped trying to close the door. "What theater?"

"The AMC theater showing *Necromaniac*."

"So?"

"So that's where the guy was murdered, as you well know."

"What's that supposed to mean?" said Grant, his voice edged.

A middle-aged woman with grizzled black hair walked down the hallway, carrying a paper bag loaded with groceries, a baguette sticking out of it.

"Do you really want me to talk about it out here?" said Mandy.

Grant didn't know what Mandy was driving at, but he figured she was right that they should keep their conversation private, since she had a sinister aspect.

"Come in," he said.

"That's better."

Mandy entered Grant's apartment. He closed the door behind her.

"What's this about?" he said, irritated. "And make it quick. I don't normally invite strangers into my home."

16

"I don't like your tone of voice. You better show me some respect, since we're going to have an arrangement between us."

"You wish."

"Change your tone, and this will go down easier for you."

"Out with it. What are you selling? What's your racket?"

"You need to dial it down a notch. I don't like your attitude."

"If you don't start explaining yourself, I'm showing you the door."

"Do you want me to go to the cops?" said Mandy, putting her hands on her hips and staring at him, her head cocked up.

"What cops? What do cops have to do with this? *I'm* going to the cops if you don't either explain or scram."

Mandy burst out laughing. "*You're* going to the cops? What a joke."

Grant grabbed her arm. "Spit it out, or I'm eighty-sixing you."

"Let go of me," said Mandy, jerking her arm free. "That's gonna cost you."

"Start talking," said Grant, exasperated.

"I saw you sitting near that murder victim. Am I getting through to you?"

Grant stood, nonplussed.

"A lot of people were sitting next to him," he said at last. "Which proves nothing."

"You're the one who did him. I know it was you."

"It was pitch black in that theater. You couldn't even see your own hand in the dark. There's no way you could have seen who killed that guy."

"You were sitting closer to him than anyone else."

"Which means nothing. How did you find me, anyway?"

"I recognized you."

It was Grant's turn to laugh.

"You recognized me?" he said, incredulous.

"You're that horror writer."

"Nobody's heard of me. You want me to believe you know I'm a writer?"

"I read one of your horror books about zombies."

"What are the chances? You must be the only one and you happen to recognize me at the theater? Hard to believe."

17

"I don't care whether you believe me or not. I know you're the killer."

"How did you find my address?"

"I knew your name. It was easy finding your address. You aren't exactly hiding. Your information is available on the Internet like everyone else's."

"I have no reason to hide."

"You might want to rethink that."

"What are you talking about?"

"If I tell the cops I saw you sitting next to the victim at the theater, they're gonna come after you as the prime suspect."

"I have nothing to hide. If they want to question me, they can. So what?"

"Then why haven't you told them you were sitting next to the murder victim in the theater?"

"Because I didn't see anything. I have no idea who killed that guy. He was alive when I left the theater."

Actually, Grant couldn't recall leaving the theater. He had been so carried away by the movie that he couldn't remember anything else that took place at that time or immediately thereafter. And he didn't know how that blood had gotten on his knife. His heart started to beat faster.

"Then you don't mind if I go to the cops about what I saw?" said Mandy.

"I mind if you tell them I had something to do with that guy's murder, because I didn't."

Mandy made a beeline for the door. "Then I guess I'll be going to the cops. Maybe they're offering a reward for information about the murder."

Grant belted to the door, got there before Mandy, and prevented her from departing.

"I don't want to be involved in this murder investigation," he said.

"That's what I thought. I'm open to a mutually beneficial arrangement. I need help with my rent."

"Join the club."

"That's not the right answer. Get out of my way so I can go to the cops."

"I had nothing to do with that guy's murder. Did you see me kill him?"

"No. But I can put two and two together. You were sitting near him, and he was murdered during the movie, according to the cops."

"That doesn't mean anything," said Grant, becoming annoyed at arguing with her.

"Then you won't mind talking to the cops. Now let me go. My boyfriend is a member of the Mongols. He's not gonna like to hear that you kept me trapped in your room. He has a short temper, and he likes to use his hands to inflict pain. I can't remember all the noses he's broken in bar fights."

"That sounds like a threat."

"It's a description of my boyfriend."

"Threats are illegal in the state of California."

"So is false imprisonment. Now let me out of here," said Mandy, her voice becoming shrill.

Grant didn't want the neighbors to hear her. He couldn't make up his mind what to do. He wasn't sure what had happened at the movie theater when he had seen the film. He had no memory of killing anyone, and yet his knife had blood on it. He had washed the blood off. It could have been the blood of an animal. Maybe he had killed a rat and forgot about it. But where had he encountered a rat? He doubted one would have been in the movie theater.

For the life of him, he couldn't remember anything happening in the movie theater. He was too engrossed with the horror movie to remember anything else that had taken place there. It was a gripping horror movie that commanded his full attention when it was running.

"If you're so innocent, why are you worried about me going to the cops?" said Mandy.

"I don't want you spreading rumors about me."

Kill her. She'll rat you out to the cops. You'll spend the rest of your life in jail. Kill her. Take the knife and cut her tongue out.

A voice in his head was sounding the alarm. It sounded like the demon from the horror movie.

Clenching his jaw Grant restrained his hand from reaching for his knife.

19

"You're stressing me out," said Mandy. She fished out her cell phone from her purse. "I'm calling my boyfriend."

Gnashing his teeth Grant moved out of her way. He didn't want to kill her. What had got into him? He had nothing to hide. Why was he preventing her from going to the cops?

"That's better," said Mandy. "A thousand bucks will prevent me from going to the cops."

"Do whatever you want. I did nothing wrong."

"Look, I'm a nice person. I'll give you another day to think it over. I really don't want you to go to jail."

Grant opened the door for her. "I'm not telling you what to do."

Kill the rat. She's nothing but a greedy bitch.

"I think you better go," he said, struggling to control his urge to knife her, a nervous tic under his right eye.

"What's wrong with you?"

"Nothing."

She walked into the hall. "I'll be back tomorrow."

He shut the door.

"You better not be," he muttered.

Chapter 5

No sooner had Grant shut the door than his cell phone chimed. It was Sherry.

"Where's the Venmo money?" she said. "I still haven't gotten it."

"Because I didn't send it. I loaned you all my money. It's gone."

"How could you do this to me?"

Grant felt like hanging up. How did he ever get involved with this woman? He knew she was trouble when he first met her. She wanted to borrow rent money from him the first day he met her, because her landlord was evicting her. He should have told her to get lost right then and there. But he felt sorry for her, and she was attractive. He gave her the benefit of the doubt and loaned her money for her rent.

That was just the beginning.

Every time he saw her she borrowed more and more money. There was no end to her borrowing. She had to move to a different apartment, because the landlady was giving her a hard time. Then she had to move again, because bedbugs infested her new apartment.

"Are you there?" she said.

"What do you want?"

"I want three thousand dollars. I need to rent a hotel room and buy a plane ticket back to LA tomorrow."

"I can't help you."

"How can you do this to me? Where am I supposed to sleep tonight? They won't let me stay at this hotel another night unless I pay them now."

"Why are you telling me this?"

"Where am I supposed to sleep tonight? Do you want me to sleep with a bunch of bums in the subway?"

"Don't you understand? I filed for bankruptcy. I'm in Chapter 7. The money's gone."

"I'm gonna get assaulted in the subway and bitten by rats because of you. Venmo me the three thousand. Or use PayPal or Zelle. I don't care which."

"Have you heard a word I've said?"

"I'm a young girl alone in the big city. How can you do this to me?"

"Stop blaming me for all your problems. I'm out of this."

"You need to send the money now. Use PayPal."

"I'm not loaning you another cent."

"Send it to my sister Jade. I still don't have a bank account, because my bank closed it when it was overdrawn. Jade will wire the money to me as soon as she gets it."

Grant terminated the call.

Her sister Jade. She must be in on the scam with Sherry. He was always sending the money to Jade as per Sherry's instructions. They were a tag team. The Shakedown Sisters.

He should have broken up with Sherry a long time ago. But she kept insisting she would pay him back with the money she was inheriting from her uncle once she got the money out of probate, which had been dragging on for years. He should have suspected it was a swindle and that she and her sister were professional fraudsters.

He would lie awake at night, cursing himself for not breaking up with her. And yet the next day when she called he would agree to see her again even though he knew full well she wanted more money. He continued to hope she was on the level about paying him back. If he hadn't been involved with her, he never would have loaned her a dime.

This was what he got for meeting a woman on a dating site on the Internet. Those sites were apparently rife with hookers and scammers.

His cell phone chimed. It was her again.

He refused to take her call.

He was barely scraping along on the royalties he made from his books.

He had become convinced she was never going to pay him back even if she had a rich uncle in the first place, which he was

22

beginning to doubt. She had never offered him any proof that she had inherited anything. Every time he had asked for proof, she had claimed her lawyer wouldn't let her show anybody any documents, because they were protected by attorney-client privilege.

He suspected now that she was a pathological liar and that hardly anything she had told him had been true. There was no inheritance, and she was never going to pay him back the hundreds of thousands of dollars he had lent her.

He cursed himself for believing her.

Chapter 6

"This could be the perfect ad for our movie," said Bill Towers, the marketing director of the film *Necromaniac*.

Clad in a trim navy blue suit, pushing thirty, the lean Towers sported cropped hair and three days' growth on his face.

"How can a murder be a perfect ad?" said Norman Kudlow, the fortysomething director of the film, his face gloomy.

He wore a bucket hat and sunglasses with black lenses even though he stood with Towers inside Towers's Century City office on the seventh floor. Under his safari jacket his black T-shirt had Movie Whore stenciled on its chest in white block letters. He had the beginnings of a potbelly.

"We can tell the public the movie is so scary someone got killed in it," said Towers, standing behind his desk, his cell phone in his hand.

"I don't see the logic," said Kudlow, shaking his head.

"Logic? There's no logic in marketing movies. It's about drama and publicity. *Necromaniac* has drama because someone got murdered watching it. Drama means publicity. Publicity sells movies. Remember. There's no such thing as bad publicity in Hollywood."

"Somebody got killed for Chrissake."

"I'm telling you the murder will help sell tickets to *Necromaniac*."

Kudlow pursed his lips. "Hyping a murder doesn't seem like the right way to go."

"Right way, wrong way. There's no right and wrong in marketing. Whatever sells tickets is right. Everything else is wrong."

"My film had nothing to do with the murder that took place in the theater showing the film."

"You know it, and I know it. But the public doesn't know it. They're gonna think the movie is so scary it prompted somebody to commit murder."

"And that's gonna sell tickets?" said Kudlow, gaping at Towers.

"Mark my words, *Necromaniac*'s gonna be all over social media. Everybody's gonna want to see it."

"So they can get killed in the audience by some psycho?" said Kudlow, his eyes popping in disbelief.

"They're gonna sit in the audience scared to death they're gonna be the next one murdered."

"Why would anyone want to be murdered?"

"It's the idea of being murdered by a psycho. You and I both know nobody's gonna kill them. But the thrill of thinking you might be murdered in the audience is what's gonna draw people to our movie. Horror fans love to be horrified. The idea of getting murdered while watching a movie is horrifying."

"I dunno."

"Let's see. How can we word the ad? '*Are you too scared to see* Necromaniac, *the scariest movie ever made? Even scarier than* The Exorcist.' How's that sound?"

"You're challenging them to go to the film."

"You see the potential? People want a challenge. We'll say the demon in the movie possessed the murderer and incited him to kill."

"I don't want my film to be blamed for inciting people to murder. Stanley Kubrick pulled *A Clockwork Orange* from English theaters when people thought it caused audience members to kill."

"Kubrick was a putz and a schlub. He wanted to be known as an auteur and didn't want to get his hands dirty with marketing his work. You can't have it both ways in the movies. They're a popular medium. They should appeal to everybody, not just to cineastes with master's degrees in film from pricy colleges nobody can afford."

"Film is an art form whether you like it or not."

"It's an art form that should appeal to as many people as possible. We can't get too snotty marketing it. We have to go for the lowest common denominator."

"Which is?"

"Fear, of course. Don't you see it? Murder is scary. An act of murder occurred at your movie, which enhances the scare factor for filmgoers. That's gonna sell tickets."

25

"My film doesn't incite people to kill. I don't like it being connected to a murder that happened to occur in its audience."

"Let me remind you, Norman. We're trying to make your movie sell tickets. If it doesn't do well at the box office, you won't get another job. You're only as good as your last picture's box office."

Kudlow heaved a painful sigh. "This business is a jungle. Whoever said those five words hit the nail on the head."

"And violence sells in the jungle. The king of the jungle is the lion, who kills all the competition. That's what we're gonna do—kill the competition with millions of ticket sales."

"I don't like it. I made a great film. It's not exploitation torture porn for homicidal maniacs."

Towers waved his hand with disdain. "Ah. Don't worry about the critics. Critics are embittered losers who vent their spleens on successful movies. They're a pack of hyenas feeding on a lion's kill."

"It's a horror film. Why do critics look down their noses at horror films? It makes no sense."

"Horror movies are too popular. Critics like only artsy-fartsy movies nobody goes to."

"I guess."

"We're gonna make the critics eat crow. Your movie is gonna do boffo box office."

"I don't like using a murder to market my film."

"Phooey to you, Norman. And you're not in charge of marketing. I am. We got a winner on our hands. I'm not gonna let you sabotage it by growing a moral conscience all of a sudden."

Kudlow snickered. "Nobody ever accused my films of being moral."

"There you go. That's the Norman Kudlow I know and love."

Towers held out his fist for a bump. Kudlow fist-bumped him without enthusiasm.

"That doesn't mean I would stage a filmgoer's murder to publicize one of my films," said Kudlow.

"I never said it did. Everybody knows you had nothing to do with the murder at the theater showing your flick."

"Even William Castle wouldn't pull a stunt like that. And he pulled a lot of stunts to market his work."

26

"The bottom line is we all love movies. It's the common bond that holds all of us movie folks together," said Towers, strutting out from behind his desk and coiling his arm around Kudlow's shoulder, a beaming grin plastered on his face.

Kudlow experienced the spine-tingling sensation of an anaconda wrapping itself around his shoulder.

"I believe in the power of art," said Kudlow.

"And so do I. So do I."

"Your god is Mammon, Bill."

"And you're my offering to him," said Towers, smiling.

Kudlow gave Towers a look.

"Not you," said Towers. "Your movie, I mean. What a fantastic film it is. It's gonna coin money."

"And if it makes nothing, it's junk?"

Towers winked at Kudlow. "We're two adults in this room. We both know how the world works. Let's face it. The key is advertising. Our dare to see a scary movie where the filmgoer might get killed is a unique marketing tactic. It's gonna be our ticket to box office gold. A psycho murder could be the best thing that ever happened to us."

"One thing is for sure. It won't do the poor guy that got murdered any good."

"Why do you always look on the dark side of life?"

"I'm an artist. I'm a victim of my imagination. This has all the earmarks of a debacle waiting to happen."

"Ah, phooey. We need to spread the word that going to *Necromaniac* could get you killed. People are gonna jump at the chance. There will be lines wrapped around the block at theaters showing our movie."

"I don't want anyone else to get killed because of my film."

"That's not gonna happen. This murder was a fluke. But it's gonna work out for us in the long run. Nobody but the brain dead believes that movies can cause violence." Towers paused. "Don't tell me you believe in demons like the one in your movie."

"You know I don't. I wanted to make a scary movie. Possession movies are scary, so I made *Necromaniac*."

Towers nodded yes. "Like William Friedkin. He didn't believe in demons, but that didn't stop him from making *The Exorcist*, one of the scariest movies of all time."

27

"The writer of *The Exorcist*, William Blatty, believed in demons."

"He was a superstitious fool, and he didn't make the movie the success it was. In fact, he wanted to change the ending because he thought it was immoral."

"He thought it made it look like the devil won."

"Friedkin didn't believe in that religious stuff. He was the one who made the movie a blockbuster by playing to moviegoers' fears. Hell, if I want a sermon, I go to church, not to a movie. We should be thankful Friedkin won out over Blatty."

Chapter 7

Dressed in jeans and a black blazer, the forty-two-year-old journalist Perkins Weaver watched the demonstrators protesting in front of the theater where the moviegoer had been murdered. Weaver didn't ask for this assignment. He went where he was told. He would just as soon be in a bar ordering another tequila with a wedge of lime, which was where he was when he had got the call from his editor.

One of the signs said, This Movie Is Unsafe.

Another said, Do Not Attend This Unsafe Theater.

Another was more to the point with Go Home or Die.

The protesters marched back and forth on the sidewalk in front of the theater marquee, flaunting their signs.

The protest had no effect on the long line of filmgoers standing in front of the theater, waiting to be let inside. They took in the demonstrators with amused detachment as if the protest was part of the filmgoing experience and was to be enjoyed as such.

Weaver marched alongside one of the demonstrators and interviewed her, his cell phone recording them.

"I'm a journalist for the *Times*," he said. "Why are you protesting this movie?"

"Can't you read our signs?" said the twentysomething woman with short frizzy black hair.

Wearing a pink T that said LA, Murder Capital of the World in Baskerville letters on its front, she sported oversized bug-eyed shades.

"What is your name?"

"Amen."

"We just started," said Weaver, offended by her curtness.

"That's my name," she said, glaring at him.

"Oh, of course. My bad. Can you elaborate, Amen?" said Weaver, overcoming his embarrassment.

"A customer was murdered in this theater yesterday. Management should close down the theater as long as the murderer is at large. It's irresponsible to do otherwise. Business as usual is not acceptable."

"Do you think the murderer will strike here again?"

"It's possible. Until they're caught, anything is possible. Why put lives at risk by keeping this theater open?"

Weaver dodged a pedestrian clad in a suit who was bustling down the palm- and magnolia-lined sidewalk, weaving his way in and out of the line of protesters, a look of impatient annoyance on his face.

"Do you think the horror movie incited the murderer to kill someone?" Weaver asked.

"This violent, sadistic movie should be pulled from theaters. It is a hateful movie filled with senseless, graphic violence. It's violence for the sake of violence. It's fucking torture porn."

"What if the theater owners removed this movie and showed a different one? Would you continue to picket this theater?"

Amen looked flummoxed for a moment.

"That's hypothetical," she said. "If you know anything about movies, it would never happen. This movie is making way too much money for them to remove it."

"Then what are you hoping to accomplish with your protest?"

"We're hoping to shut down this theater. It's an open cesspool of murder. People should be protected from hellholes that are breeding grounds of violence."

Weaver eyed the eager crowd queued in front of the movie theater.

"Nobody's forcing them to go to this movie," he said.

"Haven't you seen the ads?"

"What ads?"

"The ads daring people to attend *Necromaniac*, screaming that people are scaredy cats if they don't go to the movie and . . . ," Amen trailed off, scowling at a teenage boy making a face and sticking out his tongue at her.

"And what?" said Weaver.

"The ads are hyping the murder at the theater, saying moviegoers might get killed while watching this exercise in tastelessness and sadism."

"Did someone pay you to stage this protest?"

"Of course not. I wouldn't be a bit surprised if some Hollywood marketer paid someone to commit the murder in this theater to gin up publicity."

"You really believe marketers hired a hit man to consummate a hit here?" said Weaver, dumbfounded.

Amen's smug expression said it all.

Weaver picked up on a TV news crew on the other side of the street filming the protest. He started to wonder if the very visible protest was a publicity stunt to get people to go to the movie.

"You really believe what you're saying?" he asked. "That movies can incite violence?"

"This movie does. I can't believe management is allowing people to come here only one day after the murder that took place in these very seats at this unsafe theater showing sick and depraved torture porn day and night. This theater is a hotbed of filth and corruption."

Weaver picked up on a counterprotester marching on the other side of the street, bearing a jeering sign that said Too Scared to Go to a Movie? LOL. He flourished his sign violently up and down, taunting the demonstrators who were protesting the movie.

A vendor strolled down the sidewalk hawking hot dogs out of his mustard yellow cart to patrons lined up for the movie, marketing his wares as Horror Dogs, the two words printed in bold red block letters on the side of his pushcart.

The dog and pony show was looking more and more like a publicity stunt rather than a news story, decided Weaver, though he had no proof. A carnival hoopla atmosphere didn't necessarily mean the event was staged by PR flacks.

Out of the corner of his eye, Weaver noticed a film crew enter the theater. He wanted to know what was going on. He followed them.

31

Chapter 8

A male cameraman, a female announcer, and a male boom operator entered the theater lobby. They looked to be in their late twenties and early thirties. Weaver followed them as they made their way through a dim-lit tunnel to the theater where the filmgoer had been murdered.

They commenced filming a seat in the audience.

The statuesque black brunette announcer with bee-stung lips stood beside the seat in the as-yet-empty theater and stared at it as the longhaired boom operator held the mic over her head.

The cameraman, who was also the director, trained his camera on her.

Weaver noticed that the murder victim's seat looked cleaner than the other seats. He realized it had new upholstery.

"Action," said the director behind the camera.

The announcer pointed at the seat.

"This is the actual seat where Nicholas Briscoe was savagely murdered yesterday while he was watching the demonic horror movie *Necromaniac,*" she said. "As you can see, the bloodstains have been removed and replaced with new upholstery." She faced the camera. "Will anyone dare sit in this seat for the next showing of the scariest horror movie ever made?"

"You have to leave now," said an usher. "The movie will start soon and we're gonna let the audience in."

"The next person who sits here might not survive the movie," said the narrator, facing the camera and ignoring the usher.

"This is a perfectly safe theater. We have two security guards in the lobby in case of a disturbance."

"Many people believe viewing this shocking horror movie incited the murderer to kill," said the narrator, continuing to ignore the usher.

"We can't have you filming in here when the audience enters. You need to leave," said the usher, becoming flustered. "I don't want to have to call security to have you forcibly removed."

32

"We are being forced to leave the theater so we cannot show you the next person who will dare occupy this seat of death."

"That's enough," cried the usher. "That's a perfectly good seat."

"Will anyone be brave enough to occupy this seat?"

"Shut up. I'm calling security."

"Cut," said the director, lowering his movie camera. He turned to the usher. "You'll thank me after this clip runs on YouTube. People want to be scared, and this theater is gonna scare a lot of people to death. It'll get a reputation for horror."

"Not if everybody's too scared to come here."

"You don't understand your audience. They *want* to be scared. The more scared they are, the better." The director turned to his crew. "That's a wrap."

The film crew retreated from the theater into the lobby.

Weaver kept his cell phone recording the whole time. As he followed them onto the sidewalk under the marquee, he realized the number of counterprotesters on the other side of the street had increased and they looked surlier than they had before.

A blond longhaired twentysomething guy holding a sign that said Freedom of Speech angrily pegged his sign across the street at the group protesting the showing of the movie. The sign sailed into a middle-aged man's face, cutting it. Irate, his cheek dripping blood, he shook his fist at the assailant.

"I could've lost an eye," he screamed, his face red.

The protesters and counterprotesters yelled insults at each other.

"Banning movies is like burning books," cried the longhaired guy.

"Go back to your mommy's basement," yelled the wounded protester. "This movie is endangering lives."

"Movies don't make people kill. People like you do."

A masked short, stocky counterprotester wearing jeans with a rope belt flung his half-full plastic water bottle at the protesters marching in front of the movie theater. The bottle struck a middle-aged woman in the stomach. She doubled up in pain.

Weaver watched the film crew start filming the melee. Meanwhile, he snapped pictures of the unfolding violence with his cell phone.

Car horns commenced blasting as the counterprotesters charged across the street to mix it up with the protesters. Cars screeched to a halt as angry demonstrators charged in front of them in order to cross the street and wage battle with their opposite number.

The two security guards emerged from the theater lobby, saw the fracas, and called the police to break it up.

A traffic snarl ensued, precipitating gridlock. Enraged drivers blasted their horns in frustration. Some of them piled out of their cars and screamed obscenities at the rioters.

Enthralled by the riot, the filmgoers standing in line for the movie didn't know whether to watch the imbroglio or flee for their lives.

Sirens shrieking, blue and red lights flashing, black-and-whites descended on the rioters.

"This is the LAPD," said a cop through the bullhorn mounted on his squad car. "You are ordered to disperse."

The cops blocked the street with their cruisers, preventing cars from entering the area.

Some of the rioters threw punches as the two sides brawled in front of the movie theater.

Grumbling about a refund, several moviegoers waiting in the queue to see the film started to leave.

Cops stormed out of their black-and-whites in riot gear and, wielding polycarbonate shields and steel billy clubs, charged into the donnybrook to break it up.

The film crew shot the crackdown, and so did Weaver with his cell phone.

Weaver ducked as a full plastic water bottle hurled by a protester whooshed toward his head.

The cops fell to busting rioters and binding their wrists behind their backs with flex cuffs.

"You can't even go to a movie anymore," complained a teenage girl with black hair streaked with red highlights as she departed from the protester-choked sidewalk skirting the theater.

Protesters continued to skirmish with their opposite numbers until cops in riot gear separated them and hauled them away.

A brawny cop wearing a riot helmet made to bust Weaver.

"I'm press," said Weaver, clutching the press ID hanging from his neck and brandishing it in the cop's face.

"We're clearing the area," said the cop. "Move back."

Weaver retreated.

Admonished by the cop, the film crew retreated to their dented van.

Chapter 9

Grant's life was spiraling downward.

Sitting in his apartment he brooded over his problems.

The IRS was threatening to throw him in jail for not paying the taxes he owed even though he had filed for Chapter 7 and his bankruptcy case was still open. Although his debts to creditors were discharged, his debt to the IRS was not, and they wanted their money. The problem was he didn't have it, which was why he had filed for bankruptcy in the first place. The reason he didn't have it was because he had lent all his money to his ex-girlfriend Sherry and she had no intention of ever paying him back.

As if that wasn't enough to worry about, he was bothered by the fact he couldn't remember anything about the roly-poly guy he was sitting near at the theater when he had seen *Necromaniac*—the same guy someone had murdered during the movie. How could he have not noticed a guy getting murdered a seat away from him? He had become so enrapt in the movie that he had become oblivious to his surroundings and to anything that had happened near him.

He couldn't understand how blood had gotten on his knife. He had no memory of using the knife. All he could remember from last night was the horror movie. He kept hearing the demon in the movie talking. It was like the voice had taken up residence in his head. Which was impossible, of course. A demon couldn't jump from a movie into a person in the audience.

He didn't believe in demons. They were just agents of evil that he as a writer employed to create an atmosphere of horror in his novels. He believed they existed only in the imagination. Then how could the demon have told him to kill Mandy when she had tried to blackmail him?

His cell phone chimed. He took the call.

"I need money," said Sherry.

"Why do you keep calling me demanding money?"

"Because I'm alone in New York, and I have no place to stay. How am I supposed to fly back to LA without money?"

"I have no idea."

"What am I supposed to do?"

"What am *I* supposed to do? I'm bankrupt from loaning you all my money."

"Use PayPal or Venmo. Or Zelle. I'm waiting."

"I'm not loaning you any more money."

"I can't believe you're doing this to me."

Kill her. Kill the thankless bitch.

The demon voice from the movie was taking up residence in his head again.

"I still haven't got your Paypal," said Sherry. "I checked with my sister and she didn't get it either."

All of the PayPal payments went to her sister Jade. Sherry claimed she didn't have a bank account so she couldn't receive payments. All part of their racket. She couldn't be linked to him through electronic payments. Only her sister, who he had never met, could. When Sherry was with him in his apartment, she borrowed cash, which was untraceable—when he *had* money anyway, which seemed like ages ago.

Grant figured the two sisters were employed by an illegal gang, at least that was what he figured now. At the time he was being fleeced he thought Sherry was a woman down on her luck who needed financial help, not a con artist shaking him down. He realized now that he was a fool for believing her scam story that she loved him, had inherited from her deceased uncle two million dollars that were locked in probate, and would pay back the loans he had made to her as soon as her inheritance cleared probate.

If this wasn't a case of fraud, what was? He felt like a duped investor. What complicated the matter was his romantic involvement with her. But fraud was fraud. At this point he had no idea if the two million dollars she was supposed to inherit was genuine or part of her scam to inveigle him out of his life savings.

He had reported her scam to the local cops and to the FBI. Neither of them had done anything regarding his report as far as he knew. The proof was Sherry was still trying to shake him down.

"There is no PayPal payment," he said. "You can wait till you're blue in the face. I'm not loaning you any more money."

"My sister hasn't gotten it."

"Can't you hear me?"

37

"This is urgent. It's an emergency. I don't have anywhere to stay in New York. Do you expect me to sleep on the sidewalk?"

"I expect you to turn yourself into the cops for being a scammer."

"What?" said Sherry, outraged.

"You're a professional scammer. You're never gonna pay me back."

"After all I've done for you, how can you say such a thing?" she said, her voice catching.

She was good, he had to admit. Her throat catching on cue. She knew how to act. He had thought it was all genuine when he had first met her. But then again . . .

He had thought it odd that she didn't have a bank account, but she had said it was because she didn't have a job because of Covid. Which was plausible. He had kept giving her the benefit of the doubt in their relationship. He had been trying to be less cynical about humans while he was involved with her, hoping their romance was the real thing, and look where it had got him: the poorhouse and the IRS threatening to levy all his property, including his royalties, no matter how paltry they were, to get the money he owed them.

"You seem to have a lot of financial problems for a multimillionaire," he said.

"I told you I can't get the money I inherited. The houses my uncle owned are in probate in two different states, Michigan and Florida. Which complicates matters because each state has different probate laws. Now send me three thousand dollars on Venmo so I can stay overnight here in a hotel and fly back to LA tomorrow."

"You can't squeeze blood out of a rock."

"You're smart. You'll figure out a way to get the money."

He wasn't smart enough to see her as the scammer she really was until he was already broke and deep in debt. He thought of himself as downright stupid for falling for her and her sister's scam aided by their corrupt lawyers and whoever else was involved in the racket.

"It doesn't have to be Venmo," she said. "Use CashApp. CashApp's good."

"I don't want to keep arguing about this."

"How can you do this to me? I'm alone in New York," she said, beginning to cry.

She was good at getting him to feel sorry for her. Well, it wasn't going to work this time, because he was broke and had no credit.

He had started out dirt-poor, and here he was again dirt-poor, courtesy of Sherry. Was this what they meant by *what goes around comes around*? It wasn't a comforting thought. No matter how hard you worked or suffered to get out of the gutter, you could never escape. You might escape briefly, but it was only an illusion. In the end you would always return to the gutter. At least, that was how it had worked for him.

Was it his fault Sherry had scammed him out of his life savings? Had he allowed her to do it? Did he have *victim* written all over his face? Was he a fool waiting to be scammed? No. He couldn't think like that. She was a professional scammer who had victimized him. She never had any intention of paying back all the money he had lent her. Saying she had inherited two million bucks from her dead uncle was the hook she had used to reel Grant in, making him think that she could and would pay him back the seven hundred thousand bucks she owed him.

In fact, he would never see his stolen money again.

Get used to being broke all over again, he told himself. He felt like he was back in college as a starving student. Back to peanut butter sandwiches for lunch and hot dogs for dinner. Back to the gutter—a place he had never thought he would have to revisit, let alone live in.

He hung up on her.

She kept calling him back, but he didn't pick up.

He left his apartment, bummed out. His life was trapped in a doom loop, and its name was Sherry.

Chapter 10

Norman Kudlow and Bill Towers were riding through Century City in the back of a limo.

"Did you see the news?" said Towers, his face pale.

"What news?"

"How could you miss it?"

"I don't watch the news. It's too depressing."

Towers shook his head. "It's all over the place. Don't you get any social media?"

"I'm reading scripts for my next film."

"There was a riot on the sidewalks outside the theater where the guy watching your movie was murdered."

"Now it's *my* movie because there was a riot at it?"

"It's your movie because you directed it."

"You're the one hyping the murder in order to sell more tickets."

Towers rubbed his eyelids. "Nobody's gonna view the movie if riots erupt at the theaters showing it. The cops broke up the riot and sent everybody home, even the people standing in line waiting to see the movie."

"Who rioted?"

"People were protesting the movie because they claim it promotes violence. They say the movie made the murderer kill the guy watching it yesterday."

"That's ridiculous. Movies don't make people kill."

"These protesters are nuts. They're nervous Nellies who get their panties in a twist when they think about horror movies."

"So? Did they attack the moviegoers standing in line?"

"According to the news, counterprotesters who believe in free speech started the fight. They threw water bottles and placards at the Nellies. A brawl broke out. Cops came and told everybody to go home."

"Crap."

"Crap is right. The theater closed down for the rest of the day."

"Well, people can see the movie at other theaters."

"Yeah, but they might be worried about encountering another riot."

"You were the one that said bad publicity was good for the movie."

"I wasn't talking about a riot. Riots are bad news. The distributor is threatening to pull your movie from theaters, because it incites violence."

"What kind of an idiot is he? The rioters caused the violence, not *Necromaniac*."

Towers poured a Scotch from the miniature bar in the back of the front seat of the limo.

"We'll have to wait and see how this plays out," he said, and took a pull on his drink.

"They can't blame the riot on the movie. The rioters weren't watching the movie. You said they were on the sidewalk. So how could seeing the movie make them become violent?"

"True. They weren't watching it. But they were protesting *because* of the movie."

Kudlow shrugged. "It's a free country. Not much we can do about protests."

"Don't you see? It's gonna kill ticket sales."

"What can we do about it?"

Towers mulled it over. "We have to make it clear to people that the riot only occurred at one theater showing *Necromaniac*. The rest of the theaters showing the same movie had no problems."

"How are we gonna prevent rioters from protesting at the other theaters showing it?"

"I dunno. If only the cops would catch the murderer, this whole problem would go away."

"You think?"

"I doubt the protesters would continue protesting if the cops caught the killer."

"I'm not so sure. The protesters might believe the movie will incite a different person to kill."

"Don't be ridiculous. The protesters just want attention. They want to get their ugly mugs on the TV news. It's all about publicity."

Kudlow adjusted his sunglasses. "If they really believe movies can incite people to commit murder, these clowns could cause us a lot of grief."

"Why do you wear dark glasses when you're inside?"

"I don't have any eyes," deadpanned Kudlow.

Towers burst out laughing. "You're such a card, Norm. Don't have any eyes. Ha. Bullshit. You can see as well as me. Otherwise, you'd be falling down all over the place whenever you went anywhere. Where's your cane?"

"I'm not blind. I see what's *inside* my mind, not what's outside."

"Ah-ha. Spoken like a true auteur. You're gonna win an Oscar nod for *Necromaniac*. I guarantee it."

Towers's cell phone chimed. "Hello?"

As he listened, a smile broke out on his face. He terminated the call.

Kudlow stared at him with a questioning look.

"It's about time for some good news," said Towers. "Even though we lost money at the theater where the guy was killed, ticket sales were up everywhere else. Every other theater was sold out. I knew it. People want to see what all the excitement is about, so they're dying to see your Oscar-winning movie."

"Horror movies don't win Oscars for their directors."

"What do you mean? Look at . . . look at . . ."

"See what I mean? You can't name a single horror film director that won an Oscar."

Towers kept thinking about it. "What about . . . It's coming to me . . . What about . . ." He snapped his fingers. "The director of *Silence of the Lambs* won an Oscar. Jonathan Demme."

"It wasn't a horror movie. It was a thriller."

"You're crazy. Anthony Hopkins scared the shit out of me as Hannibal Lecter. He's scarier than Norman Bates and Michael Myers combined."

"*Psycho* and *Halloween*. Two other films whose directors didn't win an Oscar. Friedkin didn't win an Oscar for *The Exorcist*, either."

"Then you should be ecstatic. You and Demme will be the only two horror directors that ever won an Oscar."

"You're dreaming."

"To be honest, I don't care if it wins an Oscar. As long as it makes buckets of money, and *Necromaniac* will, I'll be happy. Your movie's gonna be more popular than *The Exorcist*. People will kill to score a ticket to it," said Towers, chuckling.

Kudlow gasped. "Don't say that."

"Chill out."

"We don't want any more dead bodies inside movie theaters."

"I was speaking metaphorically." Towers paused. "Oh, I get it. You were joking. You have a wicked sense of humor, Norman. Sometimes it's hard to tell when you're being serious or humorous."

Kudlow's blank expression didn't change.

"Like right fucking now," said Towers.

Chapter 11

Grant wondered how much pain and suffering a person could endure before their bodies imploded. He felt like his body was on the verge of imploding on account of his dreadful life.

He turned his cell phone off so Sherry couldn't call him and demand more money.

To escape his life he went to another showing of *Necromaniac*. While watching this movie he had noticed his problems had melted away because he had become so engrossed in the horror film.

He drove to a different theater to experience the movie this time and had to sit in the rear row because the theater was rapidly filling with eager filmgoers.

He sat in the seat at the end of the row. With her blue eyes and blonde hair the woman he was sitting next to reminded him of Sherry, which annoyed him. He wanted to escape the swindler and here she was sitting next to him. Of course, it wasn't her. It couldn't be her. She was in New York, sleeping on a sidewalk, according to her. He had determined she was a pathological liar, however. She could as easily be here in LA as well as in New York or in any other city. She could even be sitting in this theater beside him.

But he doubted it.

Still it looked like her. He didn't want her to think he was staring at her. He kept his eyes trained on the ads running on the screen. He had come to the movie to escape her, and this woman sitting beside him was reminding him of her.

Ticked off, he thought about changing seats, but the theater had filled up and he could spot no vacant seats, especially with the lights dimming.

What were the chances he would sit next to a woman who looked like Sherry? He guessed they must have been pretty good. Otherwise, how could this have happened? He hadn't even looked at her when he had sat here. This was his assigned seat, and he had grabbed it. It wasn't until later when he had started feeling comfortable in his seat and had scoped out his surroundings that he had realized she looked like Sherry.

The movie came on.

It got on his nerves that the woman looked like Sherry. He needed to concentrate on the movie. He would forget her as soon as he became enrapt in the gripping horror story. Even though he had seen the movie before, he knew he would become enthralled by it once again. The demon would appear any minute and proceed to carry out its possession of the main character, the manager of a crematorium.

Kill her. She ruined your life. Kill her.

The voice of the demon. How could it escape from the motion picture screen into his head?

Are you just gonna sit there and let her get away with ruining your life? Kill her. She deserves to die for what she did to you.

He should have been more skeptical of her and thrown her out of his apartment the day he first met her as soon as she had asked for a loan.

Woulda, coulda, shoulda. The past is dead. Time to act in the present. Kill her. Don't let her get away with it. Kill her.

How could a demon in a movie be talking to him? He must have been imagining it.

She's never gonna leave you alone unless you kill her.

Its voice kept tormenting him. Grant wondered if he himself was in the movie. He couldn't be in the movie. He was a filmgoer watching the movie. Then how could the demon be talking to him? Why was it talking only to him? The other people sitting in the audience were watching the movie too. Why wasn't the demon talking to them? Why did it pick only him to speak to?

It wasn't speaking to anyone in the audience, including him. He was imagining it. He had to be.

Kill her. She stole your life from you and left you with nothing, not even your car. How can you sit there and let her get away with it?

Sweat poured out of Grant's face. None of this made sense. Maybe he was cracking up. People *did* crack up when their lives took a turn for the worse. He could hear the demon's voice clear as day. How could he hear something that didn't exist? He had no answers.

His life was hitting the skids. That was all. There was no demon.

Kill her. Kill the swindler. You're her mark. Fight back. Take control of your life. She's destroying you. Resist her. Kill her and free yourself from the corrupt scammer.

The only demon was in the movie. Then why did he keep hearing the demon in his mind?

Stab her in the temple. Do it now.

Chapter 12

Accompanied by a thirtyish brunette, Detective Kevin Kesey of the Robbery-Homicide Division of the LAPD entered the empty theater where Nicholas Briscoe had been murdered in his seat.

Prematurely bald at the age of forty-five, clad in a tan blazer and black slacks, the stocky Kesey strode through the carpeted lobby to the twentysomething usher who was standing near the food counter watching him.

In her thirties, the brunette Detective Xochitl Rivera wore a high fade with the part on the side like a man. Beneath her baggy blazer she had a figure sculpted by a regimen of daily weightlifting.

"Can I help you, Officers?" said the neatly coiffed usher named Ted, according to his name tag.

"I want to see the seat where the decedent was killed," said Kesey.

"Certainly. Follow me."

The usher entered the theater showing *Necromaniac* and led Kesey to the seat in question.

"Other police were already here and said we could clean the premises," said Ted.

"No problem. That was forensics. I've seen the evidence they gathered." Kesey scoped out the theater. "Do you have CCTV in here?"

"No."

Kesey grunted with displeasure. "Do you have a record of the moviegoers who attended last night's showing of *Necromaniac*?"

"Uh—more or less."

"What's that mean?"

"We have a record of the people who paid with credit cards. If they paid with cash, we don't have their names."

"Did most of them pay with credit?"

"Um, about half."

"Could I see your ledger with the names of the moviegoers?"

47

"Sure."

Ted, with Kesey and Rivera in tow, retreated from the theater to the lobby. Ted crouched behind the cash register counter and retrieved the ledger, which he handed to Kesey.

"Kind of old-fashioned keeping a ledger," said Kesey. "Most people use computers for everything these days."

"That's a computer readout as you can see," said Ted.

Kesey flipped through the pages affixed to the clipboard until he found the list of the names who had attended the blood-soaked showing of *Necromaniac*.

"I need to take this ledger downtown and make a copy of the names," he said.

"Fine."

"We can probably figure the killer paid in cash," said Rivera.

"Probably," said Kesey, "but we might get lucky. We're gonna have to check out the names on this ledger and see if any of them have records."

"Do you have CCTV in the lobby?" Rivera said, scoping out the ceiling for closed-circuit cameras.

"No," said Ted. "We never have any problems. The owner doesn't see any need to buy surveillance equipment. It's not like we're a jewelry store. People come to see movies here, not rob us. We carry small sums of cash in our cash register."

"Were you here the night of the murder?"

"Yeah."

"Did you notice anyone suspicious?"

"What do you mean by suspicious?"

"Was anybody cutting up, making a scene, or making a lot of noise or something?"

Ted thought about it. "I dunno. I wouldn't say there was anything out of the ordinary. Some teenagers were a little noisy, but they shut up when the movie started."

Rivera nodded.

A newscaster's voice sounded through the lobby loudspeaker.

"Despite the shutdown of the theater where the brutal murder of a filmgoer took place, ticket sales of *Necromaniac* are breaking all records," announced the newscaster.

"A murder taking place here isn't hurting sales any," said Kesey.

48

"It hurt *our* sales," said Ted. "We had to close down yesterday thanks to a riot outside our theater."

"You're the exception to the rule, apparently. Everywhere else the movie is selling out, according to the news."

"We were sold out here before the riot shut us down."

Kesey nodded. "That's what I'm talking about."

"You would think people would be scared of going to the movie because of the murder here," said Rivera.

"You don't understand horror aficionados," said Ted. "They *want* to be scared. That's why they go to the movies, especially this one now that its notoriety has grown because of the murder."

"It's sick when you think about it. Going to a movie because somebody got killed watching it," said Rivera, pulling a face.

"We live in a sick age," grumped Kesey. "The age of serial killers and mass murderers. The heroes these days are Ted Bundy and Charles Manson."

"Do you think the killer got the urge to kill from watching this *Necro*-whatever movie?"

"*Necromaniac*," corrected Ted. "It's about the manager of a crematorium who becomes possessed—"

"I wouldn't be surprised if the killer did," cut in Kesey. "Hollywood is churning out a bunch of sick horror movies these days."

"You gotta see the movie. It's some scary shit."

"Back in the day a sick horror movie like this would ruin a director's career—"

"Like *Peeping Tom* did to Michael Powell's," said Ted, a cineaste eager to display his vast knowledge of film.

"Never heard of him."

"Because *Peeping Tom* torpedoed his career," said Ted, making a downward motion with his hand to accompany his statement.

"You sound like you know a lot about movies."

"I love movies."

"Did this *Peeping Tom* you're talking about make people kill each other?"

"Hardly anyone saw it. It did lousy box office and was pulled from the theaters. It's about a serial killer who makes movies of the people he kills as he's in the act of killing—"

"Maybe they should pull this movie from the theaters."

"*Peeping Tom* is now considered by critics to be a great film. It was the first slasher movie ever made. It was way ahead of its time. People are more sophisticated now. They like horror movies."

"I don't think *sophisticated* is the right word," said Rivera. "More like *depraved*."

"To my point," said Kesey. "We live in a sick age."

A uniform pushing thirty bustled into the lobby, his face working.

"There's been another murder," he said.

"Where?" said Kesey.

"At another theater showing this same movie."

Ted widened his eyes.

"Who?" said Kesey.

"A member of the audience," said the uniform. "That's all they told me."

"Let's roll," said Kesey, his face hectic with excitement.

He burst out the lobby door, Rivera and the uniform on his heels.

Chapter 13

Kudlow and Towers sat in Towers's Century City office. Towers was sitting behind his desk when his cell phone chimed. His face clouded as he listened to the caller.

Towers used the remote on his desktop to flick on the 4K HDTV mounted on the wall opposite his desk.

"Another murder has taken place in a theater showing *Necromaniac*," announced the TV newscaster, a petite Asian woman in her early thirties standing in front of the theater where the killing had occurred.

"Not another one," said Kudlow, craning around in his seat to watch the news.

"One helps publicity," said Towers, disconcerted. "Another could have the opposite effect. I'm not sure. This is uncharted waters."

His face registered concern as he watched the TV news, where black-and-whites were converging on the murder site, their sirens keening, their light bars flashing blue and red.

Two clean-cut young EMTs in navy blue uniforms rolled a gurney with a sheet-covered corpse on it down the sidewalk toward a meat wagon parked near the curb not far from the theater marquee.

"This is blowing up in our faces," said Kudlow, his face grim as he continued to watch the news.

"Let's not jump to conclusions," said Towers. "This thing could still work in our favor. Ticket sales could skyrocket again. People are gonna want to know what's so scary about this movie that's driving someone to commit murders. They're gonna want to see the movie."

His face brightened at the idea.

"I don't like the idea that my film's driving someone to kill," said Kudlow. "It's supposed to scare people, not turn them into homicidal maniacs."

51

Towers poohpoohed the idea. "Everybody knows movies can't turn people into killers. This serial killer is some maniac. He probably killed half a dozen people before he even saw the movie."

"Yeah. Movies can't make people killers. There's no way. This wacko's got issues. I wish he would commit his murders elsewhere. He's giving my film a bad name."

"I still say ticket sales are gonna go through the roof," said Towers, waving his hand at the ceiling.

"Hell, if I thought my film might turn somebody into a homicidal maniac, I never would have made it."

"Of course. We know that. Your movies entertain. That's what movies are all about. Entertainment. They're not instruction manuals on how to commit murder. Only an idiot would believe otherwise."

"Unfortunately, there are a lot of idiots out there."

"The name of the murder victim is being withheld by the police till they inform the next of kin," said the announcer.

"How's he killing these people?" said Kudlow.

"The cops aren't saying," said Towers. "They don't want people playing hoaxes, confessing they're the killer. And they don't want copycat killers. You know cops. They want to keep everything hush-hush."

Kudlow jumped to his feet and paced around. "They need to catch this nutbag."

"Yeah, yeah. They'll get him. Someone in the audience is bound to have seen him."

"It's hard to make out much in a dark theater especially if you're concentrating on watching the film. And my film is gripping. It grabs you by the throat and doesn't let go."

"And that's why the theaters aren't gonna pull it. They got too much to lose by dropping a multimillion-dollar blockbuster like your movie."

Kudlow came to a halt in the center of the office. "Do you think this psycho killer has a vendetta against my film and wants to make sure it tanks?"

"No, that's crazy talk. The guy's a psycho all right. But he has no idea what he's doing. The murders have nothing to do with you or your movie."

52

"What if it's not the same killer?" said Kudlow, his visage glum. "What if there are two killers?"

"Don't give me a heart attack. If there are two killers, I can hear the protesters now. The movie is creating an army of murderers. Don't even think there's more than one killer." Towers paused a beat. "Before I forget, I got an interview for you lined up on TV."

"You know I don't like doing interviews."

"We need you to make the case for your movie. Tell the people why it can't incite someone to commit murder. You're the best spokesman for your movie."

"I ought to kill you for doing this to me."

Towers chuckled. "Don't worry. You'll ace it."

"I don't like the idea of having to defend my film like it's something evil. It's a movie for Chrissake."

"That's what you'll say in the interview. People will listen to you because you're a world-famous director. You're our best spokesman."

Chapter 14

There was more blood on his knife, noticed Grant as he inspected the blade in his apartment. He had washed off the blood, and here it was back on his knife. Not only that, the blood hadn't coagulated. It was fresh.

He took the knife to the kitchen and washed off the blade in the sink.

He had no idea how the blood had got there. He must be suffering blackouts. Maybe because his life was so miserable he had to have blackouts to be able to go on living. Constantly thinking about Sherry and what she had done to him would drive him crazy if he couldn't blot it out of his mind from time to time.

But that didn't explain the blood on his knife.

He rinsed the blood off the knife and wiped the blade dry with a paper towel.

If he couldn't escape his life by going to a movie, he would go nuts. Movies were keeping him sane, especially *Necromaniac*, which he could watch over and over again and continue to get swept away by it.

He eyed the filled bookshelves lining his walls. If he didn't have movies and books, he would put a gun barrel in his mouth, squeeze the trigger, and lift the back of his skull off.

Someone knocked on the door.

Grant opened it.

His junkie brother Herb shambled into the room. Herb's life was as messed up as his. The guy couldn't keep a job. He kept shooting up skag. Emaciated, he had shoulder-length brown hair that didn't look like it had been washed for several days, perhaps weeks.

Herb used to be a private detective, but he had sampled the heroin stash of one of the drug dealers he had tracked down and had become hooked. Herb's career had gone into a tailspin as he became a confirmed junkie. He stopped applying himself to his job and instead spent his time plying himself with dope.

He once told Grant the very idea of getting another job terrified him. Herb didn't see how anyone could hold a job. The amount of work involved was unbearable. Making a living was too difficult to try doing over again from scratch. He couldn't face it. He didn't understand how other people were able to make a living. Just thinking about all the things you had to do in a job exhausted Herb. He had enough trouble getting out of bed in the morning. In the end he decided he would rather be a junkie.

"Hello, Herb," said Grant.

"Grant," said Herb, nodding.

"Long time no see. What brings you here?"

"You're my brother. I haven't seen you in a while. Isn't that a good enough reason to visit you?"

It was, but Grant didn't buy it. He wondered if Herb was jonesing. The guy was shaking and sweaty.

"How long have you been in town?" said Grant.

"A couple days."

"Want a beer?"

"Yeah, sure."

Grant retrieved two cans of Stella from the refrigerator and handed one to Herb.

"I feel sick," said Herb. "I need product."

"Why'd you come here? I don't do drugs."

"I need money. Can I borrow some dough from you? I'll pay you back."

"Do I look like a bank?" snapped Grant. "Everybody wants to borrow money from me."

"You know I'm good for it."

"No, I don't know that."

"We're brothers for Chrissake. Blood's thicker than water."

Herb was fifty-five. Grant didn't know how the guy had lived as long as he had with his habit.

"Sherry beat you to it," said Grant.

"What's that supposed to mean?"

"It means, she borrowed all my money and never paid me back."

"Why blame it on me?"

Grant took a pull on his beer. "I'm stating a fact. She turned my life into a nightmare. I'm not blaming you."

55

"Never lend money to a girlfriend. They won't pay you back. They think you owe them money for just being born."

"She got it all, and there's nothing left. I'm in Chapter 7."

"Crap. I can't believe this is happening."

"You're gonna have to get money somewhere else."

"Like where?"

"If I knew I'd be going there myself. I'm a couple months away from being evicted."

"You lent her *all* your money?" said Herb, incredulous.

"She said she inherited two million bucks so she could pay me back. But she kept borrowing and borrowing, getting me to pay all her medical and legal bills, her flights to Key Biscayne to go to probate court, her stays at hotels. You name it, she borrowed money for it. Whenever I asked her to pay me back, she came up with an excuse. The usual one, actually, that her inheritance was locked in probate."

Herb swigged his beer. "What am I gonna do? Look at me."

He was wearing an olive drab T-shirt with short sleeves, the track marks clearly visible like tiny craters in his arms. He was so far gone he could care less if anybody saw the scars.

"I'm not the guy to go to for financial advice," said Grant, and laughed at the thought.

"I promise I'll pay you back."

"You and Sherry."

"But she's not blood. We're blood. Can't you sue her?"

Grant took another pull on his beer. "The bankruptcy trustee said she has her lawyer working on that."

"Good."

"Her lawyer's been working on the case for two years and hasn't recovered a dime. He makes my cousin Vinny look like Clarence Darrow."

"Do we have a cousin Vinny?" said Herb, bemused.

"I meant the movie."

Herb smiled. "Oh yeah. Funny movie. Joe Pesci, right?"

"Yeah."

"Fire him and hire someone else."

"He's the trustee lawyer. He doesn't work for me. I can't fire him."

"Doesn't he at least give you or your lawyer updates about what he's doing on the case?"

"He never contacts me or my lawyer. I'm out of the loop even though it's my money that's at stake. He speaks only to the trustee."

"How does your bankruptcy case ever get closed?"

"When Vinny sends his bill for two years' worth of work to the trustee, I guess."

"I don't see how you get back any of the money you lent Sherry."

"I don't either."

"What's to prevent this farce going on for three or even four more years without anything being accomplished?"

"Nothing. It's how the law works. Lawyers take as long as possible to inflate their bills."

"And the trustee's OK with that?" said Herb, bewildered.

"She's part of the corrupt system. Cousin Vinny knows Uncle Sam has deep pockets and will pony up when billed. Why should the trustee care? It's not her money."

Herb threw up his hands, forgetting he was holding the Stella and spilling some of it before he realized what he was doing and put down his arms.

"It's a racket like everything else," he said, grimacing.

Grant didn't argue the point. He doubted he would recover any money from either the bankruptcy trustee lawyer or from anyone else involved in Sherry's scam.

Chapter 15

Grant heaved a sigh of frustration. "We're on our own. I gotta write and sell more books. I don't know what you're gonna do."

"I can't face getting another job," said Herb. "I don't like to work. Work is too difficult. Being alive is bad enough with all the shit that happens. You add work, and I don't see how people handle it. How do they do it?" said Herb, his visage earnest.

"They do it to survive. It's not like it's a choice."

"I'm out of it. I'm not gonna kill myself with work. I once had a job as a bus driver. It scared the hell out of me. I was certain that one day driving that big bus every day in the heavy LA traffic I would run over somebody or crash into another vehicle and kill the occupants. Or maybe one of my passengers, some gangbanger or drunken bum, would hold a gun to my head and pull the trigger."

"At least you could pay your rent."

"I went to four years of college to get a job as a bus driver? It makes no sense. I thought a college education was supposed to open doors to a high-paying job. They ought to hang the guy that said that."

Grant didn't want to think about it. He believed in a college education, but he hadn't gotten a high-paying job as a result of his BA degree. He could have made more money bagging groceries than he made from book royalties.

"At least you're educated so you can read your eviction notice," he said. *As I can mine.*

"How did we end up being misfits? Do you want to be a misfit?"

"Do we get a choice?"

Herb nodded. "Good point. Do we have any control over our lives? So how about it? Can you help me?"

"No."

"Thanks for nothing." Herb paused. "You think Sherry would help me?"

58

Grant laughed. He couldn't help it. The idea of Sherry lending money to anyone was ludicrous. Of course, if it was *his* money, she might. But he was sure she had spent all of his money, and now that the well had gone dry she couldn't count on him to pay her bills.

"What's so funny?" said Herb, offended.

Grant became serious. "She keeps calling me, trying to borrow more money from me."

"This is hell. What am I supposed to do? I need a fix."

"Maybe you could catch the psycho who murdered that guy at the horror movie. There might be a reward out for the killer."

"Yeah, sure."

"Why not? You used to be a PI."

"Not anymore. My body's falling apart. I can barely haul myself out of bed every morning."

"I'm serious."

"So am I."

Herb tossed down his beer and flipped the empty can toward the wastebasket in the kitchen. The can bounced off the wastebasket and clattered on the linoleum floor.

"Another talent I don't have," he said, shrugging at the can that lay on the floor. "Not gonna make it as a Laker."

"Self-pity gets you nowhere."

"Where am I supposed to be getting?"

"The coffin if you keep shooting up."

"I'm going back to my girlfriend's apartment," said Herb, making for the door. "You don't know nothing."

His hand on the doorknob, he halted. "You know where I can score some cheap fentanyl?"

"I hear that stuff kills you."

"Exactly."

"Don't you understand what I'm saying?"

"I don't want to understand what you're saying."

"Whatever floats your boat."

"I dare you to kill me."

"What?" said Grant, dumbfounded, not sure he had heard Herb correctly.

"Remember when we were kids we were always daring each other to do something?"

59

"We're not kids anymore."

"Are you scared to take my dare?"

"You need help, Herb."

"When I dared you to jump off a sand dune at the beach, you did it."

"And it knocked the wind out of me. I thought I broke my neck."

"But you did it. That's my point. You weren't a scaredy cat back then."

"Daring me to kill you is a whole different ballgame. Murder is against the law."

Herb licked his sweaty lips. "When we were in high school I dared you to steal a six-pack of beer from a liquor store, and you did it. It was illegal, but you still did it. And then you dared me to steal a bottle of Scotch, and I did it."

"Those were kid games. We're adults now. You don't really expect me to kill you, do you?"

"This is the first time you ever chickened out of a dare."

"If this is a joke, it's not funny."

"No joke. My life's a mess. It's not gonna improve."

"I'm not a murderer," said Grant, feeling strange when he said it. Why would Herb think he was? "Forget it."

"I can't believe you're backing down from a dare. What happened to you?"

"Life happened to me. Let's look at this logically."

"What do you mean?" said Herb, quirking an eyebrow.

"If I kill you, how can you fulfil my dare to you to kill me?"

"You know that's not the way this thing works. I made the first dare. You have to take it or you're chicken."

"I don't care. I'm daring *you* to kill *me*."

"That's not fair," said Herb, teed off. "I made the first dare. You can't dare me unless you take up my dare first."

"Life isn't fair."

Herb shook with laughter.

"What's so funny?" said Grant.

"You may change your mind about taking my dare."

"Why would I do that?"

"Because your life could take a turn for the worse. A lot worse."

"It can't get much worse than it is now," said Grant, uncertain what Herb was talking about.

"That's what you think. I'm in town, and when I'm in town, things go south fast. You really don't want me around. It's a miracle I'm still alive with my bad luck."

"Let's drop this nonsense. We're adults. We gotta solve our own problems."

"The dare still stands," said Herb, dead serious, scratching one of the unsightly track marks on his arm and departing.

Grant closed the door behind Herb.

Even though Herb was his brother, the guy remained a cypher to him.

Grant couldn't believe they had both gone their separate ways in life and ended up in the same place—the hell of destitution and despair. Did they share some weird, self-destructive gene?

Grant felt reality closing in on him like a coffin.

Chapter 16

Kudlow sat in the hot seat on a TV stage for an interview with Riley Coogan, who had a reputation as a hardheaded, take-no-prisoners griller. The bright Fresnel spotlight burned Kudlow's face. He felt like a squirming bug being skewered by the focused sun rays of a magnifying glass. He was glad he had his shades on to prevent the glare of the spotlight from blinding him.

He hated being on the other side of the camera. He was a director, not an actor. Then again, like Shakespeare said, all the world's a stage.

At least he didn't have to wear a suit. Instead, he was wearing his unbuttoned safari jacket over a white T. Towers thought it made him look more like a film director and was all for it.

Clad in a charcoal grey suit with a black silk moiré tie, the fortyish Coogan sat opposite Kudlow on stage. Swarthy-complected, Coogan had short black hair and brown eyes. His bent nose gave him a pugnacious demeanor.

Knowing Coogan liked to butter up his interview subjects before going in for the kill, Kudlow expected softballs at the beginning of the interview.

"Norman Kudlow, you have the reputation of being the best director in Hollywood today," said Coogan. "Like Hitchcock, not only are your movies good, they make money."

"We call them films, not movies," said Kudlow.

"Pardon me. Whatever you call them, they are considered motion picture masterpieces."

"Not everyone would agree with you, but thank you."

"Your future in Hollywood looks bright."

"Hollywood is a fickle bitch. Time will tell."

"Except your newest mov—uh, film, I mean. Critics are calling it a blueprint to commit murder."

"That's ridiculous," said Kudlow, starting to sweat even though he had expected Coogan to broach the subject.

"They say it can cause people watching it to commit murder."

"Art doesn't make people kill each other. And film is art."

"Can you prove this?"

"Look, Aristotle called violence in drama a catharsis. It gets the violence out of the audience's system. It doesn't motivate them to commit murder."

"Then why has your movie triggered two murders?"

"The movie didn't incite the murderer to kill. The murderer was going to kill whether he watched the movie or not."

"But there have been *two* killings at the showings of your movie. There could be two murderers out there, both triggered by your movie."

Kudlow was glad he had worn a jacket so the TV audience couldn't see the sweat pouring out of his armpits and soaking his T.

"I doubt it," said Kudlow. "It must be the same psychopath committing the murders."

"How do you know that? The police haven't said there's only one killer on the loose."

"Art does not incite people to kill. The murderer is a lone serial killer."

"Have you told this to the police?"

Kudlow shifted uncomfortably in his seat. "I don't tell the police their business, and I would hope they don't tell me mine."

"You mean, you don't want them to tell you not to make another horror movie."

"You heard what I said."

"You can't deny your movie glorifies murder."

"Of course, I can deny it. How does it glorify murder?"

"The movie's heroine kills multiple people and never is punished. Isn't that a way of glorifying murder? By saying she can get away with murder?"

Kudlow's face expressed displeasure. "You're spoiling the film for people who haven't seen it yet."

"I want to know how you defend your movie, which many claim is amoral," said Coogan, leaning toward Kudlow and pressing forward with his line of attack.

"Didn't you see the film? The heroine is possessed by a demon. I don't want to go into the details. You're ruining the movie for people who haven't seen it yet by giving away too much about it."

63

"I'm simply repeating what critics are saying of your movie."

"Fuck critics," said Kudlow, flinging out his arm in a dismissive gesture.

"And what about poor Nicholas Briscoe, the man who was murdered while watching your movie?"

Kudlow regained his equanimity. "Naturally, I'm sorry for his relatives' loss."

"Did you know his parents are considering suing you for inciting his murder."

Kudlow sat nonplussed.

"Well?" prodded Coogan.

"This is the first I've heard of it."

"Is that all you have to say about it?"

"Every filmmaker in the world is gonna get sued if they have a murder at the showing of one of their movies. Does that make sense?"

"You'd have to ask Nicholas's grieving parents."

Kudlow said nothing, refusing to allow Coogan to bait him.

Crossing his legs, Coogan kept his counsel, waiting for a response from Kudlow.

"Do you believe your movie is cursed?" said Coogan at last, realizing Kudlow wasn't going to respond to Coogan's previous line of attack.

"Of course not. I don't believe in curses."

"You believe in demons but not in curses?"

"Who said I believe in demons? I made a film about one. I made the film to scare people. Not for any other purpose."

"You're not afraid people will die because they watched your movie?"

"That's absurd."

"Not everyone thinks like you."

"Good. People should be free to think whatever they want."

"Are you worried theater owners are gonna yank your movie from their theaters because it's inciting violence?"

Kudlow felt resentment smoldering inside him. "My film doesn't incite violence. It incites fear. It's a horror movie. It scares people. It entertains them. It doesn't inflame them and make them want to kill."

64

"Still, you can't deny there are people who would like to have your movie pulled from theaters in order to protect the public."

"That's censorship. This is a free country. We have freedom of speech here."

"You're not free to incite riots. That's illegal."

"My film *isn't* inciting riots."

"Au contraire. It's ginning up protests all across the country."

"The people organizing those protests are under the delusion that viewing films can incite violence."

Somebody in the audience flung a half-full plastic water bottle at Kudlow.

Kudlow ducked the projectile, his heartbeat picking up speed, adrenaline coursing through his body. He debated whether to take cover. The problem was there was nowhere to hide on the stage, not even a desk. Only two occupied chairs furnished the stage.

A phalanx of armed security guards quickly cordoned it off.

"Cut," cried the TV director in the studio.

A voice on the loudspeaker instructed the audience to leave the building.

"Lock him up," cried one of the spectators, a middle-aged woman wearing a ball cap and pumping her fist.

Kudlow figured the woman meant him, not the idiot who had flung the water bottle at the stage. Anticipating another missile being hurled in his direction, Kudlow sprang off the stage out of the line of fire and didn't mingle with the audience as it filed out of the television studio, carping about being removed. Instead Kudlow exited backstage.

Chapter 17

Grant had never turned down a dare from his brother Herb until now. But what did the guy expect? He had asked Grant to murder him.

Herb had dared Grant to commit crimes before but nothing remotely like murder. A little harmless shoplifting here and there was about the extent of it.

Grant didn't want to be known as a coward for not taking Herb's dare, but what had possessed the guy to ask him to kill him? The smack Herb was shooting up must be filling his brain with holes like a chunk of coral.

They both had managed to land on the wrong side of the American dream via different paths, but, unlike Herb, Grant wasn't contemplating suicide (not yet anyway), which was what Herb was in effect doing by daring Grant to kill him. Grant believed the best people, the ones brutalized by the world, were strongest in their broken places. He wasn't going to allow a scam artist like Sherry drive him to suicide. She wasn't worth it. Bankrupted and broken, he would go on.

He knew his prospects were as bleak as Herb's, but Grant didn't believe in giving up. However, he wasn't optimistic. His writing career had stalled out and wasn't going anywhere. He would be a deluded fool to claim otherwise. He went to movies to escape the oppressive reality of his life. Why couldn't Herb find a legal means of escape instead of turning to narcotics like skag?

Far be it from him to give advice to people on how to live their lives. What a joke. His own life . . . ugh, he didn't want to think about the debacle. His mess of a life was what someone would get for following his advice. When it came to doling out advice, he kept his mouth shut.

Leave it to Herb to ruin his day. Now Grant felt bad about refusing to take Herb's dare—even if it was outrageous. His refusal was a first for Grant, and he didn't like it. He felt like a coward.

He popped another cold Stella.

He had to stop drinking. He was having too many blackouts. There were gaps in his memory that he couldn't account for. They seemed to happen when he went to the movies, but maybe that was because he was so caught up in the movie that he lost track of everything else around him. Of course, that must be it. A good movie could do that for you—help you escape into another world so you forgot all your problems.

Which was why he kept returning to *Necromaniac*. It was a great horror film. Terrifying and insightful. It sucked you into its horrific world and wouldn't let you escape till it was over and the final credits rolled down the screen.

He thought it odd that he had viewed the movie at the same two theaters where murders had occurred in the audience. What were the chances of that happening? Not good—unless the killer was following him around. Killer or killers. It might be two different people. The cops weren't talking, so it was impossible to know if there was more than one murderer. They hadn't given out to the media what the victims had died from. They said only that the victims had been murdered. No mention of the murder weapon.

Was the killer following him to the movie? The idea of a homicidal maniac stalking him sent a chill down his spine. Why would a psycho stalk him of all people?

Three knocks on his door startled him.

He opened the door.

Clad in her motorcycle leathers, Mandy stood in the hallway.

"We have some unfinished business to tend to," she said.

Was Mandy following him to the movies, setting him up, and blackmailing him?

He let her in, because he didn't want neighbors to overhear their conversation.

She cut to the chase. "Do you have the five grand?"

"You said you only wanted a thousand yesterday."

"I talked to my boyfriend, the guy in the Mongol gang. Remember him?"

"So?"

"He said I should get five large from you."

"You're not getting either sum."

67

"Do you want my boyfriend to come here and convince you to change your mind?" said Mandy, frowning. "He's very persuasive."

"I don't have that kind of money."

"I googled your name. You're a famous writer."

"Ha," scoffed Grant. "Not according to my royalty statements."

"The Internet says you won a bunch of writing awards. You can't fool me."

"Nobody cares about those awards. People who buy books don't, anyway. Why should I pay you a plugged nickel in the first place?"

"Because I saw you in the theater where the murder happened."

"So what? You were there too. Maybe you're the one who killed the guy."

"Are you crazy? You're the one who writes sleazy horror books, not me. You're the one who's a killer."

"That's defamation. I could sue you."

"Remember? I was at the theater. I saw you sitting near the murder victim."

Seeing red, Grant paced around the living room. "It means nothing."

"You can tell it to the cops after I report you," said Mandy, making for the front door.

"Just because I write about killers doesn't mean I *am* one."

"I don't want to listen to your tricky words. I know what I saw."

"You didn't see me kill anyone."

"I saw you sitting next to the victim. That's good enough for the cops to investigate you. And . . ."

"And what?"

"And I saw you at the other theater where the second murder took place."

Grant felt his heartbeat hammer full bore. "Bullshit."

Mandy nodded. "You were there."

"You're lying through your teeth. Which row was I sitting in?"

"I couldn't tell in the dark. Rows are badly numbered in a lot of theaters. It's hard to tell which row you're in even when the light's on."

"Shaking down someone is illegal. You can't get away with this."

"If you try making trouble, I'm calling my boyfriend," said Mandy, whipping her cell phone out of her purse like it was a gun.

"You need to leave."

"Or what? Are you gonna kill me too?"

"I don't have to listen to your lies. How do I know your boyfriend didn't kill those two people and set me up?"

"Now who's talking bullshit? That's the dumbest thing I ever heard."

"No dumber than saying *I* killed those two people."

"How soon can you get the money?"

"I can't get any money. I'm bankrupt."

Mandy searched his face. "You're just saying that so you don't have to pay me."

"Even if I had the money, I wouldn't pay you. I have nothing to hide. You can't blackmail someone with nothing to hide. This must be your first shakedown. Anyway, I don't pay blackmailers."

"You're not thinking clearly. Just getting accused of murder could hurt your career as a writer. Even without a conviction."

"What career? Nobody's heard of me."

"You can't fool me. Your books are on Amazon."

"Did you look at their sales rank?"

"I've had it up to here with your arguing." She fiddled with her cell phone, thinking about placing a call.

"I'll clue you in. My e-books are ranked at around five million. My paperbacks are at twelve million."

"I don't know what you're talking about, and I don't care."

"I'm talking about ranking books by their sales. James Patterson is ranked number one because he has humongous sales of his books. My book sales are so few that my books rank in the basement. I'm in five millionth place. Or ten millionth place. Something like that."

"I'm not listening to your doubletalk. I'll give you one more day, because I'm a nice person."

"Nice person?" said Grant, shaking his head in disbelief. "A nice person doesn't go around blackmailing people."

"I *am* nice. I was brought up in a good family. But my daddy always told me to never look a gift horse in the mouth."

"I hate to disabuse you, but I'm not a gift horse."

"No more of your tricky words. This conversation is over. I'll come back tomorrow for my money, and you better have it or you're gonna regret it."

The more Grant thought about this shakedown, the more suspicious he became of Mandy.

"Why don't you admit it?" he said. "This was a setup from the get-go. You framed me for the murders of those people in the theaters."

"Oh, no you don't. You're not blaming your mess on me."

"You followed me to the theaters, didn't you?"

"Forget it. You're not wiggling out of this one. We both know who killed those two people."

Grant stared at her. "How long have you been stalking me?"

"Give me a break. You're a psycho killer."

Mandy flung open the door to leave.

"If you tell the cops you were at the two theaters when the murders occurred, you're gonna implicate yourself in the murders," said Grant.

Mandy lowered her voice. "I could tell them anonymously."

"They won't believe you if you don't identify yourself."

"I'll cross that bridge when I get to it. You concentrate on getting the money."

Mandy stalked out the door and down the hallway, her sleek leather outfit shining under the overhead track lights.

Grant ducked back into his room and slammed the door.

If she was indeed the psycho killer, maybe he could set a trap for her.

Chapter 18

Grant strained his memory, trying to recall seeing Mandy at the theater of the first murder and, for that matter, at the theater of the second.

He didn't remember seeing her at either. Of course, he was finding out his memory was spotty at best. It retained next to nothing. Was he losing his mind? When you lost your memory, were you on the road to losing your sanity?

You would think he would recall seeing Mandy because of her striking leather outfits. Not many women went around dressed in black leather togs. How could he not remember seeing her? Maybe because he never saw her, or because she wasn't at either of the theaters.

She had to have been at the first theater. She had said she had seen him sitting near the murder victim. There was no way she could know that unless she was there.

He frowned. He couldn't recall ever seeing her until she had appeared at his door yesterday, attempting to shake him down.

Maybe she had entered the theater after the lights had turned off. Which would explain why he had never seen her. But how could she have seen him in the pitch-dark theater? It didn't jibe.

Maybe she had been sitting in the theater before he had arrived, which explained why he hadn't noticed her. That explanation made more sense than any other. But why hadn't he noticed her with her leather outfit? Maybe she had been sitting behind somebody so he hadn't been able to see her.

He couldn't remember leaving the theater. The demonic horror movie had had a profound effect on him, blotting out everything else in his mind.

Somebody knocked on the door, breaking his chain of thought.

Annoyed, Grant strode to the door and yanked it open.

A black FedEx guy wearing Oakley shades, a purple polo shirt, and navy blue bicycle pants stood in the hall with a package in his hand. Dreadlocks hung down his broad shoulders.

"I got a package for Grant Osborne," he said.

Grant wasn't expecting a package. "Hi. Do I need to sign for it?"

"Sign with your finger," said the deliverer, handing him a portable scanner with a screen on it.

The deliverer handed Grant the shoebox-sized package and booked.

Puzzled, Grant closed the door and inspected the package. The return address was that of a private mailbox rental shop and didn't have a name accompanying it.

He tore open the pasteboard box and started.

A jack-in-the-box sprang out at him, its face streaked with blood. The clown face laughed at him as it wobbled back and forth on its spring.

Overcoming his shock Grant noticed a card tucked in the box. He plucked out the card and read it.

Do you accept my dare yet? I know you can do it.

Herb wasn't going to let him forget the dare. The guy wanted to die in a bad way.

Grant didn't want to get involved in Herb's sick game. Disgusted, he tossed the jack-in-the-box and its package across the room.

As the package struck the carpet, another card fell out. Grant picked it up and read it.

I saw what you did.

Grant squinted at the card, bemused. Saw what? Who cared? Herb was trying to fuck with his mind because Grant had refused to accept the junkie's dare. The H must be rotting Herb's brain, bumming him out so he wished he was dead. Grant wasn't going to get involved in Herb's suicide wish.

I saw what you did. What did it mean? Nothing. They were the words of a junkie on dope.

Grant wondered if madness ran in their family. His mother and father were both dead. Neither of them had died in insane asylums, though that didn't necessarily mean they weren't crazy. It just meant they had not been diagnosed as crazy.

He sorted through the mail on his round pressboard coffee table. He opened yet another certified letter from the IRS demanding payment for what he owed them or they would put a lien on his property, including his bank account. If they followed through with their threat, the landlord of his apartment would evict him for not paying his rent.

He flung the letter on the coffee table with dismay.

He hadn't heard from his bankruptcy lawyer in months. He produced his cell phone and called her.

"Hi, this is Grant Osborne. Do you have any updates on my case?"

"It's not that I'm ignoring you, Grant," said Becky Ludovici, his thirty-four-year-old bankruptcy lawyer. "I just don't have any news for you."

"It's been well over a year, and the trustee lawyer hasn't sued my ex-girlfriend or her sister. At least, nobody has told me he has sued anyone."

"As far as I know, he hasn't filed suit against anyone yet."

"Isn't he supposed to let us know if he sues anyone?"

"He should."

"Doesn't he need to keep us updated?"

"No."

"I don't understand why it's taking him so long to do anything."

"He thinks you were the victim of a romance scam."

"Sherry's definitely a scammer. Telling me she inherited two million bucks so she could pay me back the money she borrowed proves it. If she hadn't told me about the inheritance, I would have stopped lending her money long ago. What else did he say?"

"He hasn't told me anything else. If he does, I'll let you know."

Grant felt anger building inside him, raging at his powerlessness to get Sherry to pay him back any of the money he had lent her.

"Doesn't he have to do something in a certain time frame?" he said, champing at the bit.

"There's no time frame."

Grant kicked the coffee table in an access of wrath.

"At some point doesn't he have to shit or get off the fucking pot?" he exploded.

"Don't raise your voice at me."

73

"I'm just trying to understand why this is taking so long," said Grant, struggling to control his fury, feeling sorry for taking it out on Becky, who had helped him file for Chapter 7.

"The trustee works for the government. She hired the lawyer. He works for her. He doesn't work for you."

"Doesn't she care that her lawyer has done nothing for over a year?"

"What's the rush?"

"I'm running out of money to pay my rent. I also owe a lot of taxes."

"Do you want me to abandon your interest in the case? Then the trustee would close your claim to any money."

"No. Of course not. I want the swindler to pay me back."

"Then we'll have to wait for the trustee lawyer to decide who to sue."

"How many years does that take?"

"As long as he needs."

"Isn't there a statute of limitations on this?"

"The federal government is in charge of the bankruptcy case. They can take as long as they want."

"Isn't the trustee suspicious of her lawyer for taking so long to try and recover the lost money?"

"I'm not privy to their conversations. They have lawyer-client privilege. As soon as something happens, I'll let you know."

She hung up.

In frustration he kicked the coffee table again. He needed a car. This was LA. You needed a car to live here. He had sold his car to loan the money to the grifter Sherry for her probate lawyers. For all he knew, she could have pocketed the money for herself instead, which seemed more likely at this point. The double-dealing parasite had told him so many lies he couldn't tell where the truth ended and the lies began.

This was what he got for feeling sorry for her and trying to help her out. No good deed goes unpunished. He had to admit it wasn't all altruism. They had made the beast with two backs many times.

But he hated the idea of being used by her and conned by her phalanx of falsehoods.

74

The hell with her. He wasn't going to do her the favor of thinking about her.

And the hell with the law.

How could anyone take the law seriously? It was a sick joke. What ridiculous sums of money was the trustee lawyer raking in as he took over a year to do squat? *Jurisprudence*. They should call it *juris stupidity* or *juris cupidity*.

Maybe he should try to write something. Why? Did his writing make even the slightest difference in the scheme of things? Plus nobody would read it anyway. His sales were microscopic.

Or how about going to a horror movie? The horror movie everybody was talking about.

Chapter 19

Kudlow sat next to Towers in the backseat of their limo. Kudlow used a handkerchief to wipe the lenses of his sunglasses that he held in his hands.

"We need to find the killer," said Towers.

"What?" said Kudlow, ceasing polishing his sunglasses.

What Towers was suggesting was ludicrous, even for Towers, who had a habit of hyperbole, which went with the territory of movie flack. Kudlow figured he must have wax in his ears. He must have misheard what Towers had said. Even Towers wouldn't—

"We need to find the killer and take him to a psychiatrist to prove your movie didn't make him kill," said Towers.

"Ha. Piece of cake. Like we're cops or something."

"What choice do we have? Right now ticket sales are through the roof, but that could change on a dime if too many murders at the movie manage to scare people out of going to it."

"I'm a filmmaker, not a detective. I know nothing about finding killers."

"Why not? You've done plenty of movies about killers."

"I don't want to meet up with this psycho. Let the cops do their job."

"Cops. They're getting nowhere. The killer's still at large."

"For all we know there could be two killers. We can't be sure it was the same homicidal maniac who struck at both theaters showing my film."

Towers shifted in his seat, worry on his face. "I hope you're wrong about that. Having two killers out there makes it look like your movie is brainwashing viewers into killing. I'm voting for a single serial killer."

Kudlow put on his sunglasses and slammed his seat with his fist. "Movies don't incite people to kill." He thought about it. "If there are two killers loose, one of them is a copycat."

"It would help if the cops would tell the public how these victims died. What was the murder weapon? If they were killed with different weapons, it would indicate more than one murderer."

"The last I heard they were still notifying the next of kin of the latest victim."

Towers poured himself a drink from the minibar mounted on the back of the driver's seat.

"You got a mind like a steel trap, Norman," he said. "I bet you can find this psycho killer no sweat."

Kudlow stared at Towers. "You gotta be kidding."

"Whaddaya mean? You got killers in all your movies. You know how they think. I'm sure you could find this maniac. He's fucking over your movie for Chrissake. Don't you want to put him out of business?"

"I thought you were cheering him on at first, because ticket sales are booming on account of him."

"*At first.* But too many of these murders could turn the tide against us. Sales could plummet if customers really believe they could be killed at a theater showing your movie."

"If you're serious about catching this nut, why don't you hire a PI?"

Drink in hand, Towers faced Kudlow. "I've seen your movies. You think like a killer. It's the only way you could create such believable horror movies. Don't sell yourself short. You can find this nutbag."

"I don't want to find him. I don't want him anywhere near me."

The limo pulled to a halt at a red light.

A thirtysomething woman with braided blonde hair wrapped around her skull was standing on the sidewalk, wearing pink spandex leggings and canary yellow Hoka sneakers, staring at Kudlow, a pink dumbbell in her hand. She saw him, glowered, and flung the dumbbell at his window. Covering his face with his hands, Kudlow pulled away from the limo window as it shattered. Fragments of glass showered on Kudlow's lap and the backseat.

"What the hell's wrong with people these days?" said Towers, taken aback. "Are you OK, Norm?"

Kudlow hated it when people called him Norm. Norman was fine or just Kudlow. But Norm, no thanks. It sounded like he was

77

bosom buddies with the speaker, in this case Towers. Kudlow didn't have any bosom buddies, certainly not Towers, His Royal Highness of Hyperbole. Kudlow never believed a word Towers said.

"I think so," said Kudlow, brushing shards of glass from his arms and lap, his face ashen.

Snarling, the blonde rushed toward the limo.

"Murderer," she screamed at Kudlow.

"Get us out of here," Towers cried at the driver, hammering the back of the driver's seat with his fist.

The limo screeched away.

Kudlow examined the jagged teeth of glass that jutted out of the steel windowsill as wind buffeted his face.

"We need bulletproof glass in this thing," he said.

"Don't worry about it," said Towers. "Most people love your movie." Grinning, he shook Kudlow's arm. "We're raking it in."

"As long as that psycho killer doesn't strike again."

"I'm telling you it would be great PR if you, the director of this top-notch movie, could find this nut and make a citizen's arrest. Moviegoers would love it."

Kudlow stared out the broken window, his face expressionless.

He hated the PR side of the film business with all its bloated hype.

Chapter 20

Grant turned on the TV in his apartment to hear the latest news about the movie maniac murderer.

A blonde newscaster in her thirties was announcing the news.

"There's a ghoulish game going on in Vegas these days," she said. "Gamblers are betting which LA movie theater the killer will strike at next. The theater nearest the last murder site is getting the best odds at two to one. In Los Angeles the mayor is considering banning the showing of *Necromaniac* in LA, calling it a threat to public safety. She has appointed a Committee on Public Safety to debate the issue and give her its conclusion before she takes any action. Up in arms, Hollywood honchos are screaming censorship and claim they will take her to court if she tries to ban *Necromaniac* from local theaters.

"Police have identified the murder victims at the two theaters as Nicholas Briscoe and Cindi Pataki—"

Three hard knocks on his door startled Grant.

He strode across the room to see who it was.

A fortyish black man in an undertaker's suit stood in the hallway. His black blazer hung open, revealing a pistol holstered on his waist. His hair cropped so tight it looked painted on, he wore a turquoise bolo tie and round wire-rim spectacles.

"Yeah?" said Grant.

"Are you Grant Osborne?" said the guy, his face impassive.

"Who wants to know?" said Grant, suspicious.

Any guy who appeared at his door with a gun on his hip warranted suspicion as far as Grant was concerned even if he *was* dressed in a suit.

"Martin Truex. I work for the Internal Revenue Service."

Grant gulped. He didn't know what to say. He didn't want any trouble with the IRS. He knew they would pay him a visit sooner or later for failing to pay his taxes.

"May I come in?" said Truex.

79

"Uh—yeah," said Grant, backing away from the open door and allowing Truex to enter.

"Am I interrupting something?" said Truex, looking around the apartment.

"No."

Truex nodded.

"Would you like a drink of water?" said Grant.

Truex shook his head no. "This won't take long."

"Fine," said Grant, though he didn't mean it. He wanted Truex gone.

Grant's heartbeat was off the charts. He knew the IRS was bad news, especially when you owed them money.

"May I use your bathroom first?" said Truex.

"Sure. It's over there."

"Thank you."

Truex disappeared for a few minutes then returned.

"Your mirror is dirty by the way," he said, staring hard at Grant.

"I wasn't expecting company."

"You weren't expecting me?"

"Of course not."

What kind of guest would tell the host his mirror was dirty? Maybe Truex was trying to knock him off balance with the offhanded non sequitur.

"Let's get down to business," said Truex. "You owe ten thousand dollars to the IRS which you have made no attempt to pay."

"Because I don't have it."

"That's no excuse."

"My ex-girlfriend swindled me out of my life savings and left me bankrupt. She borrowed seven hundred thousand dollars from me and never paid me back even though she claimed she inherited two million dollars from her uncle."

"Regardless, you owe the IRS ten thousand dollars," said Truex, his expression stony. "Your situation is serious."

"I can't pay you what I don't have. My debts were discharged by the trustee and the judge after I filed for Chapter 7."

Truex shook his head. "Your bankruptcy has no effect on your taxes. You still owe the IRS ten thousand dollars."

"It's not my fault she swindled me. *She* should pay you the money."

"It doesn't work that way. You're the one who owes the money. You're the one who has to pay. If you don't pay up, you will face punishment."

"I don't have it," said Grant, beads of sweat popping on his face.

"We have the power to levy your bank account and all of your royalties."

"What exactly does that mean?" said Grant, squinting, stalling for time.

"It means, we can take all of the money in your bank account, including your royalties."

"How am I supposed to pay for food and rent?"

"Your taxes were due over a year ago. We have given you plenty of time to pay, and you haven't paid anything."

"Because I can't afford to."

"If you don't have enough money in your bank account, you will face a jail term."

"This is ridiculous. Threatening me won't make ten thousand bucks magically appear in my hands."

"This is no joke. We can and will put you in jail for tax evasion."

His game face on, Truex retreated to the door.

"You have been warned," he said, and left.

Grant couldn't take it anymore. His life was unbearable. He needed to escape it by watching a horror movie. *Necromaniac* never failed to draw him out of his miserable life into the terrifying world of demonic possession. He needed to see the movie again.

He went to the bathroom to comb his hair and stood dumbstruck in front of the mirror over the sink.

There was writing in white block letters on the mirror.

Time to Kill

It looked like it was written with a bar of soap.

Who would write such a message? Had Truex done it? He had used the bathroom. He had also said the mirror was dirty, which would explain why he had said it was dirty. It could have been his way of getting Grant to inspect the mirror and see what Truex had written on it.

81

Had Herb used the bathroom? Grant couldn't remember. Herb could have written the message. Or what about Mandy? Had she written it? What did it mean? Was it part of the frame? She was bound and determined to frame him for the movie murders. Could one of them be the movie maniac murderer trying to make it look like he was?

The sentence on the mirror could have different meanings. It could mean, it was time to commit murder. Or it could mean, there was time to waste.

Grant tried to remember who had been in his bathroom.

His memory was so shoddy he couldn't recall much of anything.

He wasn't going to let it freak him out. He was going to the movie no matter what.

He washed the words off the mirror, combed his hair, and left his apartment.

Chapter 21

Grant strode to the nearest bus stop and waited for the next bus. He really needed a car. But just because you needed something didn't mean you would ever get it. He should be writing another book. Who knew? Maybe his next book would sell thousands of copies. In his dreams. In any case, he needed money, and writing thrillers and horror novels was his only way to get any, no matter how puny the royalties.

Sitting on the blue steel bench at the bus stop, Grant checked out passing cars, wondering if Herb was following him. Herb just happened to be in town when the movie maniac murderer had taken his first victim. What were the chances?

Grant figured maybe Herb had followed him to the horror movie and killed the roly-poly guy named Briscoe who had been munching popcorn.

Grant hadn't noticed anyone hanging a tail on him when he had gone to the theater to see *Necromaniac* the first time, but he hadn't been checking for a tail either. Also, Herb used to be a PI. He would know how to hang a tail on a guy and not be seen.

Grant had had no reason to suspect anyone was following him.

Now he had a reason. Both of the theaters where he had seen *Necromaniac* had had murders take place inside them while he was watching the movie.

He scoped out the sidewalk. He didn't see Truex spying on him. No sign of Mandy either. But Mandy could have sent her Mongol boyfriend to hang a tail on him. Grant eyed a motorcycle thunder past him, its hefty rider wearing a helmet that looked like a vintage Nazi M40 helmet from World War II.

It didn't look like the motorcyclist was paying any attention to him. The guy was looking forward through tinted goggles.

The bus driver stopped in front of Grant and opened the door.

Grant climbed into the bus, paid the fee with a clump of quarters, and found a seat.

He was going to a cineplex where he hadn't seen the movie yet. He didn't want to have to deal with the looky-loos who were attending the theaters where the murders were committed. The looky-loos were just going there to get goose bumps from watching the movie in a theater that was also a murder site.

Grant didn't understand why anyone would want to frame him for the cineplex murders. The killer must want to blackmail him. But the stupid killer didn't realize Grant had no money. Blackmailing a pauper was a waste of time. Unless blackmail wasn't the motive. Maybe the killer had a different motive.

Or was it just bad luck that Grant had happened to be in the theaters when the killer struck? Grant didn't think so. If it had happened once, maybe it could be luck. But not twice. The killer had to be following him.

Even though Herb was a former PI, he was also a junkie. His tradecraft could have deteriorated as a result of his addiction, in which case Grant might be able to spot Herb following him.

Grant had never seen Mandy's Mongol boyfriend and would not be able to recognize the guy.

Grant could recognize Truex, but the IRS had probably trained Truex how to tail people.

What about Sherry? Grant wondered with a start. Did Sherry send someone after him to frame him out of revenge for his cutting off her money spigot?

A guy could go crazy thinking about all the people who might want to harm him—all the more reason for him to see a horror movie to get his mind off his paranoid thoughts.

Craning around he inspected the faces of the passengers on the bus. None of them looked familiar. There was no way one of them could be following him. They were already on the bus when he had boarded. How could any of them know in advance that he was going to board it? He himself had known only a few minutes before he had boarded.

None of them looked interested in him as he glanced at them. They were studying their cell phones or reading a book on their Kindles, dead to the world.

His knees bumped against the back of the seat in front of him. He straightened in his seat. He had to stop thinking.

The bus stopped and picked up two more passengers.

Grant watched them as they searched for seats.

Could one of them be tailing him? It was possible if they had seen him board the bus that they could have caught up to the bus and boarded it in order to keep tabs on him.

Breaking a sweat he didn't recognize either of them. But it didn't matter. They could be working for someone who had assigned them to tail him. One of them was a Hispanic guy in his twenties with a pencil-thin mustache. The other was a college-aged Asian girl with long, straight black hair that reached to the small of her back.

This was nuts, he told himself. He was turning into a full-blown paranoid schizophrenic, fearing everyone was tailing him.

He needed to relax.

He slumped in his seat and stared out the tinted window to his left. He couldn't see out of it very clearly because there was some kind of screen within it obscuring the view like gauze.

Maybe he should hire Herb to find out who was following him, except he didn't trust Herb. Grant laughed at the thought. What was he thinking? He couldn't afford to hire Herb or anyone else. If he was going to find the killer, he would have to do it on his own.

He wasn't sure he really wanted to know who the killer was. He just wanted the guy to leave him alone. No more messages on mirrors. What was the killer telling him anyway?

If the killer was a psycho like most people suspected he was, nothing he did made sense. A psycho lived in his own fantasy world of delusion and paranoia. His motives were obscure and made sense only to him.

Chapter 22

"Drop me off at this Burger King," said Kudlow, sitting with Towers in the backseat of Towers's limo and eying him through his shades.

Towers scoped out the Burger King outside his window with disappointment.

"Are you sure, Norm?"

"I arranged to meet a private detective here."

"Is he low-rent or something? You gotta shell out shekels if you want to hire a professional who gets results. PIs in this neck of the woods don't come cheap."

"This guy's discreet. He did a little acting for me for a while. He couldn't take the insecurity of the job and became a PI."

Towers nodded. "Discretion is important. We don't want anybody to know you're trying to find the killer in order to increase ticket sales of your movie. Bad PR. It makes you look like a moneygrubber." Towers chuckled. "Of course, we *are* moneygrubbers, but we don't want anybody to know it. It's called public relations."

Kudlow opened his door and got out as the limo halted in front of the restaurant.

"You don't need me, do you?" said Towers, eyeballing the Burger King with disdain.

"No," said Kudlow, shutting the limo door.

"Thank God."

The limo pulled into traffic.

Kudlow ordered a Double Whopper, fries, and a Coke. He sat at a table and waited for the PI to arrive. Meanwhile, he ate his burger.

Fifteen minutes later Herb Osborne sat opposite Kudlow with a tray bearing a Whopper, onion rings, and a root beer.

"Do you have an acting gig for me, Mr. Kudlow?" said Herb, his face brightening.

Kudlow grimaced at the miniature craters marring Herb's arms and began to think he had made a bad decision choosing Herb as his PI.

"No," said Kudlow. "I remembered you became a private detective after you quit acting. I need to hire you as a PI."

"Oh, yeah. You don't have an acting job for me? I'm good at horror movies. I could play a mean-looking zombie."

Herb stood up and started shambling around like a zombie.

"Sit down," said Kudlow.

"No problem," said Herb, taking his seat.

"I'm not making a film at this time. I need a PI."

"How much does it pay?" said Herb, and took a bite of his burger.

"Five hundred dollars a day plus expenses."

"I'm your man."

"You still are a PI, right?" said Kudlow, glancing askance at Herb's track marks.

"You better believe it. What's the gig?"

"I want you to find the nutbag that's killing people who watch my latest film."

"Oh, yeah. I hear it's a great movie."

"The psycho killer is giving my film a bad name. Critics are blaming it for turning its audience into murderers. These same critics want to ban my film because it endangers the public."

"You think they can censor your movie?" said Herb, concern on his face.

"I don't want to find out. If these murders continue, a ban is possible. The government could call my film a threat to public safety and step in to close theaters showing it."

"Sounds like Nazi Germany. Banning movies. Wow. What's this country coming to?"

"History teaches us that anything can happen. People are perpetually miserable and therefore they perpetually want change."

"Heavy stuff."

"You gotta find this psycho killer before the government decides it must act. What they plan to do depends on the citizens. And the citizens are gonna get restless if the psycho strikes again."

Herb lowered his voice. "What do you want me to do with him when I find him?"

"Turn him over to the cops."

"What if there's not enough evidence for the cops to press charges against him?"

"Does that kind of thing happen?"

"All the time. The cops have to follow the law. They need probable cause to bust someone."

"It's not good enough just to find the psycho killer. You need to put him out of commission. You can't let him commit any more murders."

"I get your drift."

"But the public has to know the killer won't strike again so they can go safely to the movies."

Herb pursed his lips. "I don't see how I'm supposed to do that. If the cops catch him, it will become public knowledge because of the media. If I take care of the psycho by myself, nobody will know but me and you."

Kudlow frowned in thought. "This is like rewriting a script." He paused. "I got an idea. After you catch the psycho and remove him, let me know and I'll send a letter to the *Times* supposedly from the killer announcing that he's gonna commit suicide."

"Are they gonna buy it?"

"If no more killings take place, they will, so you have to remove the psycho killer from circulation before I can write the letter."

Kudlow flicked a couple of fries into his mouth. He preferred McDonald's fries to Burger King's, but the burgers were better at Burger King. He wasn't a food snob. He liked both restaurants. When he was driving his Mercedes, he drove to both places frequently, and he noticed his wasn't the only Mercedes in the parking lots.

"I'll leave the letter writing up to you," said Herb.

"But you've got to prove to me you've put the killer out of action first."

"How am I supposed to do that?"

"Uh—send me a photo of him tied up."

"No problem," said Herb, munching his burger.

"You also need to show me evidence that he is indeed the psycho killer."

"Got it," said Herb, flashing Kudlow a thumbs up.

Watching Herb's scar-riddled arms Kudlow wondered if he was making a mistake by hiring him. The guy looked like a junkie. Either he was shooting up meth or smack. Kudlow hoped the guy was tripping on the former rather than the latter. Speed freaks could get things done. Like the king of detectives Sherlock Holmes, who had snorted blow. Junkies, forget about it.

"Are you sure you can handle this?" said Kudlow.

"Positive."

"We need it done ASAP."

"You got it."

"And not a word to anyone."

"You know me, Norman." Herb pinched his lips together with his finger and thumb. "Loose lips sink ships."

Kudlow was liking this arrangement less and less.

Herb finished his meal and held out his hand.

"I need a retainer fee to start work," he said, his face sweaty.

Riddled with misgivings, Kudlow withdrew his wallet from his trouser pocket and counted out five Ben Franklins for Herb. He hoped this wasn't going to end up biting him in the ass.

Chapter 23

Herb was scared shitless about this gig. He hadn't done any PI work for over ten years. Frankly, he couldn't remember the first thing about it. Never mind, he told himself. It would come back to him in no time. He would get the hang of it as soon as he started his investigation.

Making for his car he thought about buying skag first. He was feeling bummed out. He needed a fix more than anything. However, a fix might incapacitate him for his job. He supposed he could put off the fix for a while longer.

Kudlow wanted fast results. The guy could easily can him if Herb didn't make progress nailing the psycho killer haunting movie theaters.

Herb drove his beat-up vintage VW Bug to the theater where the first murder had occurred. He parked in a multilevel public parking garage and footed it to the theater.

He bought a ticket at the box office so nobody would hassle him about entering the theater lobby. Without a cop's badge he couldn't sashay into any place he wanted, no questions asked. No PI could. In any case, the truth was his private investigator license had expired years ago.

He approached the guy who looked like the head usher, a recently coiffed twentysomething guy who was standing on the crimson carpet, watching moviegoers trickle into the theater. Since it was a weekday, afternoon business was slow. The lobby smelled like buttered popcorn.

"Hello. The name's Herb. I'm a private investigator. Would you mind answering a couple questions for me."

"About what?"

"What's your name?"

"Ted."

"OK, Ted, I'm trying to find out about that murder that took place here at the showing of the horror movie *Necromaniac*."

"You and everybody else."

"What's that supposed to mean?"

"The cops were already here."

"Of course."

"Who are you working for?"

"I can't disclose that information. My clients value their privacy."

"I don't see how I can help."

"You'd be surprised. I'm gonna ask you some questions."

"OK. Shoot," said Ted, feeling important because he knew things about the murder that others didn't.

"Was there a lot of blood at the scene of the crime?"

"The seat was soaked. We had to reupholster it."

"Was it all over the carpet?"

Ted shrugged. "Some. Not too bad."

"Did you see the corpse yourself?"

"Yeah. A fat guy."

Herb pricked up his ears. "Could you tell what kind of murder weapon was used?"

"Uh—I'm not sure. I'm not a cop."

"Did anyone in the audience hear a gunshot at the time of the murder?"

"Not that I know of."

"From the amount of blood could you tell if the guy died from bleeding out or from some other way?"

"Man, I'm an usher, not an ME."

"I realize that." Herb paused. "The human body holds ten pints of blood. Did it look like ten pints of blood was pooled around the body?"

"Ten pints?" said Ted, trying to visualize it. "I don't think there was *that* much. Not even close."

"If there was a lot of blood, it would mean it took him a long time to die."

"I don't want to think about it. You're creeping me out. Wait a minute," said Ted, becoming defensive. "Are you saying the theater's responsible for his death because we didn't call for an ambulance sooner?"

"Not at all," said Herb, trying to placate him. He didn't want Ted to worry about getting sued by Briscoe's relatives. "I'm just trying to find out what murder weapon was used."

91

"Why don't you ask the cops your questions? They know more about the murder than me."

Herb chuckled. "Cops hate PIs. They're not gonna help me. You've been a big help so far, and I thank you. I have a couple more questions, is all."

Ted glanced at his wristwatch. "I've given you enough of my time."

"Was the corpse's head deformed?"

"Deformed?"

"Like it had been crushed with a blunt instrument?"

Ted chewed it over, trying to recall. "No, I don't believe so. There was blood on his head—"

"There *was* blood on his head?" said Herb with interest.

"Yeah."

"So Briscoe died from a head wound of some sort."

"I dunno. All I know is, there was blood on his head. Now that I think about it, there wasn't that much blood on the carpet. Hardly any. We didn't have to replace it like the seat upholstery."

Herb nodded, musing. "Could've been a knife or a bullet to the brain. Death would've been quick. Very little bloodletting. But if it was a bullet, the killer must have used a suppressor, since nobody heard a gunshot."

"How do you know the killer didn't strangle him?"

"If he strangled him, there wouldn't be any blood. Now I want you to think. Did you see a bullet hole in the corpse's head?"

"No. But I didn't look very closely. It was yuk, you know. It was shit, man. It was shit."

"The hole could've been hidden by his hair," said Herb, thinking out loud, "especially if it was left by a small caliber bullet."

"So who did it?" said Ted, fascinated.

"I have no idea."

Herb booked. Now it was time to get a fix or his body would never forgive him. He had Kudlow's money so he could afford the smack. On the other hand, he could go to a showing of *Necromaniac*, the horror movie that had everybody talking.

Chapter 24

Grant stood under the marquee in front of the theater that was showing *Necromaniac* and scoped out everybody milling in the area.

He didn't pick up on any familiar faces. If someone *was* following him, the guy was a pro. Grant didn't want to watch a movie at a theater where another murder was going to take place. What were the chances that both of the murders would take place in the two theaters where he was watching *Necromaniac*? Slim and none. Nevertheless, it had happened.

He had to see the movie again, though. He couldn't stay away from it. There was something addictive about it that drew him inexorably. He had to see that demon again, the demon that compelled the heroine to commit multiple murders in the film.

He used cash to purchase a ticket at the box office window and entered the theater. He liked movie theaters. They reminded him that his miserable reality could be escaped even if for only a brief moment of time.

The theater had a pretty good crowd despite it being a weekday afternoon, he noticed. The publicity the movie was garnering from the psycho murders must have been ginning up ticket sales.

He checked out the seats in search of his assigned seat. He wondered if the psycho killer was sitting here. He whipped his head around. Was somebody tailing him? The young couple behind him didn't look familiar.

If the psycho killer had followed him here, somebody would likely end up murdered.

Grant debated whether he should leave the theater. But his urge to see the horror movie won out over his fear of another murder taking place. He found his seat in the back of the theater.

He was surprised he didn't see any rent-a-cops in the theater. He had thought the theater owners might beef up security after the psycho killings. Maybe the owners feared moviegoers would be scared off by too many security guards patrolling the premises.

Somebody must really hate him to want to frame him for these psycho killings. Grant couldn't think of anyone who hated him that much. He was an obscure writer who sold few books. Why would anyone want to frame him?

A platinum blonde sat next to him, reeking of cheap perfume.

Grant's eyes watered and his throat felt sore thanks to the overpowering odor.

She wore gobs of makeup that afforded her a white, geisha-like complexion. In her forties she had a bulging stomach under her loose blouse. She might have been pregnant. There was something strange about her. Could she be the psycho killer?

She pulled up her loose blouse to expose a rat running around in a cage on her stomach.

Taken aback, he wondered if she could tell he was looking at her. She wasn't looking at him. She was looking straight toward the movie screen, which was showing commercials.

What kind of a weird woman would smuggle her pet rat into a movie theater?

He looked around the theater to see if he could find another seat to sit in. But the theater was filling up fast as the main feature was about to begin.

Listening to the rat's claws scrape against its cage Grant felt sweat bathe his face. Maybe he should leave. The woman beside him couldn't have all her marbles. Was she carrying a weapon? He sneaked a glance toward her. He didn't see a weapon on her, but it could easily be concealed under her baggy clothing.

He didn't want her to notice him looking at her, so he stared at the movie screen. There was no telling what she might do if she saw him looking at her. He couldn't let on that he had seen the rat in a cage strapped to her stomach.

By now she had lowered her blouse to cover the rat cage. Maybe she had lifted her blouse to give the rat some air. Grant could still hear the rodent scrabbling around inside its wire cage.

Before the main feature started, there was an announcement on the movie screen that stated that anybody suspicious should be reported to management.

94

This woman sitting beside him fit the bill. He didn't like the idea of being a snitch, however. After all, she hadn't done anything to hurt anybody—not yet anyway. Maybe bringing a pet rat in a cage to a movie theater passed for normal in LA.

Any way you cut it, he didn't like sitting next to her. His eyes were still tearing from the overpowering acrid perfume she had dipped herself in before attending the movie. The scratching of the rat's claws against its cage was getting on his nerves. *Scratch. Scratch.*

Necromaniac began showing.

He riveted his eyes to the screen. The movie was an intense nerve-racking experience to sit through. Even though he knew what was going to happen, the suspense was unbearable. The movie made Friedkin's *Exorcist* look sophomoric and cartoonish in comparison. The demon inside the heroine's head filled Grant with excruciating dread.

What was spoiling the movie was the rat's claws that kept scraping against its cage on the platinum blonde's stomach next to him. It sounded like a rat crawling inside a wall. *Scratch. Scratch.*

He didn't know how much he could stand. He winced in pain. The scratching was giving him a world-class headache.

Kill her. Kill the Rat Lady. She's wrecking the movie. Impale her brain with your knife.

The usher should escort the Rat Lady out of the theater, decided Grant with frustration. Maybe if enough people complained about her . . .

But that wasn't going to happen. Grant could see that everybody was watching with rapt attention the horror movie playing onscreen. Which was what he wanted to be doing if it wasn't for the cursed scratching of the rat.

Don't be afraid. Kill her. She deserves to die for her rudeness. Kill the wacko. Trust me. I'm the only one who cares about you. Her rat's driving you crazy. Kill her.

"Calm down, baby," the woman whispered to her rat.

Kill her. She's talking during the movie. The wacko thinks the rat is her baby. Skewer her brain. Cut her creepy head off.

Grant thought he saw Herb in the audience. He couldn't be sure on account of the darkness enveloping the theater. Maybe he should leave.

Had Herb followed him here? Why would he?

He picked up on a beefy bearded guy clad in a white wife beater and a black leather vest sitting a few rows away from him. The guy had a beer belly and musclebound arms like a professional wrestler. Mandy's Mongol boyfriend? Grant had no way of knowing, but it gave him pause.

Scratch. Scratch.

He could hear the movie demon voice echoing through his mind.

Kill the Rat Lady. Kill her. Kill her. Kill. Kill. Kill.

Chapter 25

Kudlow and Towers rode in the backseat of Towers's limo and watched the TV set suspended from the headliner, the flat-panel TV screen level with and to the right of the minibar in the back of the driver's seat. Kudlow had lowered the screen from the headliner with a remote so they could watch the news.

Towers was nursing a shot glass of whisky.

"There are some commentators in the movie industry who are claiming the filmmakers of *Necromaniac* hired a professional hit man to commit the murders in theaters showing the movie in order to drum up business," said the TV talking head, a telegenic blonde in her thirties.

"What?" said Towers in stunned disbelief. "Did I hear her right?"

"Yeah," said Kudlow, his face furrowed with cynicism. "What asshole is saying this bullshit."

"I have with me today Hollywood's most famous filmmaker Bob LeBeau," said the talking head. "Is that your take on the movie murders, Bob?"

"Why, yes it is, Hillary," said LeBeau, a frail, consumptive-looking guy in his fifties with frizzy apricot hair who sported peach-tinted wire-rimmed spectacles with rectangular lenses and was wearing an open-collared white shirt under a grey herringbone blazer.

"That crook," said Kudlow, outraged. "I know for a fact he doesn't pay half his actors."

"Why do you say that?" Hillary asked LeBeau, sensing a juicy story.

"It's common knowledge in the Biz."

"Do you have facts to back it up?"

"Everybody in Hollywood knows it for a fact."

Hillary sighed noisily with frustration. "Let's move on to your inside story about Kudlow's *Necromaniac*."

97

"I'd be glad to. Look at the ticket sales of the movie," said LeBeau.

"What about them?"

"On opening day hardly anybody went to the movie. It was panned by several big-name critics in the industry. It had all the earmarks of a flop. Then somebody gets murdered at a theater showing the movie, and ticket sales skyrocket."

"You believe the *Necromaniac* filmmakers actually hired a hit man to commit the murder?" said Hillary, leaning toward LeBeau, an incredulous expression on her face.

"I wouldn't put it past them."

Disappointed, Hillary leaned back in her seat. "Then you're just saying it's possible."

"Possible?" scoffed LeBeau. "I think it's probable."

"Do you have any evidence to back up your assertion?"

"I'm a filmmaker, not a cop. I'm not required to give evidence in a court of law."

"Let's sue his ass off for defamation," Towers told Kudlow.

"It sounds like you're walking back your accusation," said Hillary.

Shrugging, LeBeau picked something out of his eye and inspected it. "I'm voicing my opinion. I'm protected by freedom of speech like everybody else in this country."

"That doesn't give you the right to make unsubstantiated charges against people."

"Any fool can see what I'm saying is true. The numbers speak for themselves. The murder at the theater boosted ticket sales for subsequent showings of the movie."

"Let me get this straight. You're saying the movie director Norman Kudlow hired a hit man to murder an innocent filmgoer in order to boost ticket sales?"

"The lying bastard," snapped Kudlow, flushing with anger.

"I'm saying it sure looks that way," said LeBeau.

"It sounds like you're walking back your accusation again."

"I'm saying what everybody else is thinking, especially people in the Business. There are guys in cutthroat Hollywood who will do anything to make a buck."

"Even hire a hit man to commit murder?" said Hillary, wide-eyed.

98

"Nothing's off the table in this business. It's jungle warfare out there. People are fighting for their lives in the Biz. They'll do whatever it takes to hit the jackpot. The alternative is starvation."

"You're generalizing now. The question is, did Norman Kudlow hire a hit man to commit murder at a theater showing his new movie *Necromaniac*?"

LeBeau mulled it over.

"You'd have to ask him," he muttered.

"In other words, you have no proof of your accusation."

"I'm entitled to my opinion."

Hillary looked irritated. "I gave you this interview because you said you were going to make a shocking revelation on my show—"

"I'm saying what everybody else in Hollywood is thinking."

"That doesn't make it true—unless you have proof."

"I said my piece," said LeBeau, shifting in his seat uncomfortably.

"I'm asking you point-blank. Did Norman Kudlow hire a hit man to commit murder?"

"I believe he did. You don't know him like I do. He will do anything to sell his movies."

Hillary fetched a sigh of exasperation. "It sounds like you're backing down from the shocking revelation you promised me."

"You're getting viewers. What more do you want?"

"What a coward," said Towers, and took a pull on his whisky. "What he's saying is speculation. Anybody can speculate. It's meaningless."

"But the damage is done," said Kudlow, his face drawn. "He planted the seed in everybody's mind that I arranged the murder in order to boost ticket sales. What kind of a sick mind would think up something as heinous as arranging a murder to make a movie financially successful? It beggars belief. LeBeau should be kicked out of Hollywood."

"That's how he got to the top—by stooping as low as you can go. He spreads vicious rumors about fellow directors and trashes their careers in order to make himself look better than his competition. Nothing is beneath him."

99

"Wait a minute," said Hillary, pressing her earphone to her ear. "I'm getting a special bulletin. A third murder has been committed in a movie theater showing *Necromaniac*."

"Unbelievable," said LeBeau, throwing up his hands in disgust at the news.

Kudlow felt his jaw drop.

"No," said Towers, dropping his shot glass, the blood draining from his face. "The pendulum of public opinion is gonna swing against us. I can feel it in my bones."

"That backbiting LeBeau is pouring oil on the fire with his spurious accusations."

"We're fucked six ways from Sunday."

Gasping for breath, his hands shaking, Towers poured himself another whisky.

"The city is on edge tonight," said Hillary, her voice somber. "I'm praying for everyone. This is Hillary Delaney saying good night. We *will* get through this."

Chapter 26

"Hello."

"Hello," said Grant, standing in his apartment, cell phone in hand.

"I don't know how, but I'm still alive," said Sherry on the other end of the line. "I had to sleep on the floor at Grand Central Station. Somehow I didn't get assaulted."

He knew what she wanted. She was softening him up, trying to make him feel sorry for her so she could spring her next question, the reason she had really called.

"Yeah," he said warily.

"How are you?"

"All right."

"Are you still having blackouts?"

"Yeah."

"You should see a doctor about them. Maybe you need a CAT-scan. You could have a tumor in your brain. Get a CAT-scan of your entire body just to be safe."

She was pretending she cared about him. She didn't, he had found out the hard way. What she cared about was money.

"I can't afford medical expenses," he said.

"Look, I need four thousand dollars. You can send it with PayPal or Venmo or CashApp. I need a place to stay and I need to get a plane ticket back to LA."

"I don't have any more money. I lent it all to you. When are you gonna pay me back?"

"The money I inherited is in probate. I can't pay you back till probate is finished."

"It's been going on for over a year."

"There are two houses involved. Houses take a long time to pass through probate to the relatives."

"Why don't you admit you're never gonna pay me back? You lied to me. This whole thing between us is a scam."

"That's not true. I love you."

"You lied to me. I lent you everything I had. Even when you get that money out of probate if there really is any, you're not gonna pay me back."

"You're the liar. You said you would support me for the rest of my life."

"What?" said Grant, taken aback. "No, I didn't."

"You can't let me die here. Don't you feel anything for me?"

"I can't help you. You bankrupted me. Remember?"

"Zelle's OK. Use Zelle. Send it to Jade's account, and she'll send it to me."

"Where am I supposed to get this money?"

"Use a credit card. You have six of them."

"My credit rating is zilch. Bankruptcy torpedoed my FICO."

"I don't know anything about that."

In his mind's eye he could see her eyes go blank like they always did whenever he said something she didn't understand.

"Don't think about those things," she went on. "They're stressing you out. Things aren't as bad as you think."

Actually they're worse.

"Just send me four thousand dollars," she said. "That's all I need."

"Just four grand, huh?" he said. "You make it sound like four pennies."

"How can you joke at a time like this?"

"I'm not joking. I don't have that kind of money."

"What am I supposed to do? I'm a young girl in the big city. I'm afraid."

"I can't help you."

"I love you. Help me."

He felt bad about not helping her. When he had first met her, he had felt sorry for her and had lent her money to pay her rent. But the borrowing had kept going on and on ad infinitum until his bank account was empty. Now he couldn't help her if he wanted. He felt angry she had put him in this position with her constant demands for money.

She started crying.

Fit to be tied, he terminated the call. She was always trying to make him feel sorry for her as if it was his fault she was having so many financial problems.

She was a professional scammer. Who knew where the money he had lent her had really gone? How could he have fallen for her scam? He felt like an idiot for letting himself be conned by her. He was always suspicious of her, but he had never pulled the plug on their relationship. He had kept letting her into his apartment every time she came to see him even though he knew she would wind up asking for another loan. Maybe he had a death wish.

He had always suspected she might be a professional scammer. There were telltale signs.

Every time they went to the bank together to get her more money, she would check the upper part of the building, searching for cameras. She went out of her way to avoid being photographed. She wouldn't even let him photograph her by herself or with him. He found her camera shyness odd. And yet he continued to see her.

Another tipoff of something hinky about her was her lack of a bank account. If she was on the level, why wouldn't she have a bank account? She had told him the bank had closed her account due to lack of funds. Which was possible. It would explain her need to borrow money from him to pay her rent. But why didn't she open a new account after he had lent her hundreds of thousands of dollars?

Despite his suspicions he continued to see her.

When he had realized he was running out of money, he had told her he didn't want to see her anymore. But she kept coming back to his apartment and telling him she would inherit the two million bucks soon and would be able to pay him back. In the meantime she kept demanding more money to pay for her medical bills, insurance bills, legal bills, trips to probate court in Key Biscayne, hotel bills, etc.

And yet he continued to see her.

He would fall asleep at night wondering why he was letting her steal from him. He knew the alternative to letting her rob him was to be left alone. He had met her in the first place on a dating site on the Internet, because he was tired of being alone all the time.

He had been faced with a dilemma. If he stopped lending her money, she would never come back to him. And this time, unlike before he had met her, he would not only be alone but broke.

Nevertheless, he kept lending her money and getting in over his head by maxing out his credit cards, hoping all the while she was telling him the truth about inheriting the two million bucks from her uncle and that she would pay him back at last when she received the money from probate. His only hope to avoid bankruptcy was that she would eventually pay him back. He had to keep believing she would. Otherwise, he was doomed to poverty.

But she never paid him back a dime of what she owed him.

And then he was broke and had no other recourse than to declare bankruptcy.

He blew out his cheeks to relieve his stress. There was no use kicking himself. His life savings were gone. She would never pay him back. It was all lies, part of her scam. He would need to start his life over from scratch—not easy when you were sixty. He would need to write another book and hope his luck would change and, in spite of his bad track record of sales, this one would sell more than three copies on Amazon.

The problem was he had writer's block.

Chapter 27

Ever since Grant had started experiencing blackouts, he couldn't get a word written on his laptop for his next book. He didn't understand how the blackouts could be stymying his writing, but he was convinced they were. Instead of getting words written on his laptop he was suffering blackouts, which were feeding on his creative output, draining him. It unnerved him. He didn't know what it meant. He didn't know how he could stop the blackouts from happening and get back to writing.

What was causing the blackouts?

He scoped out his apartment.

He didn't own much. A fifteen-year-old plasma high definition TV. Hundreds of thrillers and horror books, some in bookshelves, some piled on top of each other against the walls, many of them with dog-eared pages—in his mind's eye he could see librarians snarling at him at the idea. One ratty recliner that was shedding its stuffing. A couple of blond Ikea end tables with horror magazines like *Cemetery Dance*, *Weird Tales*, *Scream*, *Rue Morgue*, and *Fangoria* piled slipshod on them. A potted ficus that reached five feet high near his window. A full ten-dollar chardonnay wine bottle from Trader Joe's that stood on his tiny square kitchen table for one.

He picked up on the grilled vent in his wall and narrowed his eyes. Was someone pumping a knockout gas through the ventilation shaft? A government agency? The IRS kept threatening to levy his bank account if he didn't pay them his back taxes. Did their agent Martin Truex rig the ventilation system to poison the air in the room with a toxic gas to render him unconscious? But why would the IRS send their man Truex to do such a thing? Causing Grant to have blackouts wouldn't make him pay his taxes—unless he *knew* they were doing it to him, which they hoped would scare him into ponying up his delinquent tax bill. Whether he was scared or not, he couldn't pay them what he didn't have.

He inspected the vent. Maybe he was inhaling mold through the vent that was knocking him out. He knew inhaling mold could cause hallucinations in a person. Maybe it could cause blackouts as well.

He realized his sock felt wet. He rolled up his trouser leg. The charcoal grey sock looked damp. He rolled up his trouser leg farther to reveal the knife strapped to his ankle. Dumbfounded, he noticed the knife had blood on it. He shook his head in disbelief. He didn't remember using his knife for anything. Somebody must be framing him. They had used his knife the last time he had blacked out and had replaced it while he was still unconscious.

He withdrew the knife from its leather sheath and rinsed off the blood-streaked blade in the kitchen sink.

Whoever was setting him up for these murders was knocking him out somehow and using his knife to commit the murders, making it look like he had committed them. He had to be careful about not getting caught in the frame. The framer might have left other evidence incriminating him at the scenes of the crimes.

Grant knew he had no shortage of enemies. Any one of them could be behind this diabolical plot to implicate him in serial killings.

He hurried into his bedroom and removed his shoes and socks. He tossed the blood-soaked sock and its fellow into the dirty clothes hamper in his closet and put on a new pair of socks. He inspected his shoes, didn't see any blood on them, and put them back on.

He recalled the message written on his mirror in soap: Time to Kill. Somebody had to break into his apartment in order to write it, or had Truex or Herb written it when they were here? And he couldn't rule out Mandy. She had also been here.

Wired, he sat down at his desk to write on his laptop, hoping he could get something down.

He sat there for ten minutes, unable to write a single sentence.

He threw up his hands in futility.

He couldn't write. He was too consumed with anger at the person framing him for murder. And how could he forget the scammer Sherry? She infuriated him even more than the framer did. *Maybe she was the framer.* But she was in New York—at least she said she was, which meant nothing since she was a pathological liar and was using her cell phone, which could be located anywhere.

Frustrated, he bolted out of his chair and paced around his room. He felt like pulling out his hair.

Chapter 28

Eager to buy tickets, moviegoers formed a burgeoning queue in front of the theater where the most recent murder had occurred.

Squad cars were parked in front of the theater as police forensics teams inspected the crime scene, where they had strung yellow tape, cordoning off the theater. Uniforms blocked the ticket window and the entrance.

Perkins Weaver shoved a microphone in the face of the first person who stood in line, a muscular guy in his twenties wearing rose-tinted glasses, khaki board shorts with cargo pockets, and an olive drab tank top.

"Hi. I'm a reporter. Aren't you scared to go to this movie?" said Weaver, recording his questions and the answers with his smartphone.

"Scared?" said the guy, smiling. "I *want* to be scared. That's why I go to horror movies."

"What's your name?"

"Howard."

"Haven't you heard about the psycho killer who's murdering filmgoers as they watch this movie, Howard?"

"That's why I'm here. I want to see him try something. It's exciting."

"But you could end up getting killed."

"That's why it's so exciting. I like horror movies. I want to see what's driving this psycho to keep killing at this flick. It must be an incredibly scary movie."

"You think the movie is inciting him to commit murder?"

Howard contorted his face in thought. "Who knows what a psycho's thinking? All I know is, he's killing only at the showing of this movie, not at any other. So this is the flick I want to see."

"Even if he tries to kill you when you're watching the movie?" said Perkins in surprise.

"I'm ready for him. These hands are lethal weapons registered with the LAPD," said Howard, holding up his hands and chopping the air with them. "I know taekwondo."

A uniform with a buzz cut made his way to the head of the queue.

"This theater is shut down for the rest of the day," he announced.

The waiting moviegoers groaned with disappointment.

"It's not fair," said Howard. "I came all the way from Temecula to see the movie here to find out if the movie murderer maniac was gonna strike again."

"You'll have to go to a different theater," said the uniform, stone-faced. "Nobody's getting into this one today. It's the scene of an active murder investigation."

"Bummer," said a ponytailed brunette standing behind Howard in jogging shorts and a silver tube top. "I already bought my ticket online. This is a rip-off."

Protesters of the movie started gathering across the street, waving placards that condemned the movie for inciting violence.

Weaver swung his smartphone around to film them.

A thirtyish guy with a shaved head hurled a Molotov cocktail at one of the black-and-whites parked in front of the theater. As the vehicle erupted into flames, the assailant fled the scene. Guns drawn, two uniforms sprinted after him, identifying themselves and yelling at him to halt.

"Asshole," said Howard, watching the squad car become engulfed in flames. "I wish that coward would come over here. I'd show him." He turned to watch the fleeing bomb thrower. "Look at the scaredy-cat run for his life." He raised his voice. "Run, pussy, run."

"Those types hate movies," said Ponytail.

"It's the movie haters who cause all the violence."

"Can I quote you?" said Weaver, holding his cell phone close to Howard's face.

"Sure. Uh—just don't use my last name. I don't want nutbags phoning in death threats to me."

"What *is* your last name? It's just for my records."

"I'm not giving it to you."

109

"This is the LAPD," declared a uniform wielding a bullhorn. "You are ordered to disperse. Leave now or you will be arrested."

"Burn the movie," hollered a thirtyish protester standing across the street, cupping his hands around his mouth. "Burn the movie. It's cursed. It's devil's work. Burn it before it kills again."

"Our children's lives are in danger as long as this cursed movie is shown," screamed a fortysomething woman with shoulder-length white hair, a silver crucifix dangling from her neck and hanging outside her black dress. "Burn every copy of the movie and never show it again."

Clad in Birkenstock clogs, she shook her fist at the movie theater, her face a mask of wrath.

Chapter 29

Herb saw the riot unfolding. He made a beeline for the movie theater and, seeing that Perkins was a reporter, buttonholed him.

"What's going on here?" said Herb.

"Who are you?" said Perkins.

"I'm a PI."

"PI? Who do you work for?" said Perkins, pricking up his ears.

"That's privileged information. I never divulge my clients' names."

"I'd like to know who you're working for."

"You're outa luck."

Studying Herb's face, Perkins didn't press the matter. "Closing the theater sparked a riot."

"Why'd they close the theater?" said Herb, scoping out the theater entrance.

"There's been another murder. The killer struck here."

"When was the body discovered?" said Herb, animated.

"After everybody left the theater showing *Necromaniac.*"

"Do the cops have any suspects?"

"Not that they're telling us."

Three more squad cars converged on the scene, their light bars flashing blue and red, sirens howling. The uniforms already on the scene set to rounding up rioters who had refused to disperse and securing their wrists with flex cuffs.

Herb clapped eyes on the burning black-and-white. "What happened to the cruiser?"

"A rioter torched it," said Perkins. "Why do you happen to be in this area?"

"I—I'm investigating the movie murders."

"But you didn't even know there was a murder here until I told you. What brought you here?"

"I—I'm checking out all of the theaters that are showing *Necromaniac.*"

"Why?"

"It's part of my investigation," said Herb, starting to get prickly. "Why are you asking me so many questions?"

"I'm a journalist," said Perkins. "That's what I get paid to do."

"I'm usually the one asking questions."

"Since you're a PI, do you have any idea who the psycho killer is?"

"I just started working the case," said Herb.

Even if he did have an idea, a journalist was the last person he would tell.

"What's that guy doing up there?" said Herb, looking up at the fifth floor of a high-rise apartment complex across the street.

He saw a twentysomething longhaired guy standing on the balcony waving a sign that said Repent.

"He must be part of the protest demonstration," said Perkins, following the direction of Herb's gaze. "Some religious zealots are condemning the movie."

"He's pouring something on his body," said Herb, squinting in the sun, which was shining behind the apartment building.

"Repent," cried the protester from the balcony, emptying a jerrican on his body. "This movie is devil's work. Repent, sinners."

"Oh no," Ponytail cried in horror on the sidewalk, watching him. "Somebody stop him."

The protester used a lighter to set himself on fire. His body burst into flames, becoming a human torch. He screamed in agony.

"Call the fire department," a uniform yelled.

A young cop dashed into the apartment building to help the burning protester.

"Jesus," said Perkins, training his cell phone on the protester's self-immolation.

Ponytail bent over and threw up on the sidewalk.

"What's he doing?" said Howard, visibly shaken as he watched the burning man moving about on the balcony.

The flaming, charred protester managed to climb onto the balustrade, leap off the balcony, and crash into a burning heap on the sidewalk.

Howard leaned over and threw up.

The unnerving screams of onlookers rent the smoking air, echoing through the canyon of high-rises.

112

Transfixed in horror and unable to look away, Herb stared at the burning, smoking clump of flesh on the sidewalk across the street. Feeling compelled to watch he felt like he was going to pass out as well. He could smell burning flesh as the wind shifted and blew billowing clouds of smoke toward him. Sweat beaded on his face.

Out of the corner of his eye he caught a glimpse of Perkins filming the burning body with his cell phone.

"This is gonna make the front page," said Perkins, grimacing.

A uniform pelted across the street and tried to put out the fire, using only his hands to pat out the smoldering clothing of the religious zealot.

"Does anyone have a blanket?" the uniform yelled, wincing as the smoke irritated his eyes.

Carrying a particolored beach blanket, a middle-aged guy with a tonsure bolted out of his SUV that was parked on the side of the street. He threw the blanket onto the burning body and joined the uniform in wrapping it around the sizzling flesh in order to smother the flames.

As the smoke cleared above the charred body, they could see they were wasting their energy and lifted the blanket.

Half the protester's brain had spilled onto the concrete sidewalk after he had crashed into it from his fall. The other half was crushed into paste inside his compressed fractured skull. One of his eyeballs popped out of its socket and dangled from the optic nerve onto the steaming concrete.

White-faced, Tonsure retreated to his SUV.

"You forgot your blanket," said the uniform, holding out the smoking blanket to him.

Shaking his head Tonsure didn't look back. He climbed into his SUV and sat frozen in the driver's seat, staring out the windshield in a state of shock, unseeing.

The uniform produced his radio and put in a request for an ME.

An approaching fire engine's forlorn siren keened in the distance.

Herb was dying for a fix.

How did he get here in the first place? Smack did weird things to his memory. Sometimes he wondered if his brain looked like a porous chunk of pumice.

A cawing crow swooped down from the high-rise apartment building's gutter, alighted with a flutter of its sable wings near the immolated protester crumpled on the sidewalk, and pecked at the eyeball dangling from its optic nerve like a cherry.

The uniform shooed the crow away.

The crow squawked in protest and took flight.

Chapter 30

Kudlow was sitting in the backseat of Towers's limo and staring out the tinted windows when he felt his cell phone vibrate in his trouser pocket.

He took the call.

"There's been another murder," said Herb.

Kudlow gulped. "Tell me you caught the murderer."

"I didn't."

"Crap. What's all that noise I hear in the background?"

"The cops. I'm at the scene of the crime. There's a riot here."

Kudlow rolled his eyes. "Dare I ask why?"

"Protesters of your movie got violent and blew up a black-and-white."

Overhearing Kudlow, Towers flicked on the limo TV set. The scene of the riot was playing out on all of the network channels.

Kudlow could see the squad car burning on TV. A fire engine was only just arriving, a meat wagon in its wake. Police were having a hard time clearing the area of looky-loos.

"Not good," muttered Towers, watching the TV.

"What caused the riot?" Kudlow asked Herb.

"I don't know for sure. It must've had something to do with the murder that took place at this theater."

"The theater was showing my film?" said Kudlow, and held his breath waiting for an answer.

"Yeah."

"Fuck," Kudlow exploded. "Is this a different theater from the other two murder sites?"

"Yep."

"There's gonna be a backlash," muttered Towers, stroking his chin, his eyes glued to the TV set. "Too damn many murders. The novelty has worn off. This is serious. And these riots are making it worse."

Kudlow heard Herb say, "Also, some religious zealot set himself on fire and jumped to his death off a balcony. It was awful."

Kudlow narrowed his eyes. "How do people sound where you are? Are they angry at my film?"

"Uh—people were lined up to see the movie, and they were disappointed when it was canceled."

"Were they blaming my film for the murders?"

"I didn't hear anyone standing in line blaming it. The protesters across the street wanted the movie pulled from theaters for inciting violence."

"Movies don't incite violence," said Kudlow, the cords in his neck sticking out, his face turning red.

"That's what *they* were saying. Not me. I like movies, especially horror movies."

"You need to catch this psycho killer before he strikes again."

"I'm getting closer. I believe he's using a knife to kill these guys. Possibly a suppressed gun, but nobody has heard anything when the murders were committed. Of course, it might be because the noise of the movie soundtrack drowned out the gunshot."

"That's it?" said Kudlow, let down.

"Let me finish. And the killer knows how to kill his victims on the spot. None of his victims survived, which means they must have died fast—before the movie let out, in any case. The small amount of blood near the victims also indicates a fast kill. You stop bleeding when you're dead."

Kudlow took in Herb's information with mounting apprehension. "I hope you're not saying he's a professional hit man."

"It's possible."

"Is it probable?"

"He could be a doctor. Doctors know how to kill someone quickly."

"Yeah, but what are the chances? Doctor murderers are rare."

"You're forgetting Dr. Crippen."

Kudlow shrugged. "What I said before. They're rare."

"The killer could be ex-military, Special Forces, or CIA, as well."

"I see. Then not necessarily a hit man."

116

"Like I said, it's possible. There are several possibilities, including a hit man."

"Don't tell anyone your findings," said Kudlow, gripping his cell phone harder. "If the psycho killer *really* is a professional hit man, people are gonna start believing Bob LeBeau's bogus theory that I hired the killer to gin up ticket sales to my film."

"My findings are strictly privileged info between you and me."

Hollow-eyed, Kudlow stared at the TV screen showing the crime scene. "I hope the cops haven't reached the same conclusion as you for their investigation."

"As far as I know, they aren't talking."

"If people start believing that spiteful son of a bitch LeBeau, my career is over. I never met a director so unsure of himself and so full of envy for fellow directors. He loves seeing other directors' films flop at the box office. He's probably drinking champagne after seeing these riots on TV."

"I can't stop people from flapping their gums."

"Wait a minute. You said CIA. You think the CIA is out to trash my career by murdering people watching my film?"

"I said it's possible. CIA black ops agents are trained to kill their targets quickly. It's the only sure way to keep the victim from retaliating. Get it over with and sneak away without making a sound."

Kudlow brought his hand down his forehead, his expression grim, and snorted.

"You're overreacting, Norman," said Towers. "Why would the CIA want to wreck your career? The killer's psychotic. Psychos are a dime a dozen these days. They're always crawling out of the woodwork and offing someone. Don't you watch the news?"

"I feel like I'm getting closer to the guy," said Herb.

"You can't let him strike again," said Kudlow.

He terminated the call. His visage grave, he turned to Towers. "Maybe we should pull my film."

"Don't say that. This will all blow over. If we pull the movie now, we'll never be able to get it back into distribution. We'll lose our asses."

"I don't want people to die watching my film."

117

"You don't really believe your movie is turning people into murderers?"

"Of course not. I've said over and over again movies can't do such a thing. Art doesn't turn people into killers. I never would've become a filmmaker if I thought it did."

"There you go. This backlash will pass. Nobody with half an ounce of common sense believes your movie is creating killers." Towers paused in thought. "In the meantime, we're gonna have to do something to drum up sales, though. People don't want to be injured in riots when they go to a movie."

"For sure. Filmgoers want to be scared vicariously in a film. They don't want to go to a theater with protesters throwing bombs at them."

"Having one or two murders at the showing of your movie was a novelty, and it fanned interest, but now a third murder and a riot . . ." Towers shook his head. "Now it's backlash time."

"What do we do?"

"We have to convince people it's safe to go to your movie."

"How?"

Towers stared at Kudlow.

"What?" said Kudlow, feeling uneasy.

"We need you to go on TV again and assure people your movie won't turn them into killers."

Kudlow groaned. "I already did that with what's his face."

"Riley Coogan?"

"Right."

"You need to prepare for round two."

"I almost got beaned in that last interview. I had to run for my life."

"We'll ask Coogan to step up security measures for the next round."

"I'd rather eat burning coals."

Towers chewed it over. "I'm wondering which is hurting us more—the psycho killer or these riots against your movie."

"If the cops would catch this psycho, people would flock to my film, and it would stop demonstrators from protesting it."

"We gotta hope the psycho killer makes a slip and gets caught. It could well happen. They caught Son of Sam and the Milwaukee Cannibal."

118

"They caught Ted Bundy too. But his murders went on for years. And they never caught the Zodiac Killer."

"Why do you always look at the dark side?"

"That's why I'm an artist and not a salesman," said Kudlow, his face clouding. "An artist's job is to get at the truth."

"When you go on TV again, don't bum everybody out. Make the case that your movie is cathartic, or whatever you called it, and can't incite moviegoers to kill. Moviegoers don't like big words unless you explain them. Make sure they understand what you're talking about."

"It's only three syllables."

"We're not gonna let this psycho killer intimidate us. The show must go on," said Towers, pumping his fist and grinning.

The TV camera zoomed in on a stocky man with a long brown ponytail, a black beret canted on his head.

"I confess," he said. "I'm the movie killer. I killed those three people in the theaters. The director hired me to kill them."

Nonplussed, Kudlow stared at the TV screen in disbelief.

Chapter 31

Herb watched detectives Kevin Kesey and Xochitl Rivera close in on the ponytailed guy confessing to the murders.

"What a story," said Weaver, jacked up as he used his cell phone to film the killer surrendering to the cops.

"Cuff him," Kesey told a twentysomething uniform at his side.

Kesey eyed the self-confessed ponytailed killer with suspicion.

His hands cuffed behind his back, the suspect was pushing thirty with a cluster of acne scars on the right side of his face that made his flesh resemble sandpaper. He stood in front of Kesey on the sidewalk under the theater marquee as police milled around the blockaded street, rounding up stragglers and sending them on their way or busting the ones who resisted.

"What's your name?" said Kesey.

"What's yours?"

"Detective Kesey, and I'm the one asking the questions," said Kesey, teed off.

"Stewart Hogarth. I wanted to make sure I was surrendering to a cop. You're not in uniform."

"I'm a detective," said Kesey, flipping open his blazer to reveal his badge clipped to his leather belt. "And you're in my custody. Are you gonna give me a hard time?"

"No, sir. Are you in charge of the murder investigation?"

"I'm not answering your questions. *You're* answering mine. Got it? *You're* the one under arrest."

"I plead guilty."

"Did you say earlier that a movie director hired you to kill these people?"

"I did."

Kesey arched an eyebrow. "Why did he want them dead?"

"I didn't ask him. In my business I do what I'm told."

"Did he tell you which people to kill?"

"Yeah."

120

"They weren't random killings?"

"No."

"Why those three people?"

Hogarth shrugged. "Beats me."

"Are you saying you're a hit man?"

"Yep."

"How many people have you taken out?"

"Let's see. Let me think. Forty-three, including the last three."

"When you say the movie director, which one are you talking about?"

"Norman Kudlow."

"Do you believe him?" said Rivera, who was standing at Kesey's side.

"He wouldn't be the first hoax confession we've gotten for these murders," said Kesey.

"He's at the crime scene where the murder just took place. That implicates him."

"It implicates a lot of people. These hoaxers want publicity. They want their mugs plastered on TV." Kesey scoped out Hogarth's clothes. "How come you don't have any blood on your clothes if you just killed someone?"

"I want a lawyer," said Hogarth.

"Why do you want a lawyer if you're confessing?"

"I know my rights."

Kesey shook his head.

"It can't be this easy," Herb told Weaver, who was standing near him and watching the interrogation.

"Hoaxes are a dime a dozen for serial killings, especially ones that get a lot of air time," said Weaver.

"If he's really the killer, why would he confess to the cops?"

"Great minds think alike. I smell a hoax." Weaver paused a beat. "However, I've done a lot of reading about serial killers, and some of them *want* to be caught. Ted Bundy wanted to be caught, and he wanted to be executed, so he arranged to be caught in Florida, which is one of the few remaining states that have the death penalty."

Chapter 32

Grant heard knocks on his apartment door.

He glanced at the tilted chair whose back he had wedged under the doorknob to keep intruders from breaking in, namely Mandy's Mongol boyfriend. Removing the chair and opening the door Grant saw Herb and let him in.

"What have you been up to?" said Herb.

"I'm been trying to write," said Grant.

"How's your book coming?"

"Not well. I'm not getting anything down."

"Can you lend me a thousand bucks?"

"I can't lend anyone anything, because I don't have anything," said Grant. "If you need money, get a job."

"I got a job."

Grant did a double take. He found it hard to believe anyone would hire Herb after they took one look at his needle-scarred arms.

"Then you're better off than me," said Grant. "I should be the one asking for a loan."

"Eh, the job isn't paying quite enough."

"What kind of job?"

"A PI. Speaking of which, I've had a busy day."

"Oh, yeah?"

"Did you hear there's been another movie murder?"

"Not again."

"Yeah. And there was a riot at the theater. Haven't you seen the news on TV?"

"I've been trying to work. I don't have time to watch the news."

Herb spotted a strip of paper lying on the carpet and picked it up. He was planning on tossing it in the wastebasket but pulled a face as he read it.

"I thought you said you were working today," he said.

"I spent the whole day trying to write."

Herb held up the strip of paper in his hand. "This is a ticket stub for a showing of *Necromaniac*."

"Is this a frame?" said Grant, taken aback.

Was his own brother Herb the one framing him for the murders? Grant stared at Herb, scrutinizing his face.

"I just came from this theater," said Herb. "It's the scene of the most recent murder."

"What are you trying to say?"

"I thought you said you were here working all day."

"I've been trying to."

"Then how did you get this ticket stub?" said Herb, holding the ticket up near Grant's face.

"Is this your grand *J'accuse* moment?"

"What are you talking about?"

"It sounds like you're making an accusation against me."

"Not at all. I'm trying to find out if you saw anything suspicious at the theater today. My assignment is to find the movie killer. If you saw something suspicious, it could help me track the killer."

"It sounds like you're saying *I'm* the killer."

"Whatever gave you that idea?" said Herb in astonishment.

Grant retreated to a closet, opened it, and returned with a pistol in his hand. He trained the muzzle on Herb.

"I can't believe you're accusing your own brother of being a murderer," said Grant.

"What are you doing with that gun?" said Herb, knitting his brows and backing away from Grant.

"Sit down," said Grant, motioning to the sofa.

Shaking with apprehension, his terrified eyes locked on the pistol, Herb made for the sofa and sat down.

"Why would I think you're the movie killer?" he said. "Somebody confessed at the scene of the crime. If you were there, you could help identify the guy who confessed."

Grant remained suspicious. "I don't believe you."

"It's true. I was there when he confessed."

"Bullshit. You're gonna use that ticket stub in your hand to incriminate me in the murder."

Grant felt his cell phone vibrate in his trouser pocket. He took the call.

Maybe he shouldn't have.

Chapter 33

"How are you?" said Sherry at the other end of the line.

"OK," said Grant grudgingly, suspecting she was going to put the arm on him.

"Are you taking your blood pressure meds?"

"Yeah," said Grant, keeping his SIG P226 trained on Herb.

"I almost got assaulted here in New York at Grand Central Station," said Sherry, her voice cracking.

Grant contorted his face, knowing she was trying to make him feel guilty about her being in jeopardy because of him.

He said nothing.

"Don't you want to know if I'm all right?" she said.

"Are you?"

"I managed to get away."

"Did you call the cops?"

"Did you ever try to get the cops to help you? Forget it. They only come when there are dead bodies strewn on the floor in pools of blood."

"I can't help you."

"Do you want me to get assaulted? I'm all by myself here in New York. Do you know how scared I am?" she said, lowering her voice so others in the station couldn't overhear her.

She kept trying to make him feel guilty. It used to work when he started seeing her. He felt sorry for her every time she asked for a loan to pay her medical bills, car payments, insurance, rent, or whatever. But now he knew she would never pay him back. He refused to let her manipulate him into granting her another loan.

"I can't help you."

"I didn't get your Venmo for the five thousand yet," said Sherry.

"That's because I didn't send it."

"What did you use? Zelle? Zelle's good. Just let me know when you send it and I'll ask Jade if she got it."

"I didn't send Zelle. I didn't send anything."

125

"What about PayPal?"

"No."

"Where am I supposed to stay if you don't help me? I'm starving and I have no place to stay," she said, sobbing.

"My money's gone. You spent it all."

"How can you do this to me?"

Grant ground his teeth with irritation at the way she kept blaming him for her problems.

"I can't bail you out every time you have a crisis," he said. He caught sight of Herb trying to get up and head for the door. "Don't move," he said, keeping his SIG trained on Herb.

"What?" said Sherry, thinking he was talking to her.

"Nothing. Herb's here. I was talking to him."

"PayPal's fine. Use PayPal this time."

Grant would curse her to his dying day. Her constant borrowing from him had put him in his financial debacle. There was no way he was going to lend her another dime even if he had a dime to spare. He had nothing to spare. He couldn't legally declare anther bankruptcy for ten years, which meant he had to pay all the debts he was racking up now and in the future.

"I'm not using PayPal or anything else," he said.

He would never forgive himself for falling for her scam. Not that he could do anything about it now. Once money was gone, you could never get it back.

"How about CashApp?" she said. "Use CashApp this time."

"Don't you understand?" he said at his wits' end, his voice rising. "I'm not lending you any more money."

"How can you do this to me?" she shrieked.

He terminated the call, and in frustration took a deep breath to calm himself. She was good at stressing him out. His blood pressure was skyrocketing. He was better off without her. Before he had tumbled to the fact that she was a professional swindler, he had enjoyed some good times with her. But it was all a con to separate him from his money.

Still angry, he glowered at Herb.

"Chill out," said Herb, his eyes locked on the gun muzzle, raindrops of sweat appearing on his brow. "You got me all wrong. I didn't come here to accuse you of anything."

126

"Then why'd you pull that stunt with the ticket stub?" said Grant, wagging his SIG at Herb and fuming from talking to Sherry.

"It's not a stunt. I saw the ticket stub on your carpet and picked it up. End of story. I don't care if you were at the theater when the third killing took place. I'm not gonna tell anyone."

"So what if I went to that movie theater? So did hundreds of other people. It means nothing."

"Can't we forget this?"

Grant realized he was angrier with Sherry than with Herb. No one could set him off worse than Sherry. He saw Sherry sitting on the sofa. He started to squeeze the SIG trigger. No, he told himself. It couldn't be her. She said she was in New York. On the other hand, saying so didn't make it true. She was a pathological liar. But Herb was sitting in front of him on the sofa, not Sherry.

"Don't shoot," said Herb, waving his hands in front of him, his eyes starting from their sockets. "It's me, your brother."

Grant stared at him. Realizing Herb was right, Grant released the pressure on the trigger. What was he thinking?

"I never knew you had a gun," said Herb, unwinding after a fashion as he saw Grant relax his finger on the trigger.

"Self-protection. This city's crawling with crooks."

"I thought maybe it was something else."

"What do you mean?"

"Like maybe somebody threatened you."

Grant wondered how Herb could have found out Mandy was trying to blackmail him and had told him she would send her Mongol boyfriend after him if he didn't pony up. Was that what Herb was referring to when he talked about a threat? Or was he on a fishing expedition? After all, how could Herb possibly know about Mandy? Grant hadn't told him about her. Unless—had Herb sent Mandy here to blackmail him? Was it all part of Herb's framing him for the movie murders? Was Herb going to get a cut of the blackmail money when Grant forked it over to Mandy? It was hard to believe. How could Herb concoct such a byzantine shakedown? On the other hand, why would Herb say someone had threatened him, Grant?

"What makes you think somebody threatened me?" said Grant.

"Because you bought a gun. And . . ."

127

"And what?"

"It's no secret you've been having trouble with Sherry."

"You think she would send someone here to rough me up?"

"I can see where you might think so and get a piece."

"Sherry's too busy scamming people to threaten them."

Herb couldn't suppress a chuckle.

Grant's eyes flashed. "Was she the one who sent you here to frame me so she could shake me down for thousands of bucks?"

"You've been watching too many movies," said Herb, becoming antsy as Grant smoldered and continued to level the SIG at him. "Life isn't anywhere near as complicated as TV thrillers. Maybe it's that book you're writing that's messing up your head."

"Or maybe it's making things clear to me."

"You have an overactive imagination."

"I'm not writing a book now, anyway," said Grant irritably. "I have writer's block."

"Then why are you so suspicious of me?"

"Because something's not right. Why do you show up out of nowhere when all these bad things start happening in town?"

Herb shrugged. "Dumb luck. Bad luck, really. I happened to be in the wrong place at the wrong time. Sometimes I think I have a curse on me."

"Hmm," said Grant, not convinced.

Chapter 34

"I have a bone to pick with you, regarding our previous meeting," said Coogan as he and Kudlow sat on the stage in front of the TV cameras in the studio that recorded Coogan's talk show.

Kudlow hated the idea of taking part in another interview, but it was part and parcel of damage control. He needed to defend his film from trolls and protesters. Despite trying to appear calm he felt an occasional bead of sweat popping through the makeup on his face.

Supposedly this was an interview. It felt more like a police grilling before a public execution. He might as well be a French aristocrat waiting to be guillotined by the Jacobins. Kudlow couldn't wait until it was over with. He would never have agreed to do another interview with Coogan if Towers hadn't convinced him it was necessary to salvage *Necromaniac* from its naysayers who were demanding it be pulled from distribution as a threat to public safety.

"I'm waiting," said Kudlow.

"You said in our previous interview that Aristotle said violence was cathartic in drama."

"What of it?"

"In actuality Aristotle was talking about tragedy being cathartic, not violence."

Coogan's words gave Kudlow pause. Kudlow recovered his cool.

"Violence is an essential part of tragedy," he said. "Without conflict and violence in drama, there would be no tragedy."

"Let us be clear to the audience. Those are your words, not Aristotle's."

"As a fellow dramatist, I'm telling you what Aristotle meant. The violence in the art of drama is cathartic. It purges the desire for violence from the spectator."

"Except in *your* film, which incites viewers to violence," said Coogan, appealing to the TV audience to get a rise out of them.

129

The crowd grumbled.

"My film does *not* incite violence," said Kudlow. "No film does. Film is art. Art doesn't incite violence."

"Then why are so many people being murdered as they watch your film in movie theaters? A third person was murdered today at a showing of your movie."

"The killer is psychotic. My film isn't inciting him to kill. No movie incites anybody to kill. If he never saw my movie, he would still commit murders. Maybe he has, in fact, committed many murders before ever viewing my film."

"You're speculating."

"You're the one who's speculating when you say my film incited the maniac to kill," Kudlow fired back.

"This interview isn't about me. It's about you and your horror film that is inflaming the city."

Kudlow shifted energetically in his seat. "It's not inflaming the city. People like you are inflaming the city by falsely claiming that my film is inciting people to kill."

"The facts are clear," said Coogan, gloating over Kudlow's discomfiture. "Three people have been murdered in theaters that were showing your film *Necromaniac.* Do you deny the facts?"

"My film didn't kill these unfortunate filmgoers. The psycho killer in the audience did. The psycho needs to be stopped."

"Did you hear on the news that somebody confessed to the killings?"

"There you go," said Kudlow, feeling more comfortable in the hot seat. "Ask him what his motivation was. I'm sure it wasn't my film."

"I'm not gonna ask him anything." Coogan faced the audience. "It turns out the cops let him go. It was a hoax."

The audience oohed and aahed.

Kudlow tensed up again.

"The guy's description of how he murdered his victims was hogwash," Coogan went on, turning to Kudlow. "The cops could tell right away he was a phony who just wanted attention. There was no way he killed the victims." Coogan hung fire. "If this killer is a psycho like you say, why haven't the cops nabbed him by now?"

130

"Some of these psychos are clever. Just because he's a psycho doesn't mean he's an idiot."

"You're an authority on psycho killers now?" said Coogan, smirking.

"I'm a film director. I make films. That doesn't mean I don't have a right to an opinion."

"When you make a movie that incites violence, you lose your right to voice your opinion," declared Coogan like it was an edict.

Kudlow heard scattered claps in the audience, which infuriated him. How could they be clapping for the rabblerouser Coogan?

"How many times do I have to tell you my film doesn't incite violence? Art doesn't incite violence."

"It does when a movie is *cursed*," said Coogan, laying emphasis on the last word.

The audience became quiet at the shocking accusation. It was so quiet Kudlow could hear himself breathing. An ominous atmosphere filled the studio. Kudlow knew he had to break the spell, or the audience might turn rowdy.

"That's ridiculous," said Kudlow.

"Are you denying you're a satanist?" said Coogan, pointing his index finger at Kudlow.

"*What?*" said Kudlow, dumbfounded. "Of course, I'm denying it. What liar said I was a satanist?"

"Do you deny your movie is about a satanic demon that possesses people and wreaks havoc, killing anyone who gets in its way?"

"It's a film about demonic possession. Nowhere does it advocate satanism."

"Then why are murders being committed in theaters showing the movie?"

"Because there's a psycho killer on the loose."

"The media are referring to the movie maniac murderer as the Hollywood Psycho. Let's follow their example."

"Fine."

"We need to know what is inciting him to cut a bloody swath across the city. I'll tell you what. *Your* cursed movie is what," said Coogan, jabbing his forefinger at Kudlow's face as if he was identifying a criminal in a police lineup.

"I don't believe in curses. Voodoo mumbo jumbo like sticking pins in dolls to kill your enemies is bunkum, pure and simple."

"Then why did you make a movie about demonic possession?"

"Because I wanted to make a horror film. I like scary films. Roman Polanski directed *Rosemary's Baby*, which, as everybody knows, is about Satan impregnating a girl. It doesn't mean he's a satanist just because he makes a film about Satan. In fact, he's an atheist."

"There's a big difference between Polanski and you. *Rosemary's Baby* didn't incite its audience to commit murder."

"And neither does my film *Necromaniac*," said Kudlow, bolting to his feet.

"The facts say otherwise. Your movie is cursed. You need to do the right thing and pull *Necromaniac* from theaters."

"This isn't the Middle Ages. We don't believe in curses anymore, let alone cursed films."

A cell phone hurtled out of the audience toward Kudlow's head, missing it by a foot and smashing a Fresnel light. The light exploded sounding like a balloon popping near Kudlow's head. Kudlow started.

A team of armed security personnel encircled the stage on the double. Two more cell phone missiles flew from the audience toward the dais. Hunched forward, shielding their heads with their hands, Kudlow and Coogan belted backstage.

"You're the one inciting violence," said Kudlow, scared he might be attacked by the unruly crowd.

"I tell it like it is," said Coogan, his face frantic as he dodged a cell phone soaring past his head.

"No, you don't. You'll say anything to get ratings even if it incites violence."

"Look in the mirror, crypto satanist."

Kudlow lunged at Coogan and threw a haymaker with his right fist. It connected with Coogan's left cheekbone and sent him reeling backward. He stumbled and fell on his backside. If Kudlow knew how to fight, he could have knocked Coogan out with such a blow. But Kudlow had no idea how to throw a punch. His landing of the blow had surprised him even more than it had surprised Coogan.

132

"I'm gonna sue your ass off," cried Coogan, sitting on the floor, flushing.

His face a sheet of alabaster, Kudlow stalked out of the studio, gnashing his teeth, trying to bridle the rage festering inside him. If that lying buffoon said one more thing, Kudlow was going to return to him and kick his teeth down his throat.

Chapter 35

"How would you like being framed for murder by your own brother?" said Grant, aiming his SIG at Herb, who was sitting on the sofa and watching him with agitation.

"Look what you're doing," said Herb. "You're threatening to shoot your own brother. What's got into you?"

"You accused me of killing that lady in the theater today."

"I did no such thing." Herb shot to his feet. "I'm leaving unless you get a grip on yourself."

His expression determined, Grant continued leveling his SIG at him as Herb made his way to the front door.

"If you continue to try to frame me for those psycho killings, I will kill you," said Grant.

Herb shook his head. "You're losing it, Grant. You need to see a shrink. And put that gun down before I have a heart attack."

Lowering his SIG, Grant clutched his head, disconcerted. "This has got to stop. I'm not acting like myself."

"It's stress."

"We're all trying to escape reality. You're shooting dope, and I'm trying to write fiction. You got track marks, and I got bad track," said Grant with cynical amusement, thinking about his paltry book sales.

"Bad track?" said Herb, baffled.

"That's what publishers call poor sales of previous books by an author."

"The hell with those moneygrubbers."

"Actually they're right. Which makes it hard to motivate myself to write another book." Grant had a sudden thought. "Wait a minute. You dared me to kill you before and now I'm ready to shoot you, and you don't want to be shot," said Grant, bemused.

"That—that was before I got a job as a PI," said Herb, his eyelid twitching. "I didn't have enough money to buy a fix. Now I'm earning some from my job."

"So now you don't want to die. Is that it?"

"I dared you because I was desperate then. I was in a black hole of depression. Now I'm seeing a sliver of light."

"I've always accepted your dares. I don't like the idea of backing down from one," said Grant, aiming his SIG at Herb's forehead.

"You'd be committing cold-blooded murder. That's not you, Grant. You're going through rough times. I've been there. I know what you're going through, but things will get better. You know what they say—when one door closes, another one opens."

"Saying it doesn't make it true."

"But it *is* true. I was down and out without a job a little while ago, and now I got a job."

"Just because it's true for you doesn't mean it's true for everyone else."

"You're too wired to think straight. Are you tweaking?"

"I'd be doing both of us a favor if I shot you. You're the guy who tried to frame me for murder."

"You're acting paranoid."

"Are you retracting your dare?"

"You know we're not allowed to retract a dare."

"I don't want to be the first one who backs down from a dare."

"You don't have to accept the dare right now," said Herb, grimacing with apprehension. "You can accept it later. There's no time limit."

"What's the difference? Now or later?"

"You're too stressed now. You'll change your mind when you get your shit together."

"Stop trying to frame me for the movie murders."

Herb shook his head in frustrated disbelief, looking at sea.

"Why are you writing messages on my bathroom mirror?" said Grant.

"Make sense," said Herb, perplexed.

"Tell me," said Grant, motioning with his SIG aimed at Herb's head.

"I'm not writing messages on your mirror."

Grant didn't want to blow away his own brother, but the guy was trying to frame him for murder. Grant couldn't understand why Herb was doing it. Was Herb jealous of him? What did he have that Herb would be jealous of? Grant was a bankrupt writer

135

who had written several horror novels that nobody had bought. How could anyone be jealous of him? Then why was Herb trying to frame him? None of it made sense.

Bewildered and dazed, Grant lowered his SIG.

"You're pushing yourself too hard," said Herb, and, seizing his opportunity, slipped out the door into the hallway, worried Grant might change his mind and threaten to shoot him again.

Grant wasn't going to pursue him. He tossed his pistol on the sofa. He wondered if Herb had gotten the message to stop framing him.

He felt his cell phone vibrate in his trouser pocket. He took the call.

"Hi," said Sherry. "How are you?"

"OK," he said, tensing at the sound of her voice.

"Jade didn't get the PayPal you sent for me yet."

"Because I didn't send it."

"It's not much. Just four thousand dollars."

"Not much? That's a lot when you're broke."

"I almost got run over by a train last night."

"What are you talking about?"

"I was sleeping on the railroad track at Grand Central Station when I heard the train coming and woke up. I got off the track just in time before the train would have run over me."

Her lies were getting more and more outrageous.

"Why were you sleeping on a railroad track?" he said, rolling his eyes.

"I told you I can't afford a hotel and I have no money to fly back to LA. I need six thousand dollars now."

"*Six* thousand? You said *four* thousand before."

"They raised the price of the plane ticket on me. Certain days cost more."

"I can't help you."

"How can you do this to me?" she said, her voice quavering.

"Don't you understand the meaning of the word *bankrupt*?"

"I don't understand legal stuff."

"When are you gonna pay me back?"

"When my uncle's money is out of probate. I can't get any of it till it clears probate."

"How long is that gonna take?"

136

"My lawyer said it could take years."

Grant fetched a long sigh. "You owe me hundreds of thousands of dollars. You're never gonna pay me back."

Even if he was able to lend her money, he wouldn't. Her credibility had sunk to zero.

"Do you want me to get run over by a train?" she said.

"Don't sleep on a railroad track."

He terminated the call and, worked up, paced around his apartment. He wasn't going to go through this again with her. He didn't know how to get her to stop making her unending demands for money.

His cell phone vibrated. It was her. Shaking his head he didn't take the call.

Reality was suffocating him.

Something inside him was telling him to go to another showing of *Necromaniac*.

Chapter 36

Kudlow knew what the mayor wanted, and he wasn't happy. Mayor Mary Coombs had summoned him to her office at City Hall with its distinctive art deco tower located in the Civic Center.

Wearing his trademark shades he was striding behind the mayor's tall skinny aide clad in a black suit. The aide led him toward Coombs's office down a long hallway where Kudlow spotted her sitting behind an outsized desk in her office in room 300. Catching sight of him she stood up. Her hair cropped, wearing a maroon dress, she was a short, middle-aged black woman with a smooth mahogany complexion. Round-lensed tortoiseshell spectacles perched on her retrousse nose.

She smiled when she saw him, and he knew he was doomed.

The aide shut the door behind him, leaving Kudlow alone in the office with Coombs.

"Have a seat, Mr. Kudlow," she said. "You're probably wondering why I invited you to my office."

Kudlow took a seat in front of her desk, his face somber. "I can guess."

"I love movies. It's so much fun living in a city that includes Hollywood, the film capital of the world."

Kudlow stared at her, wishing she would get to the point.

"With all due respect, would you mind terribly taking off your sunglasses while you're in my office," said Coombs. "I like to see the eyes of the people I'm talking to."

"I can see fine," said Kudlow.

"But *I* can't see your eyes. Do you mind? You can put them back on as soon as we're done."

Kudlow didn't want to sit here talking about his sunglasses for the next hour. He acceded to her request and removed his shades. He narrowed his eyes in the sudden light. He hadn't realized how bright it was in here.

"Thank you," said Coombs.

"No problem," he said, his eyes adjusting to the light.

She sat down in her chair. "As you are no doubt aware, your latest horror movie *Necromaniac* is causing a major disturbance in our city."

"Good art breeds discussions."

"But your movie is also breeding violence." Coombs's face clouded. "We can't have violence in my city."

"Art does *not* breed violence, and my film *is* art."

"The fact of the matter is three people have been murdered while watching your horror movie. There are some people who even go so far as to claim it's cursed."

Kudlow snickered. "Cursed? I think not. We're not living in caves anymore, Madam Mayor. We're living in an advanced civilized society. Does anybody really believe in curses these days?"

"Why aren't any other movies at the theaters inciting murders? Why is it only yours?"

"I can't answer that."

"There must be something about it that sets people off. It triggers them. Murder is unacceptable in my movie theaters."

"It's unacceptable in any movie theater except when it's onscreen."

"Point taken. But these killings must stop." Coombs paused for effect. "To me it looks like the only sure way to stop them is to have your movie pulled from theaters."

Kudlow bolted to his feet. "Pulling my film isn't gonna get the killer off the streets. He's gonna continue to kill until the cops bust him."

"As far as we know there could be more than one killer. They only strike in a theater that is showing your movie. Therefore they won't kill if your movie isn't being shown anywhere. It's simple logic."

"It's false logic. He's a psycho killer. I don't know what's setting him off, but pulling my film from theaters isn't gonna stop him from continuing his murder spree."

"All due respect, I'm requesting that you pull your movie from distribution to avoid further disrupting my city," said Coombs, her voice becoming stern. "As I'm sure you've noticed, not only has your movie triggered murders it has sparked riots."

139

Kudlow sat down. "Good art can be controversial. I'm not arguing the fact."

"But inciting riots is illegal."

"The demonstrators protesting the film are the ones inciting riots. They're the ones breaking the law and should be busted."

"They are being arrested when they commit violence during riots, but these riots wouldn't happen if your movie wasn't being shown in theaters."

"This smacks of censorship," remonstrated Kudlow, gesturing with his hand. "We live in a free country where free speech is not only allowed it's encouraged."

Coombs didn't answer for a while, letting Kudlow chill out.

"My Committee for Public Safety is discussing even now whether to remove your film from theaters in order to insure public safety," she said at length, her voice firm. "I'd like you to pull your movie of your own accord without my ordering it."

"Your ordering it would be illegal censorship."

"I'm trying to reason with you," said Coombs, becoming angry. "We're two intelligent people in this room. Let's do the right thing."

"Censorship is never right. That's why we have freedom of speech and freedom of assembly enshrined in the Bill of Rights in this country. People have the right to assemble in front of a silver screen and watch my film."

"I don't want to argue about this anymore. I want you to pull your movie from our theaters as soon as possible."

"You're talking censorship," said Kudlow, resisting.

Coombs cleared her throat noisily.

"Are you aware that Riley Coogan has filed assault charges against you with the police department?" she said, her voice even.

Kudlow bridled. "Oh, I get it. This is a shakedown. If I pull my film, you won't have me busted. Is that it?" he said, fuming.

"A word to the wise is sufficient," said Coombs, keeping her voice low.

Thrusting to his feet Kudlow kicked his chair over and stalked out of the office in an access of rage.

Chapter 37

When Kudlow climbed into the backseat of the black limo waiting for him in front of City Hall, he clapped eyes on Towers, who was sitting inside, nursing a drink and eying him warily.

Wearing his shades Kudlow slammed the limo door behind him as he scooched onto the backseat.

"What happened?" said Towers, fearing the worst.

The limo pulled away from the curb.

"The frigging mayor wants me to pull my film from theaters," said Kudlow, chafing from his conversation with Coombs.

"Out of the question," said Towers. "We stand to lose millions if we do that."

"It's also censorship. I can't believe she had the gall to ask me."

"I hope you told her no in no uncertain terms."

"It's a violation of freedom of speech."

"We'll sic our pit-bull lawyers on her if she presses the issue."

Kudlow gulped. "She dared to blackmail me. Can you believe it? The mayor blackmailing one of her citizens? It's unheard-of."

Towers cocked his head. "Is she threatening to blackball you like the HUAC did to Hollywood directors back in the forties? Did she call you a communist?"

"No. Riley Coogan filed an assault charge against me. Coombs let it be known that she would be willing to look the other way and not pursue the charge if I agree to pull *Necromaniac* from theaters."

"Don't let her shake you down. We won't stand for it," said Towers, and took a pull on his drink.

"She seems convinced my film is inciting its audience to commit murder. *Which is insane.* It's a work of art. I grant you it's disturbing, but good horror films *are* disturbing. She's blaming me for the murders. Can you believe it?"

Towers gaped. "Did she charge *you* with three murders?"

141

"No. Not yet anyway. Maybe that's her next ploy. I wouldn't put it past her. She'll do anything to torpedo my film. She thinks it will save her political career. Her polls are lousy, as you know."

"We'll sue her if she tries anything," said Towers, setting his jaw.

"Banana republics persecute their artists. This is America. We don't persecute artists simply because we don't like their politics in this country."

"Except for HUAC."

"Those directors were blacklisted as a result of World War II. They were accused of being communists who were plotting to overthrow democracy. HUAC doesn't exist anymore."

"Yeah, well, the mayor's Committee for Public Safety sounds dangerous to me. I'm convinced she wants to take steps to censor movies."

"I refuse to believe my film is brainwashing people into committing murder," said Kudlow, hammering the air with his fist.

"The irony is the murders were helping sell tickets at first. Now we're looking at censorship. Go figure," said Towers, snickering. "On the other hand, with all this publicity the pendulum might swing back the other way and gin up ticket sales as long as we don't pull the movie."

"She's got me over a barrel."

"Don't let her intimidate you into pulling your movie. She'll set a precedent if you let her get away with this. Other politicians will try the same stunt and censor movies they don't like if she succeeds. We've got to challenge her on this."

"I don't want to go to jail for assault," said Kudlow, brooding.

"Don't worry about it. We'll get our lawyers to work out a settlement with Coogan. We can handle him. He has a reputation for suing everybody. He likes to antagonize the guests on his show and get them so worked up that they assault him. Then he sues. He just wants money. If we shell out enough to him, he'll retract his charges and the cops won't be able to bust you for assault."

"I refuse to believe my film is inciting people to kill," said Kudlow, clenching his fist at his side.

"Of course it isn't. Coombs is taking out her incompetence as a mayor on you. If she had a decent police force, this Hollywood

142

Psycho would've been caught long ago. Instead she's got the Keystone Cops and she's looking for a fall guy. That's you."

Kudlow's mood darkened. "My mother wanted me to be a dentist. Maybe she was right."

"Don't go defeatist on me, Norm. You're a great director, the best in the business now that Hitchcock and Kubrick are dead. Fuck the mayor. Don't pull your movie. It's a damn masterpiece of horror right up there with *Psycho*. Let's turn on the news. Maybe they caught the Hollywood Psycho."

Towers used the remote to turn on the local news on the flat-panel HDTV.

A thirtysomething olive-eyed brunette with high cheekbones was reading the news off a teleprompter.

"This just in," she said breathlessly. "Mayor Coombs has announced that the noted film director Norman Kudlow has agreed to pull his movie *Necromaniac* from theaters to avoid inciting more violence in the city."

Kudlow became apoplectic with rage. "I did no such thing. That lying blackmailer."

Towers produced his cell phone.

"I'm calling that station right now," he said, punching numbers on his phone. "I want you to tell them the truth." He grimaced. "Shit. The line's busy. I can't get through."

Kudlow fished out his cell phone from his trouser pocket.

"I'll post the truth on my Facebook page," he said, selecting his Facebook app.

"Good thinking. What would we do without social media? Fake news is everywhere these days. The truth *will* get out."

The mayor is mistaken, Kudlow typed on his Facebook page. I have NOT decided to pull my film from theaters.

Towers leaned toward Kudlow, read the FB post, and nodded his approval.

"Explain that, Mayor of Mendacity," crowed Kudlow, beaming with triumph. "Goddamn lying politicians."

Chapter 38

When Grant saw the news about the mayor's announcement on TV in his apartment, he freaked out. How could they pull such a masterwork of horror from theaters? It was unconscionable. It was censorship. It was downright un-American. It was obvious the mayor had bullied Kudlow into pulling his movie. Leave it to a politician to toss a monkey wrench in the works.

Grant loved the movie and wanted to see it over and over again. The idea that he wouldn't be able to see it again threw him into a frenzy.

Gritting his teeth he snagged his SIG from his sofa. He would hunt down the tinpot caudillo and take her out.

Scoping out his SIG P226, he realized it was too big to carry around as a concealed weapon. He made a beeline for his closet, replaced the P226 on the top shelf, and pulled down a SIG P365, a much smaller pistol that he could conceal in his waxed trucker jacket inside pocket.

When he had had money before Sherry had swindled him, he had bought the two handguns for self-protection. Now after she had taken him to the cleaner's, he couldn't afford to buy a water pistol. He had fantasized about using one of the guns on her . . .

He wasn't going to waste his time thinking about Sherry. He had to stop the caudillo from taking his favorite horror film out of distribution. The time had come for the censor to be censored.

On the other hand, the mayor had said Kudlow had *agreed* to pull his movie from the theaters. Grant found it hard to believe that Kudlow would agree to such an arrangement. Should he talk to Kudlow before going to the mayor? If it was Kudlow's idea to pull his movie, Grant had to get him to change his mind. Nah. It was the mayor's idea. She had used intimidation tactics to coerce Kudlow into bending to her will.

Grand felt his cell phone vibrate in his trouser pocket. He took the call.

"The trustee lawyer wants to sue your girlfriend and her sister for the seven hundred thousand dollars she borrowed from you," said his lawyer, Becky Ludovic.

"Good," said Grant.

"The problem is they can't locate them. Do you know their addresses?"

"Sherry never gave them to me."

"That makes it difficult to sue them. The trustee lawyer can't serve them with a suit if he doesn't have an address for them."

"Sherry told me she's in New York."

"Do you have an address?"

"Look, she's a pathological liar. I wouldn't believe much of what she says. She claims she's sleeping in Grand Central Station. She's been calling me to get me to send her six thousand bucks, so she can move into a hotel."

"That doesn't help us. We need a good address for her. Did you send her the money?"

"Of course not. I don't have six thousand bucks. That's why I filed for Chapter 7. I have barely enough money for food and rent. I'm living off peanut butter sandwiches and SpaghettiOs."

"There's not much we can do, then. Your case is going to remain open until the trustee lawyer finds a way to serve Sherry and her sister. Without their addresses that's impossible."

"I don't see what I can do," said Grant, at a loss.

"We'll have to keep trying to find them."

"What if she has spent all the money I lent her? What good would suing her do?"

"None."

"She doesn't even have a bank account, as far as I know. At least, that's what she told me. Maybe that's how she protects herself from lawsuits."

"Part of the scam no doubt. That's why the trustee lawyer is suing Sherry's sister too. First things first, though. We need a good address for both of them."

"Every time I asked her for one, she came up with an excuse not to give it to me."

"She's a professional scammer. She knows she's going to get sued in her racket, so she doesn't give out any personal information. She's probably working with a gang of criminals who are telling her how to protect herself from the law."

"What can we do?"

"Nothing. Unless you can get more information on her that I can pass onto the trustee lawyer."

Grant shook his head. "I've tried before. She has never given me a home address. I doubt she ever will, especially if she knows she's gonna get sued."

"Did you tell her the trustee is suing her?"

"No. She keeps telling me she's broke. What good does it do to sue her?"

"You said she was inheriting two million dollars from her uncle."

"That's what she told me, but it could be another one of her lies. Maybe it would be better to sue her sister Jade. She's the one I wired all the money to."

"Do you have *her* address?"

"No."

"Then there's nothing we can do. Your bankruptcy case will remain open until the trustee can figure out who to sue and find their address."

Making it impossible for him to get a decent credit card even though his debts had been discharged.

Ludovic hung up.

Grant had to hand it to Sherry. She had pulled off the perfect con. He wished there was some way to get her to pay back his loan, but, according to his lawyer Ludovic, there wasn't. How was he going to pay for food, rent, medical bills, phone bills, Internet bills, cable bills . . . ?

Why bother thinking about an insoluble problem?

He needed to go to a horror movie. *Necromaniac* fit the bill. He was obsessed with the movie. It was the only thing more terrifying than his own life, which explained its ability to help him escape his misery. Otherwise his mind would become bogged down with his multitude of problems. He had to go to another showing before it was pulled from theaters. Maybe it already had been, he decided with a jolt.

Chapter 39

Grant rushed out his door, locked it, and strode down the hall, wondering which theater to go to this time. Going to a different theater to see the movie helped him escape his life thanks to the different setting.

The theaters were getting farther and farther away from where he lived because of his need to keep going to a different one. Some of these theaters he had never been to before, which actually made it more of an escape from his misery. All to the good.

He wished he had his car back. Every time he thought about his car he thought about the scammer Sherry. Then he got angry. He had to put her out of his mind. He had to see the movie.

Walking through the crosswalk with a spry gait, he got the impression somebody was following him. He wheeled around after he crossed the intersection. Her head down, a woman in her seventies was walking thirty feet behind him, oblivious to him.

Why would anybody be following him? It made no sense. He must be imagining it. A block away he thought he saw Herb tailing him. Whoever it was ducked into a store. Why would Herb be following him? Herb said he was a private detective now. He was probably on a case. There was no reason for him to be tailing Grant.

Grant picked up on a black guy in a dark suit behind him. Was the IRS agent Truex tailing him? No, this guy had a potbelly. Truex didn't.

Grant faced forward again and stepped up his pace. He had to get to a showing of *Necromaniac* before they pulled it from theaters.

He would go to a theater in Marina del Rey. He hadn't seen the movie there yet.

He got on the bus to Marina del Rey and sat on a plastic seat that had no room for his knees, which kept pressing against the hard back of the seat in front of him.

He thought about something Herb had told him. Or had he said It? He couldn't remember. You're acting out of character, or something like that. Maybe Herb was right. Grant found himself angrier than usual, and he couldn't write a word of his new novel. He had never had writer's block before. Why now? He reminded himself of the crematorium operator in *Necromaniac* who was acting out of character. It turned out a demon was possessing her. Could it be possible a demon was possessing him?

He hated himself for having fallen victim to Sherry's con. He had plenty of money before he had met her. Now he was destitute. And there was no way he could get her to repay all of his loans to her.

He sprang to his feet and fell to smashing his head against the steel pole near the rear door of the bus.

"Stop it," cried a heavyset thirtysomething black woman sitting near the back door, widening her eyes with fright. "You're hurting yourself."

Blood commenced pouring down Grant's face as he continued to slam his forehead into the steel pole.

"Somebody, stop him," said the woman.

"What's wrong with him?" said a teenager clad in khaki boardshorts and a white tank top and holding an upright skateboard between his legs as he sat across from her. "Is he on drugs?"

Staring with concern into the rearview mirror, the bearded bus driver pulled the bus to the curb and halted.

Grant's blood was flying all over the bus.

Passengers covered their faces in fear, thinking he might have Covid or AIDS.

"Get off my bus," commanded the bus driver, powering open the rear door.

Grant dashed down the steps out the door and jumped onto the sidewalk, blood streaming down his face and down the front of his shirt.

Seeing he was a few blocks from the ocean, he broke into a run for the beach. A few pedestrians stared at his bloody face in horror, but most paid no attention to him.

When he reached the palisades park overlooking the beach, he pelted into a public restroom and shot the bolt of the lock on the orange-painted steel door behind him. He gazed into the mirror.

148

His face was smeared with blood. He looked like some sort of bloodthirsty fiend who had just fed on a living creature. He pressed a paper towel to the wound in his bruised forehead to stanch the bleeding. He knew that even a tiny cut in the forehead could precipitate copious bleeding. He didn't think he had done serious damage to his head. Then again, he might have suffered a concussion.

What the hell was he trying to do to himself on the bus? Acting out of character. The answer came to him unbidden.

After he had managed to stanch the bleeding with the paper towel, he washed the blood off his face. He didn't know what he was going to do with his bloodstained polo. He didn't see how he could get all the blood off it without putting it in a washing machine. He didn't want people to see him wearing a blood-soaked shirt.

He peeled off his shirt, turned it inside out, and put it back on. Now nobody could see the blood even though he looked strange wearing his shirt inside out. Anyway, it was better than walking around in a blood-smeared shirt.

What the hell had got into him? Banging his head on a steel pole? He was lucky he hadn't fractured his skull. He inspected his head in the mirror again. He didn't think it was fractured. It was throbbing with pain, but that didn't necessarily mean he had broken it.

He nearly jumped out of his skin when somebody rapped hard three times on the bathroom door.

"You got a line out here, buddy," said a gravelly, threatening voice.

Grant flung the steel door open and burst out of the restroom past a rangy homeless guy with a deep-tanned face like a football and a ragged beard who was wearing black shorts and a T with Antisocial stenciled in italics on its chest. He burst out laughing at the sight of Grant booking across the park toward the pier like a whacked-out character in a cartoon.

Grant didn't look back. He had to get to Marina del Rey and see the movie before he tried to kill himself again.

Maybe it was time to call a psychic to exorcise the demon.

And pay him how?

149

He needed to stop thinking and lose himself in the horror movie before the caudillo and/or Kudlow shelved it. Despite what the caudillo had said on TV, Grant couldn't believe Kudlow had agreed to pull it. The man was a great artist. How could he in good conscience withdraw his finest film to date from distribution? It was unthinkable.

When Grant reached Ocean Avenue, he glanced over his shoulder and thought he saw Herb following him. The guy vanished into a smoke shop selling weed and magic mushrooms.

It couldn't have been Herb. This paranoid side of him was becoming intolerable. Who would he see following him next? Which was worse—paranoia or the self-destructiveness he had displayed on the bus? He could do without either of these two new versions of himself.

He strode along the sidewalk in search of another bus stop for a bus headed south toward Marina del Rey so he could see *Necromaniac* one more time.

He had a good mind to contact Kudlow and get him to change his decision about pulling his movie from theaters if indeed Kudlow had agreed to pull it. The media were flunkies of the caudillo and would say anything she told them to say regardless of its veracity.

Chapter 40

"You can't let the mayor bully you into pulling your fantastic movie from local theaters," said Towers, sitting in the backseat of his limo with Kudlow.

"At least she didn't want me to pull it from all of California, just LA," said Kudlow, dispirited.

"You can't let her get you down. Even if she wanted to pull the movie from all of California, she couldn't. She hasn't got the power."

"What if the governor sticks his nose into this mess?"

Towers scratched his stubbled cheek. "I doubt he's eager to get involved in censorship. Look, the law's on our side. Freedom of speech is guaranteed in the Bill of Rights."

Kudlow mulled it over. "I'm of two minds. I don't want anyone to get killed watching my film, but I refuse to believe my film is inciting people to commit murder."

"Exactly. Movies don't incite violence. People do. If the stupid cops would just catch the Hollywood Psycho, we'd be in like Flynn. Nothing could stop us. Everybody would want a ticket to your movie."

"I don't want any more deaths on my hands," said Kudlow, examining his open hand.

"There aren't any deaths on your hands. Don't believe the bullshit that your movie is responsible for the psycho killings."

"It's possible my film *might* be triggering a lone psycho. But anything could trigger a psycho. Looking at a bucket of buttered popcorn could incite a psycho to commit murder. Does that mean buttered popcorn should be banned from movie theaters? Of course not."

"The psycho needs to be pulled off the streets. That's who should be pulled, not your film."

Kudlow knitted his brows. "The thing is if these killings continue, more and more people are gonna want to ban my film."

151

"It's not their decision to make. It's yours. You're the creator. You're the artist. It's your baby."

"What if we pulled my film from theaters for a week or two? Maybe the cops would catch the Hollywood Psycho during that time."

Towers shook his head no. "It makes you look weak, Norman. It makes you look like you're caving to the mayor's demands. Your fans don't want to see you in that light."

Kudlow drummed his fingers on his thigh. "I suppose."

He didn't believe any art should be censored. No artist could exist believing in censorship.

"You know I'm right," said Towers. "We gotta show some balls. If the mayor has her way with you, she's gonna issue more demands. Give her an inch and she'll take a mile. Instead of pulling your film temporarily, she'll want to pull it forever. Your name will be mud. No production company on earth is gonna want to hire you to direct another movie."

Kudlow kneaded his face with his knuckles. "My conscience is giving me a hard time. After all, three people died while watching my film even if they didn't die *because* they were watching it."

"Fuck your conscience. People die all the time. The point is life goes on. No matter what you do, the Hollywood Psycho—where do they get these names?—will continue to kill until he's caught or killed."

Kudlow glanced out the limo's tinted window. Protesters lined the sidewalk, holding placards that condemned his film for inciting violence.

"Don't those bums have jobs?" said Towers, glaring at the protesters.

"There's an undercurrent of hate in this country nowadays," said Kudlow. "Haven't you sensed it? It's one reason I made my film. I'm trying to come to grips with the riptide of hate and violence undercutting today's society."

"We can't let the forces of evil win. That's why you can't let the mayor mau-mau you into pulling your movie. I'm telling you if she succeeds, your movie could be pulled from theaters all across the country, because it means you agree with her that your movie is inciting violence. Once it's pulled, we'll never be able to get it back into distribution."

"I don't agree with her. The problem *isn't* my film. The problem is the Hollywood Psycho nutbag."

Towers gestured with his clenched fist. "That's why we need to stay strong and not cave in to the mayor."

"I never agreed to pull my film. She lied about that. I haven't made a decision yet."

Kudlow stared out the limo window at the demonstrators marching on the sidewalk, their faces contorted with anger. They were glowering at the limo as if they knew he was inside it despite the tinted windows that were obfuscating their vision.

He wanted to tell them to lighten up. In the end it was just a movie. Why go apeshit about a movie?

"Why are we slowing down?" he said. "The crowd looks ugly."

"I'll ask DeShondra," said Towers.

"Protesters are blocking the road up ahead," said DeShondra, the twentysomething black chauffeur with unruly dreadlocks.

"How do they know I'm in here?" said Kudlow, becoming concerned for his safety. "They can't see me."

"Social media probably," said Towers, staring at the agitated crowd with apprehension. "Everybody knows everything that's going on these days because of Facebook and X and Instagram, you name it." He locked his door. "Better lock your door."

Kudlow did so. "Sometimes I think there's a demon out there riling up people. Something's got them going."

The demonstrators surged toward the limo and fell to rocking it. The limo lurched violently back and forth.

Gulping, Kudlow held onto his seat.

"Can they flip this thing over?" Towers asked DeShondra, grabbing the back of the front seat, his voice urgent.

"How should I know? I'm a moonlighting actor, not a professor of thermodynamics," said DeShondra, her face sweaty as she watched through the windshield the raging mob converging on the limo.

"Not thermodynamics," muttered Kudlow, his heartbeat jacked up, his lizard brain elsewhere, thinking whether it was time to flee. "Physics."

"Physics. Thermodynamics. You think I care?"

Three demonstrators in front of the limo screamed with fury and commenced striking the hood with their placards, snarling at the windshield.

"Run the fuckers over," said Towers, his eyes bulging with fear.

DeShondra applied the brakes to the crawling limo. "No thanks. Fuck it. I didn't sign up for this gig to get hit with a murder rap. I'm an actor, goddammit. I should be acting, not running over a mob of maniacs frothing at the mouth."

"Well, act like John Wick and get us the hell out of here before they put our heads on pikes."

DeShondra crossed her arms on her chest in defiance.

"I ain't budgin'," she said.

Grimacing, Towers turned to Kudlow and grabbed him by the arm.

"Maybe if we don't say anything, they won't know we're in here," said Towers, keeping his voice down. "They can't be sure, because they can't see us."

"They shouldn't know we're here in the first place."

"Did you post anything about our whereabouts on Facebook or X recently?"

"No."

Towers thought about it, pursing his lips. "The news said you were in talks with the mayor about your movie. Somebody must have hung a tail on you when you left the mayor's office. They saw you get into the limo."

"Then we're fucked."

"I'm calling the cops," said Towers, producing his cell phone.

At that moment, one of the demonstrators swung a bat and shattered the passenger's-side window in the front of the limo.

"Shit," cried DeShondra, her eyes starting from their sockets.

Chapter 41

Herb was hanging a tail on Grant, because he couldn't understand how Grant knew the third victim of the Hollywood Psycho was a woman. The cops hadn't released any information about the identity of the victim yet. Herb only knew the victim's sex because he had heard a couple of cops talking about her when he was at the crime scene trying to trace the killer.

Herb had been following Grant in his beat-up VW Bug. Herb couldn't believe it when he had seen Grant jump out of the bus with a river of blood pouring out of his face down his shirt. Herb figured Grant must have been mugged on the bus. He wanted to help Grant, but he also wanted to know where Grant was headed. Could Grant have anything to do with the killings at the movie theaters?

Herb had watched Grant run toward the beach. Herb had followed but he didn't want Grant to see him.

It was hard to believe Grant could be involved in the murders, but the guy was acting out of character. Herb figured it had something to do with Grant's ex-girlfriend Sherry. Grant had undergone a sea change when he had met her, and it wasn't a change for the better. Now Grant was broke and resentful on account of Sherry. Could it be possible Grant was cracking up?

The two brothers hadn't been in touch with each other for many years. It could be that Grant was just getting older, rather than his personality was changing. Herb couldn't be sure. After he had seen Grant hop off the bus with his face smeared with blood, Herb was more determined than ever to find out what was going on with Grant.

If a mugger had attacked Grant, why didn't Grant report it to the cops? Then again, maybe Grant had phoned them, but then why did he leave the scene of the crime? He should have stayed on the bus and waited for the cops to arrive.

Herb had seen Grant dart into a restroom in the palisades park that overlooked the beach. When Grant had exited the restroom,

Herb could see that Grant had washed his face and had turned his shirt inside out. Staying out of sight Herb continued to tail Grant.

Grant's behavior wasn't tracking. Herb was more curious than ever to find out what was going on with Grant. Herb couldn't believe Grant would actually murder someone. Still Herb had to know the truth. And if Grant was involved in the psycho killings, Herb would have to report him to the cops even if Grant was his brother.

Spotting Grant whipping his head around to look behind him when Herb reached Ocean Avenue, Herb ducked into a smoke shop that reeked of the sweet aroma of weed. He gazed out the window at Grant, waiting for him to stop looking in this direction. Herb didn't know if Grant had made him.

In any case, Grant faced forward and kept striding down the sidewalk away from Herb, apparently satisfied he hadn't seen anybody tailing him. Herb dashed out of the shop and continued following Grant.

You would think Grant would be headed for the nearest police department to report his mugging on the bus. But Herb doubted it. None of what Grant was doing was making sense.

Herb decided he should keep following him. Could it be possible, as wild as it sounded, that Grant had had something to do with the psycho killings at the theaters? Herb didn't want to believe it. But as yet it was his only lead in the killings, slim as it was. He knew his client Kudlow wanted him to find the killer as soon as possible.

Herb had gotten his fix so he was calmer now, but he was also broke again. The pusher he got his smack from was robbing him blind with his exorbitant prices. Herb hoped Kudlow would give him a bonus if he found the Hollywood Psycho on the nail.

Herb's PI skills had never been the best in the world. He was probably missing an obvious clue that was staring him in the face, but he couldn't give up. If he gave up, he might as well be dead. He would just have to use what skills he had and do his best. He felt the black cloud of depression hovering over him.

He had to ignore it and keep tailing Grant. But did he really want to find out that his own brother was a psycho killer? Maybe he was better off not knowing. But he had to do his job. He needed the money. Always the money. There was no way to live without it.

156

And he wanted to go on living no matter how lousy his life was. Which made no sense if you thought about it. That was the funny thing about life. No matter how awful and full of suffering it was, people still wanted to go on living. He was a strung-out junkie hooked on skag, but he still wanted to see another day—as long as he had enough money to buy more junk.

What if he found out Grant was the Hollywood Psycho? Would he really turn his own brother in? Hopefully, Grant was innocent. But Herb had to know. It was his job.

Chapter 42

"I'm sick of this psycho killer terrorizing our city," said Kesey, a surly expression twisting his face, as he surveyed the most recent crime scene where the Hollywood Psycho had struck.

"I'm with you," said his partner Rivera. "Psycho killers are the worst in my book. They don't kill for a reason. It's loony-tunes time. If a murderer kills out of revenge or greed or something like that, I understand it. But loonies—no. Poor Valentine Martinelli."

"Is that the name of his third victim?"

"Yeah, but it hasn't been released to the public yet until her next of kin are notified."

By themselves they were inspecting the theater seat where the maniac had killed Martinelli. The seat had blood on it, but not a lot.

"Such a waste of humanity for no reason," said Kesey. "And the sad thing is this city's full of kooks, any one of which could wig out and go on a killing rampage in the blink of an eye."

Rivera looked at the blank theater screen. "Do you think this horror movie is triggering the nutbag?"

"Horror movies these days are pretty bloody gruesome. Have you seen any of the newer ones?"

"I don't like horror movies. I see enough horror in my job. I don't want to see more on my time off."

Kesey rubbed his nose. "I've seen a couple. Some of them are bloodbaths. Blood and gore everywhere. Gratuitous wall-to-wall blood for ninety minutes. Did you ever see *Evil Dead Rise*?"

"No."

"Blood everywhere. Unbelievable."

"I prefer comedies."

Kesey smiled. "For sure a comedy won't make you go out and knife somebody in the temple."

"Do you think it's the same killer doing these theater murders?"

Kesey nodded yes. "Same murder weapon. Same MO."

Rivera cringed when she picked up on an animal scurrying under the theater seats.

"Yuk," she said.

"What?"

"Was that a rat? It looked like it had blood on it."

Kesey looked where she was looking. "Where? I don't see anything."

Rivera walked down the aisle, peering along rows of seats at the shelving black concrete floor, watching for movement.

"There it goes," she said, pointing.

Kesey saw the blood-mottled rodent scamper toward the theater screen, squeaking.

"It's a rat," he said, and pegged after it.

"I hate rats."

"We need to catch it."

"I wouldn't want to see a movie in a rat-infested theater," said Rivera, scoping out the theater, which looked fairly new. "Maybe this movie really is cursed."

"You believe in curses and all that?" said Kesey, pausing his search for the rat to eye her, his tone skeptical.

"I believe there are evil forces in the world, and I *am* religious."

"I gave up on religion when nobody ever answered my prayers as a kid."

"My abuela once told me God only helps those who help themselves."

"In other words, he doesn't exist. The proof is he does nothing."

Rivera ignored him. "I believe this movie is cursed. A lot of these horror movies Hollywood cranks out like sausages should never see the light of day."

"If people would stop going to them, Hollywood would stop churning them out."

"Just because people go to them doesn't make the movies worthwhile. They're not good for people."

"I lost it. Where did it go?" said Kesey, casting around the theater near the screen curtain for the rat.

"Why do you care? Let it go."

"I saw blood on it. It could've been near the murder when it was committed and gotten the killer's blood on it."

Rivera jogged over to the screen and joined Kesey hunting for the rat.

"You really think the rat was next to the murder when it happened?" she said.

"I'm chasing every clue we can get. Right now we got squat. If the killer's blood spilled onto the rat, we gotta get that rat," said Kesey, sweeping the floor with his gaze.

"It could be the victim's blood."

"The point is we gotta find out. There it goes."

Its back hunched, the rat scampered under a seat in the first row.

"It's heading toward the back row again," said Rivera.

"We can't let it get out of the theater or we'll never find it," said Kesey, bopping down the aisle after the rat.

He whipped out his Smith & Wesson 4506 from his shoulder rig.

"Are you gonna blow it away?" said Rivera with surprise.

"If I have to."

"You still use that old S&W 4506?" said Rivera, pulling out an FN 509 from the holster on her waist.

"I like it. It's solid stainless steel. It'll last forever. And I prefer its .45 ACP rounds to 9 mils. More stopping power."

"You don't need a lot of stopping power for a rat."

Kesey shot her a dirty look.

"Look at us," Rivera said dryly, gun in hand. "On safari for rats."

"Where did it go?"

"You're gonna turn that rat into mincemeat with a .45 ACP round."

"We can't let it get out of here. It has evidence on its fur."

"Rat blood will get mixed with the human blood on the fur if you blow away the rat."

"The ME can separate them. We humans don't have the same blood as rats."

"How do you know?"

"Do you really believe you have rat blood running through your veins?" said Kesey, staring at Rivera in disbelief.

160

"Blood is blood. I don't think we should mix the rat blood with the human blood. Maybe the DNA will get contaminated."

Kesey fired a round at the scampering rat. The rat screeched, did a somersault, and kept running. Kesey cursed. As he pursued it he tried to acquire the moving target in his sights again.

"That's our best piece of evidence," he said, chasing the rat. "We can't let it get away."

"What about fingerprints near the chair where the victim sat?"

"Forensics got a bunch of prints, but there's no guarantee any of them are the killer's."

The rat scrambled under a row of seats, disappearing from sight.

"The doors are closed," said Rivera. "How can it get out? We just have to corner it."

"Then what?"

"Do you have a box or something?"

"I don't carry boxes around with me," said Kesey, trying in frustration to locate the rat underneath the theater seats. "Where'd it go?"

Rivera confronted the rat standing near the wall that skirted the seats.

Feeling trapped, the rat twitched its whiskers, snarled at Rivera, and charged her.

She screamed and kicked it in the head, sending it flying into the wall. It slid down the Sheetrock and lay in a senseless heap on the carpet.

"Good work," said Kesey, belting after the rat. "We gotta grab it before it comes to."

He lifted the rat by the tail.

"You're not supposed to do that," said Rivera, watching him.

"Do what?"

"Lift it by its tail. It hurts the rat."

"Fuck the rat. I don't want it to bite me. Where are we gonna put it till we can get it to the ME? It might come to any minute."

Rivera chewed it over. "I'll think of something."

"Hurry," said Kesey. He sniffed the rat. "It smells like cedar chips."

"Maybe it's already dead."

"I don't have a stethoscope on me to find out."

161

"I'm thinking. You know, Valentine Martinelli had an empty cage on her stomach. Maybe this rat was in the cage. The cage had cedar chips in it."

"You're saying this rat was the victim's pet?"

"Why not?"

"Sounds weird to me."

The rat twitched.

"Oh, shit," said Kesey.

"Maybe it's just a reflex," said Rivera, watching the rat.

"We need a container."

"I know," said Rivera, snapping her fingers. "I'll get my duty bag from the cruiser. You can put the rat in there."

"All right. Make it fast," said Kesey, dreading the rat would regain consciousness any second.

He glanced with disgust at the rat dangling by its tail from his hand.

"Don't let go of it," said Rivera.

"I don't want rabies."

"I'll be right back."

Rivera sprinted out the theater.

Kesey felt a strong urge to stomp on the rat to make sure it was dead. However, he didn't want to contaminate the blood DNA on the rat fur with rat blood, because it might belong to the psycho killer, so he bridled the urge.

The rat twitched again.

"Don't."

The rat went still.

"Good boy."

162

Chapter 43

Grant reached his movie theater of choice in Marina del Rey, jumped off the steel steps leading from the rear door of the bus, landed on the sidewalk, and strode toward the marquee.

He was surprised to see people gathered in front of the marquee milling around the sidewalk. They looked confused and ticked off.

"What's happening?" Grant asked a longhaired guy pushing thirty, wearing a white T with Black Sabbath printed in black gothic letters across its chest.

"The usher told us they're shutting down the theater until they hear from the LA mayor about her and Kudlow pulling *Necromaniac* from distribution."

"Kudlow would never agree to pull his film."

"I don't believe it either, but the usher wants to wait till Kudlow makes an announcement on TV about what the mayor said."

"Marina del Rey has its own mayor, and it's not Coombs."

"The owner of this theater is gonna follow Coombs's example."

"That's a ridiculous overreaction."

"I'm with you, dude. I want to see this movie. It's supposed to be some scary shit."

"It's so real you feel like it's happening to you."

"You saw it?" said Sabbath with interest.

"Yeah."

"Do you think it makes people kill each other?"

"No way." Grant noticed a frosty crowd gathering across the street. "Who are those guys across the street?"

"Idiot protesters. They think the movie promotes violence. They want to shut it down."

Grant gazed through the closed plate-glass doors into the theater lobby.

"Is there some way we could sneak into the theater and see the movie?" he said.

"I'm right behind you, dude," said Sabbath with an eager visage. "Do you know how to work a digital video projector?"

"Isn't the movie already in the projector? It shouldn't be that difficult if it's ready to go."

Its light bar flashing red and blue, a black-and-white tooled down the street.

"Forget it," said Sabbath. "Five-O. I'm not busting into the theater with them here."

Out of the corner of his eye Grant caught sight of Herb approaching on the sidewalk. Grant wheeled around to confront him.

"Are you following me?" said Grant, seething.

"No," said Herb. "I heard they shut down *Necromaniac* at this theater. I wanted to see if there's been a murder here."

Grant narrowed his eyes. "I thought I saw you following me."

"It wasn't me. Has there been a murder here or not?" said Herb, surveying the closed theater.

"No murder," said Sabbath. "The owners got cold feet and won't let anybody in. They told us the mayor and Kudlow are pulling the movie from theaters."

"Bullshit," spat Grant.

"I'm convinced this movie's cursed. What about you guys?"

"It's a great movie. People think it's cursed because it seems so real. Which proves it's a masterpiece of horror. It deserves an Academy Award. Instead, the powers that be want to censor it."

Grant picked up on a sign that said Burn This Movie popping up across the street. More signs sprouted up like weeds in an untended garden. Save the Children. Horror Kills. Horror Promotes Murder.

"Those people are scarier than any horror movie," said Herb, eyeballing the protesters.

"Why doesn't Kudlow make a public announcement that he's not gonna pull his movie?" said Grant. "What's taking him so long? There's no way he's gonna let the blowhard mayor steamroll him into submission. He's the best living director. He won't cave."

"He made an announcement on Facebook and X that he wasn't gonna pull his movie," said Sabbath.

164

"There you go. Then what's the problem?"

"This theater owner wants to see him say it on TV. That's what I heard."

"So nothing is true unless you see it on TV?"

"The way things are, Kudlow's lucky they don't throw him in jail," said Sabbath, furrowing his brow with worry.

"Like this is some third-rate banana republic? It can't happen here. We don't jail our artists in this country."

"It's getting so it's not safe to live in this city."

Grant eyed the protesters. "Lighten up, people. It's just a movie."

He doubted they could hear him. The chanting demonstrators were stirring up too much of a ruckus for them to hear anyone but themselves, drowning out everybody who disagreed with them.

"The movie's cursed," they roared, shaking their fists. "Burn it in hell."

"Do-gooders scare the shit out of me," said Sabbath.

"The horrible thing is they think they're doing us a favor by censoring the movie, saving us from demons," said Grant.

"Who's gonna save us from the do-gooders?" said Herb.

"The road to hell is paved—"

An explosion rocked the sidewalk, buckling it. The bombed theater burst into a conflagration, sending searing flames billowing across the street. The crowd panicked, screamed, and ran for cover.

Chapter 44

Starting at the blast, Grant, Herb, and Sabbath scrambled away from the theater as masonry and jagged chunks of concrete rained down on the sidewalks and street, smashing several fleeing people in the head and killing them while gravely wounding dozens of others.

The blast hurled the marquee into the air and dumped it into the middle of the street, smashing its neon lettering tubes and light bulbs.

"It's the cursed movie," a middle-aged woman cried, cradling her white poodle in her arms, fleeing for her life through the smoke, blaze, and raining debris. "It's killing everyone."

"They're not even showing the movie," said Grant, watching her from the doorway of an apartment house in bewilderment, his heartbeat racing. "Why is everybody blaming the movie?"

He coughed on the smoke that was stinging his eyes and spotted a length of rebar cartwheeling through the air, hurled by the force of the blast. The rebar impaled the eye of a ponytailed middle-aged man with a receding hairline, pierced his brain, and blew out the back of his skull, which clattered and fragmented on the sidewalk. A piece of skull in the shape of a china saucer held an oozing portion of brain.

Grant winced watching the impaled man scream in agony, clutch his head, and crumple on the sidewalk. When the remaining back of his skull struck the concrete, the protruding end of the rebar hit the concrete as well and was jammed backward through the man's brown eye, skewering it and popping it from its socket like a shish kebab. The man's body shuddered on the sidewalk then became motionless.

Grant felt the blood drain from his face. He looked away from the corpse.

An upholstered steel theater seat catapulted by the explosion rocketed through the air and crashed into the head of a seventyish, crabby pedestrian with a bushy white mustache who was wearing a

166

pale green gimme cap and was trying to flee. The steel back of the seat fractured his skull and decked him. His brains seeped out of the fissures in his skull like albumen out of a cracked eggshell and slicked the sidewalk, where a fleeing teenage brunette in distressed jeans slipped and fell on her face, breaking her nose and shattering her front teeth.

The dead were everywhere. Screams, sobs, and the groans of the wounded filled the smoky air, turning the area into a war zone.

"A demon didn't destroy the theater," said Grant. "A saboteur did. They planted a bomb in it."

"How do you know it wasn't the Hollywood Psycho?" said Herb, standing on the same steps leading to the apartment house doorway where Grant was standing.

"Why would he suddenly change his MO?"

"Good point."

"This movie's getting a bum rap," said Sabbath, his elbows bloody, coughing on the swirling smoke as he approached Grant and Herb.

"Are you OK?" said Herb.

"I'm fine as a frog's hair," said Sabbath. "Just smoke in my lungs." He went on a coughing jag. "I got lucky," he said between hacks. "Look at all those dead bodies strewn on the street like rag dolls."

A dazed brunette in her twenties approached them from the street, her gait unsteady, her dress charred and in tatters. She had lost one of her red pumps when she had fled from the explosion. Pieces of plaster nestled in her full head of hair like spiders in a web.

Sabbath helped her off the street onto the sidewalk. "Are you all right?"

"My ears are ringing," she said, her eyes unfocused. "I can't hear. I'm fucked. The blast knocked me over. I skinned my hands."

She showed him her barked palms, which dripped blood.

Its siren blaring, a fire engine shrieked down the street toward the burning theater, two black-and-whites with flashing light bars on its heels. A boxy red van carrying EMTs wasn't far behind.

"I'll take you to the paramedics," said Sabbath, escorting her toward the EMT vehicle.

167

"Who would do such a thing?" said Herb, eying the bombed-out, blackened husk of the burning theater with some of its broken two-by-fours still standing. "Nobody bombs movie theaters. It's crazy."

"The rabblerousing mayor is stirring up the public by telling them Kudlow said he would pull his movie from distribution, but Kudlow never verified her announcement," said Grant. "*Necromaniac* is a work of art. It shouldn't be banned or burned. It should be enshrined for future generations to see and enjoy."

"I haven't been able to see it yet."

"You gotta see it before the mayor gets her way. I hope Kudlow fights her tooth and nail to keep his movie in theaters."

"Where is Kudlow? I haven't heard anything about him since the mayor's announcement."

"Maybe he's hiding. I wouldn't blame him. I bet he's getting death threats from these jacked-up protesters with a hard-on for him."

"Why did you come here to see this movie again?" said Herb. "You already saw it."

"Because it's good. If I like a movie, I go to it more than once." Grant glowered at him. "Is that a problem?"

"Of course not."

"Why are you following me anyway?"

"I—uh—need more money. I don't want to get evicted. I wanted to ask you for a loan."

"I thought you got a job."

"It doesn't pay that well. I don't want to go cold turkey," said Herb, brushing beads of sweat from his forehead. "Can you spare five hundred bucks? I'll pay you back."

"Where have I heard that before?" said Grant, thinking of Sherry, his expression jaundiced.

"I mean it. As soon as my client pays me, I'll pay you back."

Firemen sprayed the burning theater with hissing high-pressure water hoses.

Damaged by the blast, a palm tree growing out of the sidewalk near the demolished theater cracked loudly and fell across the street. The palm fronds struck a bank's roof, leaving the trunk canted at a forty-five degree angle spanning the boulevard.

"I think we should beat it," said Grant. "I don't want to get pumped by cops about what I saw here."

Especially since he was packing a gun. If the cops found out he was carrying, there would be hell to pay. All sorts of suspicion would be directed his way. He couldn't remember why he was packing heat. The damn terrorist explosion had scrambled his brains.

"Me either," said Herb, glancing furtively at the uniforms piling out of their squad cars.

Grant and Herb stole away from the bomb site, hugging the shadows as they departed.

Chapter 45

"The cops came just in time," said Kudlow, disheveled, mulling over his close shave with the demonstrators who had trashed the limo he had shared with Towers.

The demonstrators had been in the process of dragging DeShondra out of the limo driver's seat when the cops had arrived and busted them for assault and for vandalizing the limo.

Kudlow was riding in another limo now with Towers in the backseat, DeShondra at the wheel, looking nervous, anticipating another assault by demonstrators.

"You guys don't pay me enough for this job," said DeShondra. "I should get hazard pay."

"Relax," said Towers. "Nobody knows we're in here. The windows are tinted. You worry too much."

"How did they know we were in the other limo? It had tinted windows too."

"They must have seen Norman get in it outside City Hall after he met with Coombs."

"I don't want to die in no riot over a movie I never seen," said DeShondra.

Towers made a dismissive gesture toward DeShondra and faced Kudlow.

"I hope those animals helped you make up your mind about what to do with your movie," said Towers.

Kudlow poured himself a glass of pinot noir from the minibar attached to the back of the front seat and quaffed it.

"My mind's made up," he said. "Before I wasn't sure, because my conscience doesn't want anyone to die because of my film. I still feel the same, by the way."

"Your movie's not causing any deaths," said Towers, putting up his hands in front of him and patting the air, trying to calm Kudlow down.

"Let me say my piece. However, I refuse to be bullied into pulling my film from distribution."

Towers ripped loose a hoot of joy and flashed two thumbs up. "*All right.* I knew you wouldn't cave."

"I'm not gonna let a pack of harebrained hyenas with AI-generated signs tell me what kind of film I can make."

"Right on."

"And I'm not gonna let a lying double-dealing mayor put words in my mouth about me pulling my movie." Kudlow tossed back his drink. "Fuck her."

"I'll drink to that."

Brimming with optimism Towers poured himself a glass of Scotch from the minibar.

Drink in one hand, a remote in the other, he turned on the flat-panel TV that hung suspended from the headliner.

"I'm gonna enjoy every minute watching her eat her words when you tell her to shove it," he said.

A picture of the smoking bombed-out remains of the theater in Marina del Rey appeared on the TV screen.

"Jesus," said Towers, awestruck.

"It looks like something out of World War II Berlin," said Kudlow, overcome. "I know that theater. It's one of my favorites."

"I'm telling you the news scares me more than any horror movie. I see dead bodies."

"And the demonstrators think my film's too violent with its demon horror? Gimme a break. Look at that debacle. How many innocent lives were lost?" said Kudlow, his eyes morose.

"What happened? That's the Marina theater. We get good sales there."

On the screen EMTs removed corpses and blood-streaked, wounded bodies on gurneys from the smoking rubble.

"What kind of depraved nitwit would bomb a movie theater?" said Kudlow. "When these cancel culture maniacs start bombing film theaters, they've crossed the line. This isn't just vandalism. They're committing mass murder."

"The politicians are inciting this violence," said Towers. "They get everyone worked up, telling them the movie is making people violent, and look what happens. They're incentivizing people to commit violence. Egged on by demagogues, a headcase blows up a theater showing your movie."

171

"You can bet Coombs is gonna make me the fall guy for this bombing," said Kudlow, squirming in his seat, hot under the collar.

"That's how pols gain power. By scapegoating."

"This is getting worse by the second."

"Look at it this way. The news says the theater was closed when it got bombed, because the owner didn't want to show your movie. So they can't blame the bombing on your movie."

Kudlow gave him a long look. "Listen to what you're saying. Any theater associated with my film is gonna get blamed for deaths, first psycho killer victims, now terrorist bomb victims."

"But they *weren't* showing your movie at the time of the bombing. That's the important thing."

"My film is the film they would have shown if they'd been open. I can see my detractors blaming it and me for the bombing," said Kudlow, tugging at his collar.

"I'm not so sure. There could be a backlash against these protesters after the public finds out they bombed a theater and killed dozens of innocent people."

"Whoever did this not only hates films but humanity itself. What kind of sicko hates humanity? How can anyone get off on blowing up people? The loss of life is staggering . . . ," said Kudlow, his voice faltering.

"These stupid demonstrators, that's who. This is how they protect us from movies they don't like. Blow everybody to kingdom come."

"People who hate movies should be called out. It's inexcusable. They're the same people who burn books."

Towers put his forefinger to his lips. "Shh. Don't give people any ideas. They'll start throwing films in bonfires."

"Do they really think banning certain films is gonna make society better?"

"Nobody's forcing anybody to go to your movie. Filmgoers are going because they *want* to go. I don't see how anybody can blame you for the violence racking the city. Put the blame where it belongs. On the protesters and bomb throwers."

"Coombs is the one painting a bullseye on my back. She wants me dead if I don't agree to pull my film from distribution. It wouldn't surprise me if she was the one who ordered the theater

172

bombed to put pressure on me to knuckle under to her demands to withdraw my film."

Towers scratched his cheek stubble with a pensive visage as he studied the demolished theater on screen.

"How are we gonna handle this?" he said.

"Pull a Polanski and flee the country," said Kudlow.

"I'm not joking."

Kudlow pursed his lips with displeasure. "What makes you think I was joking?"

"Polanski raped an underage girl. You didn't commit a crime. There's no comparison."

"The mayor is portraying me as a bloodthirsty monster who makes films that incite violence. In other words, I'm a criminal in her eyes."

"Listen to me. We need you to appear before the cameras and make a statement that you're appalled by this tragedy, that your enemies are responsible for the devastation and loss of lives. Your movie and your fans had nothing to do with the bombing."

"If I make a public appearance, it might touch off violence."

"You could make your announcement in a studio without an audience." Towers paused. "Or you could appear on Riley Coogan's show."

"No way. That slimy snake would do everything he could to put me in a bad light—"

"Did you hear that?" said Towers, holding up his hand.

"What?"

"The newscaster said the Committee for Decent Movies has claimed responsibility for the terrorist explosion."

"Never heard of them. What are they? A violent updated version of the Hays Code?"

"Whoever they are they need to be jailed. The movie business is in a slump as it is because of Covid and recent strikes by the actors and writers. Now no one is gonna feel safe going to a movie because of these terrorists. Movie theaters are gonna be empty."

"I can see the mayor now blaming my film for their act of terrorism."

"These assholes are gonna do more to wreck the movie business than Covid," said Towers, put out.

173

"I wonder if they have anything to do with the mayor's Committee for Public Safety."

"The mayor and the muckraking media are working hand in glove to whip the public into a feeding frenzy."

"I'm not gonna let terrorists push me around. I don't cave in to intimidation."

"That's what I want to hear," said Towers, smiling.

Chapter 46

Grant rode shotgun in Herb's VW Bug as Herb drove. Herb glanced at him.

"Why don't you make amends with Sherry?" he said.

"Are you kidding? She defrauded me out of almost a million bucks."

"Have you listened to her side of the story?"

"Her side of the story is she wants me to loan her more money, which she will never pay back."

"Having a hate on for her solves nothing. Don't you want to get back with her?"

"I don't want a relationship with a scammer, a liar, and a fraudster," said Grant, incensed by the way Sherry had used her romantic relationship with him to inveigle him out of his money.

"Maybe she is gonna pay you back when she gets her inheritance from probate."

Grant laughed. He couldn't help it. The idea that Sherry would ever pay him back was farcical.

"Believe it or not, that's what I used to think," he said. "*Boy,* was I wrong. It was a scam from the get go, and I fell for it."

"You're too cynical about people."

"That's what I kept telling myself when I was seeing her. I told myself I was too cynical, so I kept giving her the benefit of the doubt because I was involved with her, and I kept loaning her hundreds of thousands of dollars. Stupid me," said Grant, slapping his forehead and feeling like kicking himself.

"You make her sound like a demonic monster."

"She's a scammer, pure and simple. A professional crook. And what steams me is there's nothing I can do about it to get any of my money back."

"Holding a grudge against her won't do you any good. Forget about it and move on."

"I don't have much choice in the matter."

"You know what they say. Time heals all wounds."

"How can I forget about it when she keeps calling me and trying to borrow more money?"

"We're all hurting," said Herb, staring out the windshield as he drove. "We're all damaged goods."

Grant whipped his head toward Herb. "*She* isn't hurting. She scammed me and she got away with it."

"If you really believe she scammed you, why don't you sue her?"

"With what? I can't afford a lawyer. She got everything from me. Helping her was like stepping into quicksand. The more money I loaned her and the deeper I got, the harder it was for me to escape. I kept loaning her more money and maxing out my credit cards in the hope that she really would pay me back." Grant hung his head. "My hope turned out to be a delusion."

"I'm hearing she's homeless."

"I doubt it. I'm sure she's found another victim for her scam. She's a pathological liar. She'll tell any lie to get money. I don't know how she could spend almost a million bucks in a little over a year. It's mind-boggling."

"I dunno, but it sounds like you miss her."

Grant did at double take. "How do you figure that? What I miss is the woman she pretended to be, the woman who was down on her luck and needed to borrow money and would pay it back, because she was going to inherit a fortune from her uncle. That's the woman I miss, not the lying scammer who never had any intention of paying me back. For all I know she inherited zilch. The inheritance story could have been part of her scam. She could be running a racket with her cohorts, like her sister, and probably others."

"Did you tell the cops?"

"I did. I told them she defrauded me."

Herb eyed him. "What'd they do?"

"They took my report and did nothing."

Herb shrugged. "Cops. What do you expect?"

"Apparently there's no legal protection against women like Sherry. There must be a lot of them, because they can get away with it. They don't face any legal consequences for their criminal acts."

"Not all women are scammers if that's what you're saying."

"Of course not."

"Maybe you need to get out more and meet new people."

"I'd be a big hit with the girls with my empty bank account," said Grant, smiling wryly.

"Some of your books might start selling. You never know."

"It sounds like you're trying to cheer me up. Why?" said Grant, searching Herb's face, which was concentrating on driving.

"I still need a loan, and I promise I'll pay you back. You can't go around angry and bitter all the time. It's not good for you."

"Why should I loan you anything? You're gonna spend it all on smack."

"Do you want me to go cold turkey?" said Herb, grimacing, his face sweaty.

"Don't blame your junkie ways on me."

"I'm not blaming you. I'm asking for five Ben Franklins."

"You're as deaf as Sherry. I'm broke."

"I wouldn't ask you this if it wasn't an emergency. Cold turkey sucks."

"Maybe a bank will lend you money now that you got a job."

Herb pulled a face. "I just got the job. A bank won't give me the time of day, and you know it."

"I'm not in a good place financially."

"I know you inherited money from Mom."

"We both got the same amount. You spent all of yours on dope. And I had the misfortune to meet a professional scammer who I felt sorry for—"

"Felt sorry for?" said Herb in disbelief. "You wanted to jump her bones."

"I'm no saint. That entered into it."

"That's putting it mildly."

"So here we are stuck in the same leaky boat. Two brothers going nowhere. The Brothers Karamazov except we don't have an Alyosha for a brother."

"You and your literary bullshit. I have no idea what you're talking about."

"We don't have a religious brother. Just two nonbelievers, you and me."

"I believe in smack. It gets me though the day. I have no idea what floats your boat."

177

"I wish I knew," muttered Grant, expressionless. "I guess I'm still trying to find something to believe in."

"You're making life too complicated. Just enjoy what's there."

"Then why do you shoot up?"

"Because—because it's there," said Herb, proud of himself for coming up with an explanation.

"It's not gonna be there if you can't afford it."

"That's where you come in if you can lend me five hundred bucks," said Herb, eying Grant expectantly. "It's your good deed for the day."

"No good deed goes unpunished. I learned that from Sherry," said Grant, his face glum.

"I'm your brother. Can't you help your own blood?"

"Nothing's changed since the last time you asked me. End of story."

Herb fetched a long sigh, his hands on the steering wheel at three- and nine o'clock.

"Maybe you should mend fences with Sherry," he said. "You seem bummed out without her."

Grant shot Herb a death stare. "Not gonna happen. She scammed me. She's a professional crook. She doesn't give a damn about me. All she wants is money."

"Then help her out. Maybe you'll feel better about yourself."

Grant said nothing. Tired of arguing, he gazed out the windshield at the cars up ahead.

Chapter 47

A talking head on TV was explaining why he thought Kudlow's film *Necromaniac* was cursed.

Kudlow and Towers were watching the show from their limo backseat, Kudlow with his trademark shades on.

"Where do they get these idiots?" said Kudlow.

"He's supposed to be some parapsychologist or something," said Towers, unimpressed.

Towers's cell phone chimed. He answered it and listened.

"The mayor wants to talk to you," said Towers, holding his hand over the phone transmitter.

"I don't want to talk to her," said Kudlow, folding his arms on his chest. "I know what she wants. I'm not gonna pull my film."

"I don't know where he is," Towers said into his phone.

Nodding, Towers listened to the mayor.

"I'll tell him you called when I see him," he said, and terminated the call.

"She says there's gonna be more violence if you delay in agreeing to pull your movie from theaters," he told Kudlow. "She wants you to make a public announcement of your decision."

"Did she mention Coogan?"

"Something about he was going to drop assault charges against you if you announce you're pulling your movie."

Kudlow nodded. "She's still trying to shake me down, holding the Coogan charges over my head. I don't respond well to blackmail."

"The thing I don't understand is why people think your movie is cursed."

"There's a long history of cursed horror films in Hollywood."

"But they're just movies, after all."

"There's some truth to the matter. Look at the child star of *Poltergeist*, Heather O'Rourke. She made three of those horror films and died of a heart attack at the tender age of twelve."

179

"Wow. I didn't know. That *is* weird. Kids don't have heart attacks when they're twelve."

"That's not all. The actress Dominique Donne, who played O'Rourke's sister in the movie, was murdered by her boyfriend soon after the premiere of *Poltergeist.*"

"She was the daughter of Dominick Dunne and the niece of the writer Joan Didion, wasn't she?"

Kudlow nodded yes. "And then there's *Twilight Zone: The Movie.* One of the stars, Vic Morrow, was decapitated by a helicopter while he was acting in the movie."

"Oh yeah. I heard of that. They put the director John Landis on trial for homicide—"

"Involuntary manslaughter."

"Yeah, right. And found him innocent. The two kids Vic Morrow was holding in the scene were also chopped in half by the helicopter. Well, accidents happen. What can you do?"

"And then there's Richard Donner's *Omen.* The IRA blew up the hotel where Donner was staying the day after Donner checked out."

"But he didn't get hurt."

"I'm not finished. Gregory Peck starred in the film. His son committed suicide two months before the film started production. That's not all. Peck's plane to London where he was gonna start production on the film was struck by lightning."

"But he didn't get hurt."

"Right. Lightning strikes on planes are common, and passengers don't usually get hurt. The writer David Seltzer's plane was also struck by lightning."

"Hmm. That's a lot of lightning."

"We can't leave out *Rosemary's Baby* from the list of cursed films. A year after Roman Polanski's horror film about a coven of devil worshipers debuted, his pregnant wife, the actress Sharon Tate, was murdered in grisly fashion by the notorious Manson Family, the evilest, sickest cult in American history."

"This is just PR. I'm in the business. I should know. This kind of thing sells movies." Towers hung fire. "Remember, nothing bad has happened to any of the actors in your film or to the writer or to you, for that matter—"

"Not yet, anyway," Kudlow cut in.

"Because there isn't a curse on it."

"Tell that to the filmgoers."

"You don't really believe in cursed movies, do you?"

"I don't. But plenty of others do. And they're the ones fomenting these riots against my film. They want blood."

"I'll tell you what they want. They want your movie to tank at the box office."

"That too."

"We both know there's plenty of schadenfreude in Hollywood. Other filmmakers are jealous of you. They want your movie to fail."

"I can't argue the point. Hollywood *is* a pit viper's nest of envy. But I can't believe other filmmakers would set off a bomb in a theater that was showing my film, because they're jealous of my film."

"That reminds me," said Towers. "The mayor told me to tell you that you have the blood of the bomb victims on your hands."

"Bullshit," exploded Kudlow. "Their blood's on *her* hands for inciting the people with her incendiary rhetoric. Her vicious attacks on my film and her demands to pull it from theaters are triggering the violence."

"I wish you'd tell her to her face. We might get some good PR out of it. I'm sure a lot of people out there feel the same way and would side with you. Movie lovers don't like politicians messing with what they can see at the theater."

"I'm a film director, not a debater," said Kudlow, dismissing the idea.

"We need you to help advertise the movie. You as its director are the best spokesman."

Kudlow wiped his brow. "I'd rather eat broken glass."

"If this movie tanks because of the mayor's war on you, directing offers are gonna dry up for you like milk from a witch's tit. Your future's riding on this movie."

"The psycho killer started this mess. Then the mayor made it worse."

"There's no use crying over spilt milk. It is what it is. You need to keep pushing your flick." Towers paused in thought. "Maybe you should go on TV and attack this bloodthirsty

181

Committee for Decent Movies. They're the ones who killed scores of people with their bomb."

"They're fanatics. They're not gonna listen to me."

"We want the *public* to listen to you. Screw the Committee for Decent Movies. We have to expose them for what they are: censors and terrorists. Nobody likes censors and terrorists in this country. Americans love freedom."

"Where are we heading?" said Kudlow, peering in confusion past DeShondra's right ear out the windshield.

"We ought to return to the mayor's office so you can defy her to her face and have a film crew there to record it."

Kudlow's head jerked forward and to the side as a speeding pickup T-boned the limo.

The limo all but flipped on its side thanks to the violence of the collision, triggering the deployment of airbags in the front and back.

Chapter 48

"I think we should go to the mayor's office," said Grant, riding shotgun in Herb's VW Bug.

"Why?" said Herb, driving.

"To convince her to change her mind about pulling *Necromaniac* from theaters," said Grant, withdrawing his SIG P365 from the inside breast pocket of his jacket.

"Jesus," said Herb, taking his eyes off the road. "Are you gonna shoot me?"

"Look where you're going."

Herb slammed on the brakes as an SUV slowed in front of him on the 10.

"I should shoot you for trying to frame me for the movie murders," said Grant.

"I'm not framing anyone. I'm trying to find the Hollywood Psycho. It's my job."

"Anyway, the frame would never stick. The mayor's the one who's even more dangerous to the movie than the Hollywood Psycho. We need to teach her a lesson."

"They'd bust you in a New York minute as soon as you tried to enter her office with that piece in your hand."

"Sometimes we can't play it safe in life. If we want to stand up for what we believe—freedom of speech—we need to take risks. Nothing is more important than art. Art is truth. We have to save art even if we have to risk our lives to do it. Kudlow's film is a beautiful work of art."

"I thought it was a horror movie," said Herb, his eyes bugging out at the sight of Grant's SIG.

"It's terrifying, all right, but also beautiful."

"They're gonna lock us up if we go to City Hall with that gun."

"Who's gonna save the movie if we don't? The mayor's getting ready to censor it so it'll never see the light of day again. We can't let that happen."

183

"She was just talking. You know windbag politicians. Talk, talk, talk," said Herb, manipulating his hand like a duck quacking. "She's not really gonna pull the movie. Nobody would vote her back into office when election day rolls around."

"She has to do something to make it look like she's trying to stop the violence surrounding the movie. People are scared and want her to act."

"Could you put that gun down? I don't want to get pulled over by cops."

Grant returned the SIG to his inside jacket pocket. "The point is we can't let her ban *Necromaniac*. We gotta stop her. We need to go to her office and persuade her not to pull the movie."

"We're not gonna get within six feet of her when her security guards see that gun. They got metal detectors in City Hall."

"We gotta stop her," said Grant, grinding his teeth, a fixed look of ruthless determination in his eyes. He turned on the news on the car radio. "First, we need to locate her. She might not be in her office now."

"I need a fix," said Herb, his face stippled with beads of sweat that rolled down his cheeks.

"The movie director Norman Kudlow and his PR flack Bill Towers have vanished after a collision with a pickup in Century City," said the radio newscaster. "Their chauffeur has also vanished."

"What?" said Grant, taken aback.

"Maybe they fled the city because they were taking so much heat for his movie," said Herb.

"No way. Kudlow would defend his movie to the death. He wouldn't cut and run. It's not like him. Somebody else is behind this." Grant tapped his fingers on his thigh. "It might even be the mayor."

"The mayor kidnaped him?" said Herb, widening his eyes. "Are you crazy?"

"I wouldn't put it past her. She'll do anything to stay in power."

"He's an internationally famous movie director. Maybe it was aliens from outer space who kidnaped him."

Grant gave Herb a look. "This isn't a joke."

184

"We gotta lighten up. I can't believe the mayor would kidnap Kudlow. He's her favorite scapegoat. With him gone she has nobody to blame for the murders and riots."

Grant narrowed his eyes. "It could be the Committee for Decent Movies."

"I bet Kudlow hightailed it to Mexico. He couldn't stand the heat so he split."

"I refuse to believe he would abandon the fight to keep his movie in theaters."

"The strange disappearance of one of Hollywood's most famous directors has sent shockwaves through Hollywood," said the newscaster.

"We need to find him," said Grant. He turned to Herb. "You're a PI. How do we find him?"

"I'll have to think about it."

"We don't have a lot of time. His life could be in danger. In fact, I'm sure of it. Hell, the mayor could've sent goons to kidnap and rough him up in order to get him to agree to pull his movie."

"I still think he beat it to Mexico or somewhere else where nobody could find him. He'll show up when the heat over his movie dies down."

"He's been kidnaped. I'm sure of it. We have to save him."

"I need a fix first."

"Don't look at me. I don't have any money. Why does everybody think I'm loaded? You and Sherry."

"Then my dare is still on."

"What dare?"

"I dared you to kill me. Remember? You've never backed down from a dare before."

"Concentrate on driving. Look where you're going," said Grant, grabbing the dashboard and bracing himself for a collision, his heartbeat ratcheting up.

Herb hit the brakes to avoid rear-ending a Prius.

"Maybe I should deliberately crash into a car and end it."

"Not while I'm sitting beside you. I don't get off on being in car accidents like James Ballard."

"Who the hell is James Ballard?"

"In the novel *Crash* he . . . Never mind."

"You read too many books."

"We have to concentrate on saving Kudlow."

"I can't drive when I'm strung out."

"Do you want me to drive?"

"No," said Herb, swiping his hand at Grant to keep him away from the steering wheel. "Tell me how you avoid getting bummed out."

"I—I go to a horror movie."

"And that works?"

"If I go to *Necromaniac*. Now let's go to the mayor's office and see if she knows where Kudlow is. He's the only one who can stop her from pulling his movie."

Herb searched Grant's face. "Why do you want to be a writer if none of your books sell?"

"Because that's what I am. Writing is the only thing I have any interest in."

"But you can't make a living at it."

"Maybe I can't do anything else. If I don't write, I feel nothing but anger. Why do you shoot up?"

"I hate reality. I don't know how people deal with it. I guess . . . I'm a nihilist."

"I can understand where you're coming from after dealing with the legal system, trying to get justice after being swindled by Sherry. The legal system isn't about justice. It's about enriching lawyers. Sherry's never gonna face the music for being a scammer. Justice is a joke."

"You need to move on." Herb paused. "Do you sleep well?"

"No."

"Neither do I. Do you take pills?"

"I used to take Halcion, but it bums me out when I keep taking it."

"I can't sleep a wink. Did you ever try Ambien?"

"No. Maybe if you stopped shooting up, you could sleep better."

"Or worse. More like worse. Maybe if *you* stopped hating Sherry, you'd sleep better."

"Let's drop the subject. We got work to do." Grant eyed the slowing traffic and the accompanying smog. He coughed. "Where's all this traffic coming from?"

"This is LA. What do you expect?"

"We need to get the lead out and convince the mayor to stop scapegoating Kudlow."

"Too many cars," muttered Herb.

He stared out the windshield at the traffic ahead of him, his gaze blank.

Grant felt annoyed at him because Herb didn't seem to understand how dire Kudlow's situation was and how urgent it was to save Kudlow's movie from being censored. If the movie was censored for even one day by the mayor, it would set a horrible precedent that would set back on its heels the right to freedom of speech in this country.

But, then again, why should he be surprised Herb didn't care about Kudlow's movie? His brother, the junkie, had admitted he believed in nothing, not even art. The only thing he cared about was his next fix and enough money to pay for it.

Chapter 49

Scores of angry demonstrators dressed like Leatherface congregated in front of City Hall, gripping chain saws and bearing signs that said Horror Movies Forever. A guy wearing a Michael Myers mask stood in front of them, shaking his fist. A woman wearing a Jason Voorhees hockey mask stood next to him and shouted at the crowd.

"We want horror movies," she cried. "Give us horror movies."

"Nobody can take away our right to see horror movies," cried Myers.

Behind the Leatherfaces a sprawling milling crowd of people cheered on the speakers.

"Horror, horror, horror," chanted the crowd in response.

"We want the mayor," cried Myers, facing City Hall.

"We want the mayor," the crowd roared in unison.

"Where is she?" Myers asked the crowd. "Maybe she can't hear us. Let's make some noise. Leatherfaces, what do you say?"

The Leatherfaces each placed their chain saws on the ground, adjusted the chokes, got a firm grip on the front handles, and kept yanking the start cords until the saws roared to life. They wielded the churning blades above their heads, swiping the air and raising an ear-splitting, nerve-grating din that permeated the air.

With long chestnut hair a twentysomething jeans-clad woman standing in the crowd raised a sign above her head that said Noise.

"Get the message, Mayor?" hollered Myers.

Mayor Coombs gazed out her office window at the protesters gathering below.

"Who's paying those bastards?" she asked the middle-aged police chief, Ed Gutierrez, who sported cropped hair and a thick black mustache that curved down at the ends.

Volcanic black eyes peered from under his bushy eyebrows.

"Want me to break it up?" he said, standing in his uniform at her side taking in the scene in the courtyard, his cheeks sheets of acne scars, his breath reeking of stale tobacco smoke.

Coombs adjusted her tortoiseshell spectacles. "I believe in free speech. Let them protest. But if they turn violent, send in the riot squad to kick ass and take names."

"They're getting ugly if you ask me. Those chain saws are deadly weapons in my opinion."

"Not unless they attack people with them."

"Somebody could lose an arm or worse the way those idiots are brandishing those things."

"I don't want to get the reputation of a tyrant who doesn't allow free speech. I'm already taking heat for wanting to pull Kudlow's horror movie. But his movie is a threat to public safety. It has to be removed from theaters," said Coombs, hammering the air with her fist.

"Especially since terrorists blew up a theater showing the movie."

"That's why I'm demanding that Kudlow pull his movie from theaters. Where is he, anyway?"

"We don't know. All we know is a pickup T-boned his limo. When first responders got to the scene, they found the limo empty."

"We need Kudlow to make an announcement that he's pulling his movie from theaters. I don't want to announce it and get tarred as a censor. Kudlow has to do it. He can't possibly condone this horrible theater bombing that took place."

"These movie people. Some of them will do anything to get publicity. They got the morals of alley cats."

Coombs stared at him. "I can't believe they would resort to killing people to gin up ticket sales to their movie."

"I wouldn't put it past them. Look at those chain saw maniacs. I bet the producers of *Necromaniac* hired those creeps to demonstrate here."

"I hate the sound of chain saws," said Coombs, wincing at the racket. "It's worse than fingernails screeching on a blackboard."

"Want me to tell them to shut those damn things off?"

"Not yet. Let them protest. But I don't want anybody to get hurt."

"That's what I'm talking about. Those chain saws are deadly weapons. They're as bad as guns if you ask me."

Coombs agonized over her decision. "I don't want a confrontation."

"If we don't do something now, somebody's gonna get hurt. Look at those maniacs with their chain saws."

"They're just waving them in the air."

"So far. Did they get a permit to protest here?"

"Not that I know of. It was spontaneous."

"Then we have every right to round them up for illegal assembly."

"The city's already a tinderbox with the psycho killings and the bombing at the theater setting everybody on edge. We don't want more violence."

"You're looking at another tinderbox if you don't disperse those wackos," said Gutierrez, inflating his chest and hooking his thumbs around his belt.

"They're not advocating violence. They're showing their support for horror movies."

"What if they attack City Hall?" said Gutierrez, champing at the bit to see action.

"Arrest them. I will not stand for vandalism or personal injuries."

Gutierrez glowered at the boisterous mob. "They're lucky I'm not mayor. I'd be busting heads right about now. And if some idiot lost a hand to a chain saw in the bust, too bad for them."

"I have nothing against people who like horror movies. I'm not waging war on horror movie fans. It's this one movie that is inciting violence that needs to be taken out of circulation."

"It's those chain saws that are bothering me. They can wear their funny masks all they want, but get rid of the chain saws."

"They're referencing *The Texas Chain Saw Massacre*, a famous horror movie."

"I'm with the folks that call that stuff torture porn even though my son wouldn't agree. He loves the stuff."

"I wish Kudlow was here. He could calm these people down if he agreed to pull his movie. These horror aficionados respect him."

"*Horror freaks* is more like it. I doubt Kudlow could calm them down. I believe he would pour oil on the fire."

"They respect his views, because he's a famous movie director."

190

"I don't care what kind of big swinging dick he is in Hollywood—"

"Chief, we need him. Do whatever you can to find him."

"OK. As soon as we find the guy, we'll bring him here. Right now nobody knows where he is."

"He could be hiding on account of death threats."

"You've been getting death threats too, but you're not hiding."

"I'm not hiding from anyone. I got a job to do, and I'm doing it. I'm not gonna let death threats stop me from doing my job."

Gutierrez took in the demonstration, his expression becoming darker. "The media jackals are out there now, filming the protest. Just what the demonstrators want, I'm sure. They want all the media coverage they can get."

Coombs changed the subject. "Do you have any idea who the Hollywood Psycho is?"

"Not yet. He hasn't left behind any DNA at the murder scenes. No DNA we can trace, anyway. As you know, not everybody's DNA is in our database of criminals. If this guy doesn't have a hot sheet, he's not gonna be in our database."

"Do you think it's just one person?"

Gutierrez nodded. "The MO's the same. We believe the same weapon was used in each murder, but we haven't found it."

"We need to get the psycho off the street. It would go a long way toward calming the public. It's horrible that people don't feel safe going to the movies. I can't believe this is happening. Hollywood is an essential part of LA. The movie business helped make this city great. Now look what's happening."

Chapter 50

In search of an interview the journalist Perkins Weaver circulated through the mob of protesting Leatherfaces. The problem was he couldn't hear himself think what with the racket the thundering chain saws were making.

He flashed his Press badge in the face of one of the Leatherfaces and motioned the guy to follow him away from the ruckus. Interested, keeping his chain saw cranking, Leatherface followed Weaver.

Weaver pointed at the chain saw with his forefinger and swiped his finger across his throat to signal Leatherface to cut the power.

Leatherface got the message and killed the chain saw motor.

At last they stood far enough away from the cacophonous chain saws that Weaver could hear a human voice.

He flicked on his cell phone to record the interview.

"Would you give me your name for my interview?" he said.

"Is that necessary?" said Leatherface, his voice muffled by his mask.

"Never mind. Let's continue. Do you agree to be interviewed on the record?"

"Yeah, sure. On the record. Off the record. Whatever."

"Why are you here today protesting?"

"I'm—*we're*—protesting the censorship of *Necromaniac*. If nobody says anything, the mayor's gonna pull it from theaters. The only way to change her mind is to protest."

"Do you think she'll agree to your demands?"

"What she's doing is illegal. I love horror movies. I see every horror movie I can. Doesn't she know we have freedom of speech in this country? And that goes for movies as well as for books. Movies cannot be allowed to be censored."

"Certain scenes can be edited out so a movie won't get an X rating. Isn't that a kind of censorship?"

"That's a totally different situation," said Leatherface, angered by the comparison. "This isn't about rating. It's about censoring. The mayor wants to prevent the entire movie from being shown anywhere. That's censorship, and it's illegal, according to the law of the land."

"Do you believe in the rating system?" said Weaver, jostled by a protester who was wearing a Michael Myers mask and making for the chain saw wielders, who seemed to be getting rowdier if that was possible.

"I don't believe in it, but I can tolerate it. What I don't believe in is censorship of any kind, be it in print or in the movies. No American should believe in censorship. Next thing you know we'll have book burning like Nazi Germany."

"The Committee for Decent Movies is already advocating burning movies they don't like."

"Fuck them, and tell them I said that," said Leatherface, flourishing his chain saw.

Weaver hoped Leatherface wasn't going to crank it yet, because he had more questions. Leatherface didn't crank it.

"What if the mayor doesn't agree with you and wants to go ahead with pulling the movie?" said Weaver, eager to fire off more questions.

"I'm telling you I love horror movies," said Leatherface, raising his voice. "I'm not letting her censor *Necromaniac*."

"What do you plan on doing about it?"

"I'm protesting till she changes her mind and agrees with us. We love horror movies and we want to go to theaters and see more horror movies. What gives her the right to stop us? She makes us sound like criminals for liking horror."

"Would you like to hear what the director Norman Kudlow has to say about censoring his movie?"

"I sure would. Five'll get you ten he'd tell the mayor to shove it. There's no way he'd agree to pull his movie from distribution. He's the greatest living director, and he's not gonna stand for being intimidated by a tinpot mayor with delusions of grandeur."

"What do you think happened to him?"

Leatherface glanced at his chain saw. "I heard he was in an accident and disappeared. Which is suspicious as hell."

193

A new Leatherface who had just arrived at the protest, cranked his chain saw six feet behind Weaver. Weaver started and wheeled around at the sudden noise of the two-stroke, his heart doing a somersault. A sudden whiff of chain saw exhaust greeted his nostrils.

"Reinforcements," said the Leatherface being interviewed, his voice pleased. "We need all the protesters we can get."

The newcomer waved his smoking chain saw at his comrade in acknowledgment then joined the other Leatherfaces who were brandishing their clamoring chain saws at City Hall.

Regaining his composure Weaver turned back to his interviewee, trying to remember what he was going to ask next, having lost his train of thought thanks to the newcomer's racketing chain saw.

"What do you think happened to Kudlow?" asked Weaver.

"I'd bet the farm the mayor had something to do with it. She's imprisoned him somewhere, trying to brainwash him into agreeing to censor his movie."

"You think she would go that far?"

"Even farther. I'm telling you she could have taken out the guy."

Weaver was all ears. "You're saying she would hire someone to kill Kudlow?"

Leatherface nodded yes. "That whole accident scenario makes no sense. It sounds like a put-up job. Somebody ambushed Kudlow's limo and kidnaped him. There's something hinky going down, you can bet your life on it."

"That's a serious accusation."

"You betcha. With Kudlow dead, there wouldn't be anybody to resist the mayor's censorship of his movie."

"I find it hard to believe our mayor would do such a thing. She's a high-profile mayor of one of the largest cities in the US. Her censoring a movie is gonna be front-page news."

"She's crazy for power. She resents anybody who stands up to her like Kudlow did. She hates Kudlow because she thinks his movie is inciting violence in her city. She will do anything to take him down a notch. Taking him out is the final solution."

194

Weaver raised his voice and winced thanks to the grinding chain saws serenading the mayor. "It sounds to me like you people would riot if Kudlow was murdered."

"We sure would."

"Then I don't see the mayor risking killing him."

"It's true she might just disappear him like the caudillos do in Latin America. Then nobody could be a hundred percent sure he was dead. Or she could blame the killing on somebody else."

Leatherface lowered his chain saw like he was getting ready to restart it and join his fellow demonstrators.

"Could I ask you a couple more questions?" said Weaver.

"I wanna get back to protesting. I love horror movies. I'm never gonna let anyone take them away from me," said Leatherface, taking a step toward the mob of other Leatherfaces who were swinging their cacophonous chain saws above them, the blades churning the air like scores of moiling shark fins slicing the ocean.

"Do you plan on rioting if Kudlow can't be found?"

"I'm not sure. It depends on the mayor. If she pulls Kudlow's movie without his OK, we riot."

"And if she doesn't act?"

"We might wait a while for Kudlow to show up. But not long, mind you. If the mayor can get away with censoring a movie for even one day, we're doomed. We *cannot* let her get away with it. It's our duty as private citizens to stop her. We know Kudlow would want us to stand up for his movie."

"It sounds like you're giving the mayor an ultimatum with your threats to riot if she censors the movie."

"Call it whatever you want. I gotta get back to protesting," said Leatherface, returning to the vociferous mob of chain saw wielders.

Weaver figured he knew the title for his next article. "Riots Threatened if Mayor Censors *Necromaniac*."

Chapter 51

Grant and Herb sat in Herb's VW Bug in gridlock.

"If I don't get enough sleep, I'm very irritable the next day," said Herb.

"Join the club."

"Can you get a prescription for sleeping pills from your doctor?"

"I lost my insurance. I can't afford it anymore."

"Do you have any leftover Halcion I could use?"

"It's probably expired. Why is there so much traffic?" said Grant. "This isn't normal."

He flicked on the car radio to the local news station.

"You must not drive much," said Herb. "The freeway's always jammed."

"How can I drive without a car? I sold it to loan Sherry money for her probate lawyers. I have no idea where the money really went. She lies about everything."

"That's why you don't know how bad traffic always is."

"What are you talking about? I used to have a car."

"There's a huge throng of protesters in front of City Hall demonstrating against censorship of Norman Kudlow's new horror movie *Necromaniac*," said the newscaster through the staticky dashboard radio. "Be advised that traffic is a mess downtown as a result. Motorists are advised to stay away from the area."

"No wonder," said Grant, hangdog. "We might as well turn back. We're never gonna get to see the mayor with all those protesters around. She must have an army of cops surrounding her every move."

"I doubt we would've gotten to see her anyway," said Herb. "And I'm sure she wouldn't have listened to us even if we did."

Herb turned off at the next exist and headed for Grant's apartment.

"We gotta do something," said Grant. "We can't let the movie get censored."

196

"Do you want me to turn back and join the protest?" said Herb with an expression of disapproval.

Grant shook his head no. "It'll take us hours to get there at this rate. Forget it."

When they got back to Grant's apartment, Grant was dumbfounded to see Kesey and Rivera standing in front of his door, their faces somber. Even though they were dressed in plainclothes, Grant pegged them for cops.

What were cops doing at his door? He broke into a sweat. He was carrying a gun and a knife. He didn't have a carry permit for either. He told himself to calm down. The cops weren't going to frisk him. They didn't have probable cause. The question was, what did they want?

"Five-O," whispered Herb.

Grant wasn't going to turn back. It would look too suspicious if he turned around at the sight of cops at his door.

"Hello," he said to them with a smile.

"We're looking for Grant Osborne," said Kesey, opening his unbuttoned blazer and exposing his shield clipped to his belt. "I'm Detective Kesey and this is Detective Rivera. We're with the LAPD."

"I'm Grant Osborne."

Grant saw no reason to deny it. He didn't know what this was about.

Kesey eyed Herb and took in the tracks on Herb's arms, which Herb never made any attempt to hide. Kesey knew what they were on sight.

"And who are you?" said Kesey, a trace of disdain in his tone.

"I'm his brother Herb," said Herb, showing no reaction to Kesey's eying the track marks.

"We have a couple questions for you," Kesey told Grant. "Mind if we go inside? We don't want to attract attention out here."

"Sure," said Grant, got out his key, and opened his apartment door, hoping he could eighty-six the cops quickly.

Chapter 52

They entered Grant's apartment single file behind Grant.

Grant didn't look forward to getting grilled by cops. He tried to settle his nerves by telling himself he had nothing to be afraid of. There was no way the cops were going to find out he was carrying as long as he kept his cool.

"Have a seat," he said, gesturing to his ratty sofa with a busted spring peeking through the threadbare upholstery.

"No thank you," said Kesey, glancing at the sofa. "You can sit down if you want."

Grant figured Kesey wanted to be standing above him, acting like he was superior because he was an agent of the law. Kesey's thin-lipped mouth had a downward cast because he didn't smile much. His dark eyes looked like they were stones staring out of the bottom of a stream, eroded by the water until they were flat and dull.

"Fine," said Grant, and sat down, trying to appear relaxed, wondering what was going on. "Do I need a lawyer?"

"We simply want to ask you a few questions," said Rivera, trying a disarming smile.

"About what?"

Herb sat beside Grant on the sofa, which made Grant's side of the sofa bounce up for a moment.

"You have a nice apartment," said Rivera, scoping it out, smiling, ignoring Grant's question. She took in his bookcase full of hundreds of DVDs. "You must like movies."

"I do."

She approached the rows of DVDs and read some of the titles.

"You own a lot of horror movies," she said.

"I like horror movies."

Grant covered the exposed spring in the sofa by draping his thigh over it. He didn't like showing off his modestly appointed apartment. He didn't always used to be broke. He had been well off until he had met Sherry. There was no sense in letting nosy cops know about his current lack of means.

"Do you prefer Fulci or Bava?" said Rivera, inspecting some of the titles, acting like she knew what she was talking about, which Grant doubted.

"Mario Bava," said Grant, figuring Rivera was playing the good cop trying to soften him up for the sword wielded by the matador Kesey. "I particularly like the way he uses lighting, and he's good at depicting psychotic killers as he did in *Hatchet for the Honeymoon.*"

"You're into psycho killers, Mr. Osborne?" said Kesey, cocking an eyebrow.

"Horror movies are full of psycho killers."

"What is your profession?"

"I'm a writer." *With writer's block who hasn't written a word for the better part of a year.*

"That's an insecure business, isn't it?"

"It has its ups and downs." *Mostly downs.* "Why are you so interested in my life?"

"I'm just wondering how you make a living. What kind of car do you drive?"

"I don't own a car."

"You live in LA and don't own a car? You're one of a kind. How do you get around?"

"I take the bus."

"I guess business is slow if you can't afford a car."

"What of it?"

"Do you fill your time by going to horror movies?"

"I like to know what's selling."

"Have you seen *Necromaniac*?"

"Yeah, I have."

"Did you see it yesterday at the Hammond Theater at three o'clock?" said Kesey pointedly.

Grant felt his heart skip a beat. How could the cops know that? He had used cash to pay for his theater ticket. There was no way they could have traced a ticket to him.

"Why?" he said.

"As you know, a murder was committed there yesterday during the showing of *Necromaniac*."

"I heard about it on the news."

"You didn't see it happen?"

"Of course not."

"Even though you were at the theater when the murder occurred?"

"What makes you think I was in the theater?"

"A little birdie told us."

It sounded weird coming out of his somber face, like a stand-up comedian telling a joke and dying onstage as the joke bombed.

Grant debated whether to answer honestly about his presence at the theater yesterday. He doubted the cops had any proof he had been there. Yet somebody could have seen him there and tipped off the cops. Grant couldn't think of any other reason they would be here. So what if he was there? So were over a hundred other people. Was it a crime to be at a movie where a murder took place?

"All right," he said. "I was there."

"Why didn't you come forward and testify to the police as to what you saw at the theater?"

"I saw the movie. Nothing else."

"Nothing suspicious?" said Kesey, frowning.

"Nope."

"Even though a murder occurred in the theater while you were there?"

"Did any of the other theatergoers notice anything?"

"I'm not asking them. I'm asking you."

"I didn't see anything suspicious in the theater when I was there."

Grant felt the sofa spring dig into his flesh under his thigh, possibly opening it as he felt tension in his body thanks to Kesey's third degree.

"You should have come forward and told the police at the crime scene what you saw," said Kesey.

"I didn't see anything untoward. Are you gonna arrest everybody at the theater who didn't talk to the police?"

"We have every right to, you know. Everybody at the theater at the time of the murder is a suspect."

"That doesn't mean they're guilty."

200

"We start with suspects. Then we narrow them down to the actual killer. You're not telling us our job, are you?" said Kesey, adopting a menacing look and taking a step toward Grant.

"No."

"Which seat were you sitting in at the theater?"

"I don't remember."

"You didn't think very hard about it."

"I don't remember such things."

"I thought writers were supposed to notice details as part of their profession."

"Are *you* telling me my job?" said Grant with a slight smile playing on the corner of his lips.

Kesey didn't see the humor in the remark. "Were you sitting on the right side of the theater or the left?"

"I'm not sure. Am I facing the screen when you're talking about right and left?"

"Yeah."

Grant shut his eyes and thought about it. "Left, I think."

"Now that wasn't so hard, was it?" said Rivera as if proud of him.

"I'm getting the feeling I need a lawyer," said Grant, feeling whipsawed by the cops.

"We're just asking you questions. Not a problem."

"The types of questions are a problem."

"Not if you're innocent."

"You said I'm a suspect in a murder."

"Calling a lawyer would make you look guilty," said Kesey.

"Better to look guilty than to get busted."

201

Chapter 53

Kesey turned to Herb. "What about you?"

"What about me?" said Herb, caught off guard.

"Did you go to the movie with him?"

"No."

"You don't like horror movies?"

"I like some of them."

Kesey turned back to Grant. "What do you think about the mayor's plan to ban *Necromaniac* from theaters?"

"Is it official? I haven't heard an official announcement from her."

"Not yet."

"I didn't think so."

Kesey didn't say anything for a few moments.

"I'm waiting for your answer," he said at last. "Do you agree with her?"

"Not at all. It's a great movie. I don't believe in censoring any movie."

"Because the psycho killer won't be able to murder at another showing of it?"

"That has nothing to do with my belief. I resent your implication."

"What implication?"

"You're trying to make it look like I don't want the movie censored because the psycho killer won't be able to kill at a showing of it anymore."

"Are you saying that's not true?"

"It's not true," said Grant, having to watch every word he said to Kesey, who liked to twist his answers into admissions of siding with criminals or worse.

"You really like *Necromaniac*, don't you?"

"I do, indeed. It's a masterwork."

"How many times have you seen it?" he said offhand while inspecting his fingernails as if just trying to make conversation.

Grant saw where this line of questioning was leading. He had seen *Necromaniac* many times, but he didn't think it a good idea to admit the same to Kesey. After all, the three murders had occurred at showings of *Necromaniac* at three different theaters, the same three theaters where he had seen it.

"Once," lied Grant.

Kesey raised his eyebrows. "Only once for a *masterwork*. Your word, not mine."

"I've never gone to any movie at a theater more than once."

"Even if it's a masterwork?" said Kesey, jacking up his eyebrows in disbelief.

"I might watch it several times when it comes to cable. Are you gonna charge me with something? If not, I think we should end this."

"Am I wearing you out with my questioning?"

"I don't see the purpose. If you're gonna charge me, let me know and I'll call a lawyer."

Which was a bluff. Grant had no lawyer. Only people with money had lawyers.

"You're officially a person of interest in the Hammond Theater murder," said Kesey.

"Just because I was at the theater when the murder took place?"

"Yep."

Kesey made for the door but halted before he got there. "Just one more question. What do you think about rats?"

"Rats?" said Grant, becoming irritated by the constant onslaught of questions.

"Did you happen to see a rat at the Hammond Theater when you were there?"

"I wouldn't go to a theater that had rats in it."

"Oh," said Kesey, and reached the door.

"Why do you ask such a question?" said Grant, standing up, the underside of his thigh sore from sitting uncomfortably on the sofa spring.

"It's probably nothing, but we found a rat running around the theater and it had blood on its fur. It was human blood. Probably the killer's."

Rivera reached Kesey at the door.

"I prefer Fulci to Bava," she told Grant when she passed him. "I like *Zombi 2*."

She and Kesey piled out the door.

Grant doubted she liked Fulci. She only knew his name because she had seen it on Grant's *Zombi 2* DVD. She was still trying to ingratiate herself with him. Which suggested they weren't done with him. They would be back with more questions.

The blood on the rat could be the victim's blood as well as the killer's, but the cops hadn't said as much. They had mentioned the rat because they had wanted to see him squirm, since they suspected him of the Hammond Theater murder. They had looked disappointed when he hadn't reacted.

Grant didn't remember much about being at the theater. He had experienced blackouts during his visit there. He didn't notice the audience, because he was rapt in the horror movie. The demon in the movie seemed more real to him than did the audience. The demon transcended reality.

"A rat in the theater with blood on it," said Herb, getting to his feet. "Some weird shit. How could the killer's blood get on it?"

Grant said nothing, his face expressionless.

He recalled the woman sitting next to him had had a rat cage strapped to her stomach. The rat must have escaped at some point. Maybe the woman had deliberately let the rat out. How had the rat gotten blood on its fur?

"Why did they tell *us* about the rat?" said Herb.

"You heard him. Because I'm a suspect."

He felt Herb's eyes staring at him.

"What?" said Grant.

"Have you changed your mind about the loan?" said Herb.

"Nothing's changed. I don't have any money."

Grant started when he heard a knock on the door. Hoping it wasn't the cops returning, he answered it with apprehension.

204

Chapter 54

"Remember me?" said Mandy in her leather biker outfit.

Grant had forgot about the blackmailer Mandy. He was glad she hadn't been here when the cops had questioned him. She could put him at the site of another *Necromaniac* murder—or claimed she could. It would be her word against his without proof. He didn't think she had proof. She had seen a chance for easy money and was shaking him down. She didn't believe he was broke.

On the other hand, maybe Mandy would have clammed up in the presence of cops, since she was a blackmailer and she knew he could rat her out for attempted blackmail.

"You just missed the cops," said Grant.

"I was waiting for them to leave," said Mandy. "Did you call them here?"

"No."

She must have been worried he had ratted her out to the cops. He wasn't going to tell her he was suspected of being the Hollywood Psycho. She would probably increase the amount of her shakedown money if she knew.

"Have you been holding out on me?" Herb asked Grant with a lopsided grin.

"I barely know this woman," answered Grant.

"Who's that?" said Mandy.

"My brother."

"Are you gonna let me in or do you want me to talk out here where all your neighbors can hear?"

Grant didn't want her inside his apartment. However, the alternative of having the neighbors eavesdrop on her was unacceptable.

"Come in," he said.

"That's more like it."

Mandy clomped into the room in her black patent leather biker boots.

Grant closed the door behind her.

"Is he OK?" said Mandy, cutting a glance toward Herb.

"He's not a cop if that's what you mean."

"Does he know you owe me money?"

"No. And no, I don't owe you money."

"I'm not fooling around with you anymore. You need to start paying me or I go to the cops and blab my mouth off."

"I don't like your methods."

"Do you want me to call my boyfriend?" said Mandy, producing her cell phone. "He has a talent for persuasion, a talent you're not gonna dig."

Grant felt his pulse speed up. He didn't know how to deal with her.

"I'm sure he has better things to do," he said.

"How about I go to the cops?" she said.

"What makes you think the cops will believe anything you say?"

"Why would I lie?"

Grant had to think of something. "Maybe you want to make a name for yourself, making your accusations at a police station. There are plenty of hoaxers who lie to get attention regarding a crime."

"This sounds interesting," said Herb.

"It has nothing to do with you."

"At least make a down payment," said Mandy, holding out her empty hand. "I'm not fooling around. I can put you at the scene of the cri—"

"This is outrageous," cut in Grant, "and it's illegal. I should report you this minute to the cops for attempted blackmail."

"You're too scared to call the cops," she said, calling his bluff. "Gimme the money, honey. I'm waiting."

"They were just here."

"But you said you didn't call them."

"Can you be absolutely certain I didn't tell them about your little shakedown attempt?"

His question gave her pause.

"If they come after me, for sure I'm ratting you out, and you *will* be a suspect in the Hollywood Psycho mur—"

Grant cut her off again, not wanting Herb to hear her accusation.

"If you don't leave, I'm calling the cops," said Grant, fishing his cell phone out of his trouser pocket.

"You wouldn't," she said uncertainly. "You got too much to lose."

"Try me."

"I'm gonna let you think about your situation overnight and let it sink in, because I'm a nice girl. But I'll be back tomorrow, and if you don't pony up tomorrow, the cops will be all over your bony ass after I talk to them."

She retreated to the door, her face surly.

"You made the right decision to leave," said Grant, following her.

"Don't get too full of yourself. I'll be back tomorrow with my boyfriend. He's not gonna put up with any of your excuses. I tried being nice to you but not anymore. You want to play hardball, you got it. You're not gonna want to meet my boyfriend instead of me."

Relieved he had gotten rid of her for the moment anyway, Grant caught up to her at the door.

"Why not?" he heard Herb say.

"Because he rides with the Mongol biker gang," said Mandy, standing in the doorway. "And he used to be a member of MS-13."

"MS-13?"

"Mara Salvatrucha. You know, the guys with the shaved heads covered with tattoos that stand for all the people they've taken out."

Mandy stalked down the hall, exuding arrogance.

Chapter 55

Grant didn't think Mandy would return, but he couldn't swear to it.

For all he knew, she might not even have a boyfriend. But it would be a surprise given her arresting looks. Her testimony about seeing him at another murder site for the psycho killings combined with the evidence of his ticket stub to the Hammond Theater would put him at two psycho murder scenes, increasing suspicion of him by the cops if they found out.

What did he do with that ticket stub? Did Herb keep it? Grant couldn't recall. He had to find and destroy it. He didn't want to be considered a suspect in these killings. Just because he liked *Necromaniac* and had seen it several times shouldn't single him out as a prime suspect. However, he knew Kesey and Rivera would disagree with him on the matter.

Grant couldn't let Mandy get away with blackmailing him for one very good reason. He had no money to pay her.

He caught Herb staring at him. Grant figured Herb was trying to figure out what Mandy had on him.

"Are you sure she's not a new girlfriend?" said Herb, an ironic smile playing on his lips.

Grant could not tell if Herb was trying to be funny. It was more likely Herb was trying to get under his skin, seeing as how Herb had seemed to eat up Grant's argument with Mandy.

"Forget her," said Grant. "We need to figure out how we're gonna save Kudlow before his kidnapers decide to kill him."

"You really think they'd kill him?"

"They have to be desperate to kidnap him. People *that* desperate could resort to murder if their terms aren't met."

"What *are* their terms?"

"We have to find out."

"My client wants me to find the Hollywood Psycho. That takes priority."

"I can't believe you'd allow Kudlow to be killed."

"We can't even be sure he's been kidnaped. How can we possibly know he's being threatened with being whacked out?"

"People don't just disappear. Somebody kidnaped him."

"Jesus," said Herb, slapping the side of his head. "If I had a brain I'd be dangerous."

"What?"

"Kudlow is—I—I can't tell you."

"Stop acting so mysterious. If you can help us save Kudlow, you gotta tell me."

"I have his cell number. I can use it to track him."

"How the hell did you get his private number? There's no way he has a listed number. He's an internationally famous film director."

"I can't tell you."

Grant eyed him skeptically. "All right. Forget it. How can you track his cell phone?"

"I'll send him a text. Then I have an app that can track a test message to its destination. Piece of cake. I did it all the time when I was making a living as a PI."

"Before you got hooked on horse."

"You should talk. You can't even help out your girlfriend with a loan."

Grant scowled. "Don't talk about her."

"Why not? Because you treat her like crap?"

"She's a professional scammer and a pathological liar."

"There you go trashing her."

"She's got a lot of people fooled with her lies. She had me fooled for a long time too. It shows how skillful a liar she is."

"Maybe she really will pay you back. Probate can drag on for years, especially if it's disputed."

"I used to think she would pay me back. But her claim that she was gonna inherit two million dollars was a hook to catch a sucker like me. Now I believe she inherited nothing and will never pay me back. How is that not fraud?"

"Girlfriends aren't cheap."

"I gave her a lot of money besides the money I loaned her. I get so angry whenever I think about it. There's absolutely no way I'll ever get back any of the money I loaned her, and there's fuck-all I can do about it. It's the perfect scam."

209

"How did you get so cynical? I think you should give her the benefit of the doubt. She's your girlfriend, man."

"No, no, no," said Grant, steaming. "Never again. That's how I got into this mess, giving her the benefit of the doubt."

"I'm just saying you may be misjudging her."

"I don't want to talk about her anymore. We don't have time to talk about her, anyway."

"Maybe you're taking out your own shortcomings on her."

"What the hell is that supposed to mean?" said Grant, confronting Herb.

"You're blaming her for everything that's going wrong in your life."

"She borrowed hundreds of thousands of dollars from me and never paid me back. That's on her, not on me. How many times do I have to tell you?"

"I think you're being hard on her."

"How can I be hard on a professional crook? I can't believe you're taking the side of a crook."

Herb paused in thought. "I've been noticing changes for the worse in you since I last saw you. You seem angrier."

"Because she swindled me out of my life savings," said Grant, exasperated. "I gave her a helping hand, and she helped herself to my life savings. Let it die." He paused. "Do you have my ticket stub to the Hammond Theater?"

"Nope."

Grant searched Herb's face, trying to detect a tell indicating a lie.

"Then where is it?" said Grant.

"You must have it. It's *your* ticket stub. What would I want with it?"

"You're the one who found it on my carpet."

"I did, and I gave it back to you."

Perplexed, Grant rubbed his forehead. "What did I do with it?"

"What do you want it for?"

"I was just wondering what happened to it. It seems to have vanished."

"Then it's lucky it's not important. Why worry about it?"

Grant nodded. Still he wondered what had happened to it. He didn't like forgetting where he had put things. It bugged him. He

210

had probably thrown it in the trash. Unless Herb still had it and was lying. But why would he keep it?

"We got work to do," said Grant. "We need to find Kudlow. Text him, so we can save him from his kidnapers."

Chapter 56

Herb hated making a living. He had hated it all his life and he still hated it. Facing all the things that could go wrong on a job overwhelmed him. He would much rather be shooting up. But he needed more money for dope. And the only way he could get money—if Grant wasn't going to loan it to him—was to work.

Herb wondered if Grant was really broke or pretending to be. Grant always seemed to have money hidden away for a rainy day. No matter how hard Herb tried, he couldn't get Grant to make him a loan. Which meant Herb had to work.

Herb resented Grant for making him work.

Herb didn't want to tangle with kidnapers to save Kudlow. Herb had never seen *Necromaniac* and didn't care to see it. If the mayor had her way, nobody would ever see the movie again. And that was fine with Herb. He couldn't understand why Grant was getting his panties in a twist about freedom of speech and saving Kudlow. The guy was just a movie director.

The problem was Kudlow was also Herb's client. If Herb didn't save the guy, Herb was out a paycheck.

Even if Herb had no desire to confront the kidnapers, he needed another paycheck from Kudlow.

It was an insoluble dilemma. Herb needed more horse. The only way he could get more horse was to get more money. Kudlow had the money. Therefore Herb had to save Kudlow from a bunch of terrorists who were probably the same terrorists who had blown up the Marina theater and killed and wounded scores of innocent bystanders.

Herb was beginning to suspect that Grant had something to do with these Hollywood Psycho killings and the resulting demonstrations over free speech versus public safety. Herb couldn't figure out how Grant fit into the turmoil.

It was Herb who had ratted out Grant to the cops about Grant's presence at the Hammond Theater when the Hollywood Psycho had struck. Herb was lazy. He wanted the cops to do the business of investigating suspects. Herb was a lone PI. He didn't have the resources the cops had to investigate homicides. And Herb was scared of work. He was scared of all the things that could go wrong. So many things could go wrong during an investigation. He might even manage to get himself killed.

Herb wanted nothing more than to be back in bed shooting up. Instead Grant wanted him to confront a gang of kidnapers who were no doubt armed and dangerous.

Then again maybe Kudlow hadn't been kidnaped. Maybe he was in hiding thanks to all the demonstrators protesting his movie. And Herb couldn't forget the mayor, who had put Kudlow on her enemies list by, in essence, declaring him public enemy number one for directing a horror movie where filmgoers in the LA audience were getting murdered by the Hollywood Psycho. The mayor had a city to protect. If it meant censoring Kudlow's movie, Herb figured she was going to take action to censor it.

No good could come of this mess.

Yet Herb had to do something to get money so he could get more smack. The problem was it might end up with his getting killed saving Kudlow.

Herb wanted to escape back into the dreamworld of smack. But his desperate need for money took pride of place. He had to accompany Grant to save Kudlow.

Maybe he was exaggerating how bad things were, Herb told himself. Maybe there were no kidnapers. Maybe Kudlow had holed up because he knew the mayor had made him a marked man unless he agreed to pull his movie from theaters. Kudlow could have staged the accident to make it look like foul play might be involved, because he didn't want people to think he was in hiding. It was bad PR to hide like a chicken from your enemies. And for sure Kudlow, being in the movie business, knew all about PR.

"What are you waiting for?" said Grant. "Text Kudlow."

Herb produced his cell and did so.

Maybe this would work out. Maybe Kudlow would text back and say where he was hiding. Then there wouldn't be any overzealous armed kidnapers to deal with.

"Do you have a gun?" said Grant.

"How can I afford a gun?" said Herb.

213

Grant strode to his closet, pulled down a SIG P226 from the top shelf, and handed the piece to Herb.

"You're gonna need this when you kill me," said Grant.

"What?" said Herb, bewildered.

"I dared you to kill me."

"No way. I dared you first. You're the one who has to accept the dare before I can even consider your dare."

"I was kidding."

"It didn't sound like it."

"Take the piece. You're gonna need it when we find Kudlow."

Herb accepted the SIG, realizing Grant was right. They were probably heading for the OK Corral.

"Maybe we're both gonna end up dead without killing each other," said Herb, feeling the SIG in his hand.

"You're thinking like a junkie loser. We're gonna win this one. We gotta win for Kudlow's sake. Remember we're fighting for Kudlow's life and for freedom of speech."

"Spare me the fancy words. I just want another fix. This thing called life has way too many things that can go south. Everything's a fight to get nowhere."

"If we don't protect free speech, we lose the country."

"Are you running for office now?"

"Have you seen *Necromaniac*?"

"No."

"You need to see it. I've never felt so much horror. It was like the demon in the movie entered me. It was so real I lost track of everything else. The demon was the only thing that existed."

"I want to be happy. I don't want to be scared."

"The world kicks you in the teeth and knocks you on your ass every chance it gets. What's happy got to do with it?"

Herb looked down, lost in thought. "I guess that's why I want to shoot up all the time."

Which meant he needed Kudlow to pay him for his PI services so he could afford more smack.

"The thing is we gotta keep getting back up with or without teeth," said Grant.

"Maybe we should let the cops handle this," said Herb. "I can give them Kudlow's whereabouts, and they can save him."

214

"I doubt the cops like Kudlow, since it's *his* movie that's fomenting so much turmoil in the city. The mayor definitely doesn't like him. And, like I said before, she may be behind his kidnaping. She could have told cops to kidnap Kudlow and persuade him to pull his movie."

"Mayors don't do that kind of thing. You watch too many movies."

"People in power will do anything to stay in power."

Herb checked his cell phone and looked disconcerted. "Kudlow hasn't answered the text I sent him."

"Not good. Somebody must be preventing him from answering."

Herb checked his tracking app. "I got a signal on my app."

"Let's go," said Grant.

"Where am I gonna put this piece?" said Herb, holding up the SIG P226.

"I'll get you an ankle holster."

Grant made for the closet, retrieved a leather ankle holster with Velcro straps, and handed it to Herb.

"Are you one of these survivalists with all your weapons and military paraphernalia?" said Herb.

"I don't trust people. When push comes to shove, people will do anything to survive. Come Armageddon it's everybody for themselves."

"I'll do anything to get high."

Including jeopardizing his life to get money from his client Kudlow for drugs.

Chapter 57

From her office window Mayor Coombs watched with concern the tumultuous crowd throbbing on the concourse below. Chief Gutierrez stood at her side, taking in the mob with a sour visage.

"This protest could get out of hand real easy," said Coombs, knitting her brows.

"We want Kudlow," cried a female protester through a bullhorn.

Her hair dyed a vibrant scarlet, she was wearing a matching T-shirt that said Horror Rocks in white Gothic letters.

"Why do they think we have Kudlow?" said Coombs.

"Who knows?" said Gutierrez. "They're on drugs. They don't know what they're saying."

"Those chain saws bother me," said Coombs. "Look at how the protesters are brandishing them in the air while they're running. Somebody could get hurt."

"You're preaching to the choir," said Gutierrez, his mouth turned down at the ends.

"It may be time to disperse the crowd. I don't want anybody to get hurt. I believe in the right to assemble and free speech, but not when they endanger people's lives."

"Do you want my forces to move in?"

"I want these people to be careful with those chain saws."

"We want Kudlow," cried Horror Rocks again.

The demonstrators joined her, chanting, "We want Kudlow. We want Kudlow."

They shook their fists at City Hall.

"They look like they're getting angrier," said Coombs.

"I got a squadron of armed riot-control officers with shields lined up on the top of the steps guarding the building. Want me to tell them to break up the protest?"

"I don't want violence," said Coombs, fretting.

216

"Those idiots with the chain saws could kill and maim a lot of people if we don't do something."

"Don't those chain saws run on gas?"

"Most of 'em. Some are electric, but the ones they got are gas powered. That's why they make so much noise."

"They're gonna run out of gas pretty soon."

"Unless they're carrying spare jerricans of gas, their chain saws won't last longer than forty minutes at the most. Probably just half an hour."

Coombs glanced at her platinum wristwatch with a diamond-studded dial. "They should run out of fuel in five minutes or so."

"They could keep this up for hours if they brought enough jerricans with them," said Gutierrez, scoping out the boisterous crowd.

"How much gas does a chain saw hold in its fuel tank?"

"Can't be more than a gallon."

"Then they wouldn't need much gas to refuel."

"How many chain saws are out there? Twenty or so?" said Gutierrez, narrowing his eyes at the mob. "Those chain saws are all different sizes with different fuel capacities. They probably could get by on ten spare gallons for gas to refill them once."

"You think they're gonna refill them more than once?" said Coombs in surprise.

"I dunno what they're gonna do. It depends on how prepared they came."

"Explain."

"If this is a spur-of-the-moment protest, they didn't bring any jerricans of gas with them."

Coombs mulled it over. "Let's wait five minutes and see if they go home."

"I thought I saw a red jerrican of gas carried by a demonstrator."

"Maybe it's a container of food they brought with them."

"If it's a jerrican, they could be here for another hour. If we let them stay there for another hour, we could have violence on our hands."

"We want Kudlow," Horror Rocks yelled through her bullhorn.

The chant continued.

217

"Where *is* Kudlow?" said Coombs, becoming anxious as she watched the lathering crowd.

"I haven't a clue."

"He could help defuse the situation if he was here. Tell him to come here at once. His presence could settle down the mob."

"He disappeared after his accident. We can't find him."

Coombs confronted Gutierrez. "You're the police. If anyone can find him, you should be able to."

"I got people working on it. We'll get him sooner or later."

"Getting him tomorrow won't help us. We need him now."

"What good would having him here do?"

"He could tell the crowd to disperse because he's gonna cooperate with us and pull his movie from theaters."

"The protesters aren't gonna like that."

"If I say it, they won't. But Kudlow's their hero. If *he* says he's pulling his movie, I believe they'll cooperate and go home."

"The point is moot if we can't find him."

"Wait a minute. I think I have his cell number," said Coombs, retreating to her desk and picking up her phone from the desktop.

She scrolled through her list of contacts and found Towers's number.

"No," she said. "I have his PR flack's number."

"Maybe he knows where Kudlow is."

Coombs called the number. Waiting for Towers to answer, she scowled.

"He's not picking up," she said.

Gutierrez grimaced with disdain. "They both may've skipped town for all we know. They don't want to deal with the mess Kudlow's movie has made of our city. Typical irresponsible filmmaker. All they care about is turning a buck. They don't want to accept the consequences for their actions."

Coombs left a message on Towers's voicemail. "This is the mayor. I have an urgent message for Kudlow. Tell him to call me back ASAP. We need his help to defuse a volatile situation. Without his help it's Katy bar the door."

"We're wasting our time calling him if you ask me. These Hollywood types are all the same. Take the money and run. He's not gonna call back."

218

Chapter 58

Coombs returned to the window and gazed down at the unruly throng of protesters, beads of sweat popping on her face. She withdrew a handkerchief from her purse and wiped her brow.

"What is that red container they're passing around?" she said.

Gutierrez inspected the crowd and picked up on the container. "That's one of those gas jerricans I told you about. The rioters are passing it around and refueling their chain saws."

Compressing her lips Coombs shook her head with displeasure.

"We need to get them out of here pronto," said Gutierrez. "This is going south, and people are gonna get hurt."

"We need to wait a little longer." Coombs glanced at her blank cell phone on the desktop. "Kudlow could call back any minute."

"Even if he calls back, how can he help settle down the crowd if he's not here?"

"We could go outside and put his voice on speakerphone. The protesters would recognize it and disperse."

"What if he says he's not gonna pull his movie?"

"He won't do that. He has to help us," said Coombs, fidgeting as she eyeballed the mob.

"We're gonna have a riot on our hands if we don't get these bums out of here on the double."

"I don't want anybody to get hurt."

Gutierrez harrumphed. "We're in damage control now. It's not a question of nobody getting hurt but of how many are gonna get hurt when this mob of maniacs gets through trashing this place. We can limit the bloodshed if we start moving on these thugs this minute."

Coombs blew out her cheeks in distress. "Why doesn't Kudlow call me back?"

"'Cause he's a coward. He's scared shitless the mob will turn on him and tear him to pieces if he tells them he's pulling his movie." His face clouding, Gutierrez watched one of the

219

Leatherfaces refuel his chain saw with the five-gallon red jerrican that was being passed around. "They're already starting to refuel. They're not leaving soon. We're in deep shit if we don't act now."

Coombs eyed her cell phone on her desktop, willing it to start buzzing and vibrating. The cell remained silent. She brushed sweat from her brow with the back of her hand.

"I can't believe Kudlow would allow a riot," she said.

"Why not? He allows murders to be committed every time a theater shows his sick horror movie."

Coombs clenched her fists at her sides and gnashed her teeth, agonizing over her decision.

"They have the right to peaceful assembly," she said, conflicted. "It's in the First Amendment."

"They're carrying weapons of mass destruction."

"What?"

"Those chain saws they're brandishing. It's not a peaceful assembly."

"Nobody has gotten hurt yet."

"It's only a matter of time. Half of those whackos are drunk or on drugs."

Coombs considered it, realizing the possibility of violence flaring up in the demonstration was strong. It wouldn't take much to transform the peaceful protest into a full-fledged riot with all hell breaking loose, unleashing a possible bloodbath at City Hall.

"Send in the riot squad," she said. "Get the crowd to disperse before they can finish refueling their chain saws."

"Now you're talking," said Gutierrez. "Those drugged-up freaks are gonna rue the day they came here."

Setting his jaw with determination, he bolted out of the office.

Coombs had never seen him move so fast.

Chapter 59

On the top landing of the steps to the entrance of City Hall, Chief Gutierrez gestured to the rambunctious throng of protesters to calm down. He raised a bullhorn to his wedge-shaped jaw and directed his burning gaze at them.

"By decree of the mayor, you are hereby ordered to disperse," he announced, his throaty voice booming out of the bullhorn.

Horror Rocks used her own bullhorn to fire back. "We have the right to free speech. We have the right to peaceful assembly guaranteed by the First Amendment. We're not budging."

The crowd cheered, their cheers punctuated by the racket of chain saws flourished by Leatherfaces.

"Give us Kudlow," she went on.

The crowd picked up the chant. "Give us Kudlow. Give us Kudlow."

"We don't have Kudlow," said Gutierrez.

"We want Kudlow," said Horror Rocks.

"You have lost the right to assemble when you commit violence. You have only the right to *peacefully* assemble."

"We haven't committed violence."

"You're carrying weapons."

"What weapons?"

"Those chain saws are weapons of mass destruction, and you're brandishing them in a threatening manner."

"They're not weapons. They're gardening equipment used for trimming trees."

"They can also lop off people's heads."

Several of the chain saws burped and racketed behind Horror Rocks.

"You don't have a permit to protest here," said Gutierrez.

"The First Amendment doesn't say anything about requiring permits."

Gutierrez was losing his temper, his face flushed with anger.

"The mayor has declared this an illegal assembly," he bellowed into his bullhorn. "This is the LAPD. You are ordered to disperse this minute."

Wearing visored helmets, scores of riot squad officers, composed of both men and women bearing polycarbonate plastic shields and steel batons, stood in three solid rows in back of him.

The chief's thirtysomething clean-shaven adjutant approached Gutierrez.

"The officers are grumbling that their shields won't protect them from chain saws," he said.

"I know, Juanca. Wait."

Gutierrez put his bullhorn to his mouth.

"You are ordered to drop your weapons and disperse," he told the demonstrators.

"We have no weapons," said Horror Rocks through her bullhorn.

"Your chain saws are weapons. Drop them."

The Leatherfaces flourished their belching, screaming chain saws in protest even as several of the chain saws ran out of fuel and became silent.

Gutierrez lowered his bullhorn and spoke to Juanca. "Tell the officers to fire rubber bullets at the Leatherfaces to get them to disarm and retreat."

"Yes, sir."

The demonstrators stood their ground, waving their placards that protested censorship.

"You have been warned," said Gutierrez through his bullhorn.

He and Juanca retreated behind the riot squad.

"Advance and prepare to fire," Gutierrez commanded the riot squad.

The squad stepped toward the head of the concrete stairs and halted.

"This is your last warning," said Gutierrez through his bullhorn to the protesters. "Drop your chin saws and disperse."

"We love horror," the protesters chanted, waving their signs and chain saws. "We love horror."

"Prepare to fire rubber bullets at the demonstrators," Gutierrez ordered his officers.

Raising their rifles the officers obeyed.

222

"Fire."

The riot squad opened fire on the protesters. Many of them dropped their signs and fled.

"Advance one tread at a time and drive them back," said Gutierrez.

As his officers descended the steps Gutierrez realized that some of the Leatherfaces were wearing body armor and were not retreating while those without armor had retreated under the hail of rubber bullets peppering them.

The ones wearing the body armor were going to be a problem if they held their ground. The rubber bullets weren't hurting them. The use of real bullets by his officers might be required. Gutierrez didn't want to have to kill anyone. The mayor would become livid if he did. But he didn't know how to disperse the Leatherfaces with body armor without using real bullets.

Gutierrez counted four Leatherfaces wearing body armor who were continuing to brandish their roaring chain saws despite the rubber bullets bombarding them. The rest of the demonstrators had discarded their placards and scattered under the barrage of rubber bullets.

Gutierrez ordered his officers to halt their advance but to continue to fire rubber bullets at the four Leatherfaces. He knew the riot shields would not be able to fend off chain saw blades if the Leatherfaces counterattacked. For now, the Leatherfaces were staying put.

Gutierrez didn't know if these four Leatherfaces had refueled or not. If they hadn't refueled, their chain saws would become inoperable soon. If they had refueled, their chain saws would operate for another thirty or forty minutes before running out of gas.

He picked up on a red jerrican standing near the Leatherfaces, suggesting they might have refueled already. Waiting them out might be the best course of action and then moving on them when they needed to refuel.

The fact they were wearing body armor bothered him. It meant they had come prepared to engage in hand-to-hand combat. These guys could be ex-military. They might also be packing. Gutierrez didn't want to lose any of his officers.

The four Leatherfaces saw that the riot squad had halted their advance down the steps. The Leatherfaces let loose with a whoop, brandishing their chain saws in triumph.

"Throw down your weapons and disperse," Gutierrez commanded through his bullhorn.

The Leatherfaces jeered and gave him the finger.

Gutierrez hated disrespect of any kind. Their actions inflamed him. Before he realized what he was doing, he whipped out his service pistol. He wanted to kill them.

The thing was, if they were wearing body armor, ordinary bullets weren't going to harm them unless a lucky shot managed to sneak between the gaps in the armor. He would need armor-piercing rounds with tungsten cores to deal with these four clowns. The rubber bullets were as ineffective as houseflies.

The mayor didn't want violence, but how was he going to get the four remaining Leatherfaces to disperse? Maybe they would get bored and leave. Or maybe they had guns and would attack City Hall and try to kill the mayor. Gutierrez couldn't take the chance.

The four Leatherfaces waved their chain saws menacingly at the riot squad.

Gutierrez motioned to Juanca, who approached him.

"We need a rifle with armor-piercing rounds and a sharpshooter," said Gutierrez.

Perkins Weaver belted toward the four Leatherfaces and commenced filming them on his smartphone.

Gutierrez widened his eyes. "Who the hell is that idiot?"

Juanca gazed at Weaver. "He's got a Press badge. He's a reporter."

"That's all we need," said Gutierrez, fit to be tied. He raised his bullhorn to his mouth. "Everyone is ordered to disperse by declaration of the mayor of Los Angeles."

Perkins glanced in the direction of Gutierrez.

"Press," cried Perkins.

"Including the press," bellowed Gutierrez. "Back away from the rioters."

"I'm covering a story."

"You're too close. Back away."

"Want me to fire rubber bullets at him, sir?" asked Juanca.

"Where do they get these idiots who call themselves reporters?"

"Want me to get Carter? He has a Remington 700 .30-06 bolt-action rifle that fires armor-piercing rounds with tungsten cores."

Gutierrez grimaced. "That reporter is too close to the rioters, and he's getting closer."

Weaver approached one of the Leatherfaces in order to interview him.

"Fuck," said Gutierrez. "We can't fire live rounds at the rioters with that moron reporter there."

"He'll leave if we shoot him with rubber bullets," said Juanca.

"I don't want to be the target of a lawsuit for firing on a reporter."

Waving their chain saws above their heads, the four Leatherfaces commenced approaching the riot squad.

"Looks like they want to play rough," said Gutierrez.

"What do you want us to do, sir?" said Juanca. "Our live rounds won't penetrate their body armor."

"Get Carter."

Chapter 60

Juanca spoke into the radio on his shoulder and summoned Carter with his Remington 700.

"I'm not gonna let any of my officers get hurt by those chain saws," said Gutierrez.

The Leatherfaces, accompanied by the reporter trying to get an interview with one of them, kept advancing on the riot squad.

"Fire rubber bullets at the reporter," said Gutierrez, lowering his bullhorn.

"Yes, sir."

Juanca started firing his pistol at the reporter.

"Ow. What are you doing?" cried Weaver, rubbing his wounded arm. "I'm press."

"Get out of there," said Gutierrez through his bullhorn.

Weaver prepared to retreat when the Leatherface nearest him snagged Weaver's arm and prevented him from leaving.

"Let him go," commanded Gutierrez.

The Leatherface refused to comply and pumped his chain saw over his head in protest while holding onto Weaver's wrist.

"This is turning into a clusterfuck," muttered Gutierrez through his teeth.

Their chain saws racketing, the four Leatherfaces kept advancing toward the steps where the riot squad stood.

"We want Kudlow," hollered the Leatherface using Weaver as a shield.

"He's not here," said Gutierrez. "Throw down your weapons and leave. Or we will fire on you. I will not jeopardize the lives of any of my officers. Disperse now."

Carter ran up to Gutierrez, bearing his Remington 700 bolt-action rifle.

"We're not leaving without Kudlow," screamed the Leatherface above the din of his chain saw.

The riot squad uniforms looked nervous as the Leatherfaces approached them, brandishing their chain saws.

"Stand your ground," Gutierrez ordered his squad. He turned to Carter. "Take out the leader."

"The hostage is in the way," said Carter, concern creasing his brow.

"I hate reporters," said Gutierrez. "They're always getting in the way and lying about us in their rags."

"Sir?" said Carter, uncertain what to do.

"Train your rifle on one of the Leatherfaces without a hostage."

Carter obeyed.

The Leatherface who Carter was aiming at realized he was the target, threw down his chain saw, and fled. The other two Leatherfaces copied his actions, leaving the leader and his hostage to confront the riot squad.

The remaining Leatherface kept advancing on the riot squad, his chain saw churning above his head.

"Take him out," ordered Gutierrez.

"What about the hostage?" said Carter.

His eyes hard, Gutierrez stared at Carter. "I thought you were a sharpshooter."

"The hostage is in the line of fire, sir."

"Take the shot. That's an order. The reporter has no business being there."

His face tense, Carter gulped.

He trained his Remington 700 on the Leatherface, who kept advancing on the riot squad, his chain saw wailing above his head.

"I'm not leaving without Kudlow," cried the Leatherface. "Get out of my way, or I'll cut a path through you."

Sweat broke out above Carter's lip as he drew a bead on the Leatherface's shoulder that remained exposed behind the reporter. Carter slowed his breathing in preparation for squeezing the rifle trigger. The Leatherface and his hostage were now six feet from the riot squad, who were shifting their feet apprehensively.

"Take the shot," said Gutierrez. "That's a direct order. My officers are in danger."

"I can't get a clear kill shot," said Carter. "The hostage—"

"Fire."

Carter slowed his heartbeat again.

"We don't have all day," said Gutierrez.

227

Carter fired.

The bullet caught the Leatherface in the shoulder. The impact spun the Leatherface around, forcing him to lower the chain saw, which sliced through Weaver's arm, severing it at the elbow. Blood spurted out of the stump as Weaver's forearm fell to the concrete.

Weaver howled in agony and broke away from the Leatherface, who reeled backward, landed on his back, and squirmed in his body armor like an upended turtle, flailing his limbs trying to get up but impeded by the weight of his armor.

"Call an ambulance," Gutierrez told Juanca then turned to his men. "Arrest the rioter."

The riot squad converged on the writhing Leatherface.

Sobbing, Weaver picked up his bloody severed arm, stared at it, aghast, then passed out in shock, his face white.

"He won't be writing any more lies with that arm," said Gutierrez.

Prepared for a violent confrontation, a pair of EMTs in navy blue uniforms had been waiting on the premises. They trundled a gurney toward Weaver. Another pair of EMTs made a beeline for the wounded Leatherface.

"I couldn't get a kill shot," said Carter, his Remington 700 in hand.

"Don't worry about it," said Gutierrez. "You took him down, and the hostage is alive."

Gutierrez wasn't eager to get called on the carpet by the mayor. He figured she would blow her stack when she found out he had used violence to put down the riot. He headed for her office in City Hall, prepared for the worst.

Chapter 61

Coombs was waiting for Gutierrez as she stood behind her desk, her face stern, when he strode into her office, his spine erect.

"I heard a gunshot," she said. "I told you not to use violence."

"It couldn't be helped, Madam Mayor. We had no alternative."

"Explain."

Gutierrez stood in front of her desk, clasping his hands behind his back, trying to appear calm even as his recalcitrant heartbeat was kicking like it was on steroids.

"Four Leatherfaces were wearing body armor," he said. "Our rubber bullets had no effect on them."

"So?" she said, continuing to stand, her eyes riveted on his face.

"So the four Leatherfaces didn't retreat when we pelted them with rubber bullets even though the rest of the rioters did."

"The protesters dispersed? That's what it looked like from my window while I was watching them."

"Except for the four who continued to brandish their chain saws in a menacing manner. They refused to disperse. I told them to throw down their chain saws and leave. They refused."

"Why did you open fire on them?"

"They demanded Kudlow and advanced on my officers, threatening to cut a path through them if my officers didn't allow them to pass into City Hall."

"Then what?"

"I told the Leatherfaces you had ordered them to disperse, that my squad would not allow them to pass."

"What did they do?"

"They ignored me. Then a nosy reporter filming the Leatherfaces on his cell phone approached them to get an interview."

"A reporter? How did a reporter manage to get to them? I thought you said everyone else had dispersed."

"I thought so. This idiot reporter showed up, trying to score a scoop. One of the Leatherfaces took him hostage when I called for my sharpshooter."

"Sharpshooter? Are we talking real bullets now, not rubber ones?"

"We are. Rubber bullets will not penetrate body armor. Neither will regular bullets, for that matter. When the Leatherfaces saw my sharpshooter and his Remington 700, they threw down their chain saws and fled—all except one, that is."

"The one with the reporter hostage?"

Gutierrez nodded yes. "He kept advancing on my officers, who stood their ground even though the threat to their lives was real and immediate due to the chain saw the Leatherface was wielding in a threatening manner as he approached them."

"Did he hurt anyone?"

"He didn't hurt my officers. But he would have once he reached the front line. He would have chopped up anybody in his way. Guys with body armor and chain saws aren't joking around. They mean business."

"Let me get this straight," said Coombs, planting her fists on her desktop and leaning toward Gutierrez. "You shot the victim even though he hadn't harmed anyone?"

"Actually, he did harm someone. His falling chain saw lopped off the arm of the reporter."

"That explains the two men I saw rushed away on gurneys by EMTs," said Coombs as if to herself.

"Yes, Madam Mayor."

"I expressly ordered you not to use violence," said Coombs, glowering at Gutierrez.

"The four Leatherfaces refused to retreat. I had no choice but to use force against them."

"Why didn't you order your officers to charge the Leatherfaces with their batons and subdue them?"

Gutierrez didn't like being second-guessed. "Because the Leatherfaces had deadly weapons in their hands and would have used them against my officers, probably killing some of them. I didn't want to jeopardize even one life of my officers."

"Commendable. But didn't they have riot shields to protect themselves from blows?"

230

"Those riot shields are polycarbonate. They won't stand up to a chain saw."

Her visage darkening, Coombs turned away from him. "The media is gonna have a Roman holiday with this. They're gonna say I overstepped my authority by ordering you to put down a peaceful protest with violence."

"You can't have a peaceful protest with demonstrators brandishing chain saws."

"That's not the way the media will see it. And the protesters will go out of their way to make us look like the heavies."

"Just tell the media the truth. We were attacked, and we put down the attack without losing a single officer."

Coombs wheeled around to confront Gutierrez. "Couldn't you have waited for this assailant's chain saw to run out of gas, Chief? Then we could have avoided violence altogether."

Gutierrez stood motionless, grinding his teeth. "My officers were in immediate danger. The assailant's chain saw was working fine when he advanced on them, swiping it at them in a threatening manner."

Coombs turned away again. "It's that damn Kudlow's fault. Him and his cursed movie that's fomenting death and destruction in our city. He needs to be called to account."

"Want me to arrest him?"

"For what?"

Gutierrez shrugged. "You said his movie is fomenting death and destruction."

"Freedom of the press handcuffs me," said Coombs, crestfallen. She chewed it over. "The only thing I can do is censor his movie. Which will cause an uproar—unless we can convince Kudlow to pull his movie. If *he* decides to pull it, nobody can blame me for censoring it."

"Once he hears about this riot, he might agree to pull it."

"He wouldn't play ball when I talked to him before, but he might change his tune now. The thing is he hasn't returned my calls. I have no way to get in touch with him."

"You're the mayor. You can make a public announcement asking him to contact you."

"Where the hell is he, anyway?"

"If he doesn't want to be found, he has the resources to stay hidden."

"On the other hand, he's a famous celebrity. His face is well-known. Somebody is bound to spot him. We have to find him. We can't afford another riot on my watch. The city is already in turmoil."

"I'll put more officers on the job of locating him."

"And I'll make an announcement on TV that we're looking for him and want to be notified immediately if anybody sees him."

Chapter 62

"She said she was my partner," said Grant, riding shotgun in Herb's VW Bug. "Does a partner take all the money and spend it on herself?"

"You said she was gonna pay you back," said Herb at the wheel as they drove down a side street populated with warehouses.

"She's been saying so for over a year and hasn't paid me back a nickel. She said the millions she inherited from her uncle are in probate, and she can't access them."

If you could believe her. At this point Grant didn't.

"There you go," said Herb. "Probate's a bitch when real estate's involved."

Grant watched Herb glance at his smartphone that he had placed in the cup container on the dash so he could follow the map on his app that was displaying where Kudlow's cell phone signal was transmitting from.

"It's all lies," said Grant, hangdog. "And I believed them. I should kick myself for believing her scam."

"Why is Kudlow's cell phone signal coming from around here?" said Herb, scanning the neighborhood.

"She's the Scam Queen. I'm sure she's gotten away with it before. I'm not her first or only victim. Or her last. The cops'll never put her out of business. She'll just keep on scamming new victims and getting away with it."

"Holler if you see Kudlow. We're getting closer to him."

Every time Grant thought of Sherry he became irate. He wanted to get back at her, but he had no idea how. The only thing he could do was to stop loaning her more money. However, it wouldn't get any of the hundreds of thousands of dollars back that he had already lent her. He saw no way to get any of it back. He figured she had pissed it all away.

He had no legal recourse to get his money back. He felt powerless and became frustrated thinking about it. There was no solution. The Scam Queen had won. He just had to suck it up.

233

Herb tooled down the street. "Are you paying attention? Kudlow must be near."

Grant knew it was a waste of time getting angry. He would be better off doing something else, like writing, except he couldn't write a word. The real world was the Scam Queen's world where conning people out of their money was the main occupation, and in her world writing a true sentence accomplished nothing.

Herb slowed the Bug to a halt on the side of the street.

"The signal's coming from that warehouse," he said, gazing at a hangarlike one-story building in the middle of a vacant parking lot.

"How could I be so blind to her scam?"

"Are you paranoid or what?"

"Telling the truth is paranoia?"

"You sound like you think everybody is a scammer."

"Sherry is. I never encountered anyone in my whole life like her. She's the worst of the worst."

Herb rubbed his brow. "Do you want to save Kudlow or not?"

"Every time I think of Sherry I become furious and I want to hurt people."

"Then don't think about her. Think about your favorite director Norman Kudlow."

"She wrecked my life. She bankrupted me and wants more money," said Grant, smoldering with rage.

"You got a one-track mind. She's probably gonna get her inheritance from probate any day now and then she can pay you back."

Grant exploded with laughter. "Fat chance."

Herb broke a sweat. Transparent, glittering liquid beads popped onto his flesh and streamed down his gaunt face.

"I need a fix," he said. "Can you lend me some money?"

Grant stared at him, speechless.

"I can pay you back after Kudlow—I mean, my client pays me for my work."

"Kudlow? You're working for Kudlow?"

"Don't tell anyone. I never tell my clients' names."

"No wonder you have his cell number. I can't believe he would hire you."

"I played an extra in one of his movies. He remembered I became a PI, and he hired me."

"That doesn't change the fact I can't lend you any money. Haven't you been listening? The Scam Queen wiped me out."

"What am I gonna do?" said Herb, his hands shaking on the steering wheel of the parked Bug.

"Where's Kudlow?"

"My app says he's in that warehouse," said Herb, nodding to the expansive drab building with grey paint peeling like curling cadaver fingers.

Several broken windows, not to mention the spray-painted graffiti around them, gave the building an abandoned aspect.

A rusted chain-link fence surrounded the warehouse.

"Do you have your piece?" said Grant.

"Why?" said Herb, worried.

"I can't imagine why Kudlow would be holed up in a deserted warehouse that should be condemned. Something's wrong."

Grant withdrew his SIG P365, ejected the magazine, and inspected it to make sure it was loaded. Satisfied, he slammed the magazine back into its well.

"You look like you know what you're doing," said Herb.

"As a writer I need to know how things work. You used to be a PI. You should know how to fire a pistol."

"It's been a while," said Herb, inspecting the pistol in his sweat-smeared hand.

"It's not something you forget."

"Now what?"

"We need to find the warehouse entrance."

Chapter 63

In a program that had been taped earlier, Riley Coogan sat in his studio, interviewing the director Bob LeBeau, who was sitting opposite him in front of a live audience, the TV cameras rolling, their red lights lit.

"It is my understanding you are blaming Norman Kudlow for the riot at City Hall," said Coogan.

"There's no question that he bears the responsibility for the riot and the violence that took place there. He is also responsible for blowing up the theater in Marina del Rey—"

"Wait a minute. Let's return to the riot at City Hall. How can that be Kudlow's responsibility? He wasn't even there."

"I know. But the protesters wanted him to come out of City Hall and talk to them about his latest movie."

"How could he come out of City Hall if he wasn't there?"

"It doesn't matter. The protesters were rioting in front of City Hall because they thought Kudlow was there."

Coogan hiked his eyebrows. "I don't understand your reasoning. How do you blame Kudlow for the violence if he wasn't there?"

"It's his movie that's triggering the violence in our city, including the riot. Three murders have taken place in theaters showing his dangerous and reckless movie *Necromaniac*, a movie in my humble opinion that should be withdrawn immediately from theaters. It is irresponsible of Kudlow to continue to allow it to be shown."

"It sounds like you're advocating censorship, which is strange coming from a movie director," said Coogan, surprise registering on his face.

"I'm an artist. I'm never in favor of censorship—"

"And yet what you're saying about pulling Kudlow's movie from distribution is censorship. There's no getting around it. How is it not censorship?"

"Let me explain," said LeBeau, gesticulating with his hands. "You obviously don't understand the meaning of *censorship*—"

"Now hold on—"

"Let me continue, please. *Censorship* is when someone else censors your movie. It is not censorship if you remove your own movie from theaters."

Coogan adopted a smug expression. "It sounds like you're splitting hairs."

"I'm not. A creative artist *cannot* censor his own work. Let me give you an example that I'm sure you're familiar with. When Stanley Kubrick pulled *Clockwork Orange*—I'm sure you're familiar with the movie—"

"Of course, but—"

"Let me finish. When he pulled *Clockwork Orange* from UK theaters, it was not censorship. He did it because he was concerned the movie was instigating violence. There were several examples reported in the papers of teens committing copycat violence after they watched the movie. Kubrick did what he thought was right and pulled his movie from UK theaters. This was the official line anyway."

"What do you mean 'official line'?" said Coogan, looking perplexed.

"The truth came out later that Kubrick's family had received death threats because of his movie."

The studio audience gasped.

"That's the real reason Kubrick pulled his movie from theaters in London," LeBeau went on. "The movie was continually banned in the UK for twenty-seven years until Kubrick's death."

"And that's not censorship, according to you?" said Coogan, puzzled.

"Of course not. Kubrick was free to do as he wished, and in his case he did the right thing by pulling his movie from UK theaters."

"The 'right thing' meaning, he didn't want his family to get killed."

"The motivation doesn't matter. What matters is the end result."

"The ends justify the means."

LeBeau crossed his legs. "The point is he did the right thing, the responsible thing. Which is exactly what Kudlow must do. If he was a really great director like Kubrick, he would pull his dreadful movie from theaters, realizing it turns people into killers."

"You mention Kubrick. I read a book by his wife that said he didn't believe movies could transform a good kid into a violent thug. Thinking otherwise smacked of the Salem witch trials, according to an interview he gave."

"I don't get the connection."

"I believe he meant that he felt like someone accused of witchcraft during those times. If you were accused of witchcraft, there was no way you could prove you were innocent. Isn't that what you're doing to Kudlow by accusing him of making a movie that should be pulled from theaters? He has no way he can prove he's innocent."

"He's *not* innocent. He directed *Necromaniac*, a movie that triggers violence in its audience."

"I doubt Kubrick would agree with you."

"Well, he never saw *Necromaniac*, did he? This horror movie is an assault to common decency. It violates every code of ethics in history."

Coogan widened his eyes. "I saw it. It creeped me out, but I didn't want to commit homicide afterwards."

"Of course, no movie can transform everybody into a raging homicidal maniac. That goes without saying. But this movie is inciting a person, or maybe many persons, to commit murder. Just look at the three theaters where murder victims were found. All three theaters were showing the movie when the murders took place."

"It sounds like you're blaming Kudlow for the murders."

"I am indeed," said LeBeau, crossing his arms. "He bears full responsibility for these dreadful murders, just as Kubrick bore responsibility for the copycat murders committed after audiences watched *Clockwork Orange* in the UK."

"But Kubrick never believed movies can incite violence. He removed his movie from circulation in the UK because he and his family received death threats."

"My point exactly. His movie caused him to get death threats. Therefore, his movie precipitated violence."

238

"Wait a minute. I grant you his movie caused him to get death threats, but it didn't incite violence against him."

"Because he yanked it from theaters before anyone tried to kill his family," said LeBeau, opening his arms, figuring he had won the argument.

Coogan pulled a face. "He never said movies incite violence, because he didn't believe it."

"I don't care what he believed. What matters is he pulled *Clockwork Orange* from UK theaters. And Kudlow should follow Kubrick's example and pull *Necromaniac* from US theaters."

Astounded, Coogan bridled. "All US theaters?"

LeBeau nodded yes. "If it can incite murder in California, it can incite murder in other states in the US as well. We're talking about people's lives here."

Coogan paused. "Are you a member of the Committee for Decent Movies?"

"What does that have to do with anything?" said LeBeau with astonishment and disdain.

"Just saying."

"The answer is no."

"I'm trying to understand your hatred for Kudlow."

"It sounds like you're trying to connect me to the bombing of the theater in Marina del Rey," retorted LeBeau, his hackles rising.

"I didn't say that," said Coogan, all innocence.

"It was obvious you implied it."

"You inferred it, you mean. Let's move on. Do you believe Kudlow should be arrested for murder because his movie incited three murders?"

"I'm not a DA. I believe Kudlow should do the right thing. He should pull his dreadful, cursed movie from distribution before more murders are committed by people watching it."

Several members of the audience booed.

"We want Kudlow," they commenced chanting.

"Settle down, settle down," said Coogan, pushing his hands down in front of him several times. "I would be glad to have Kudlow back on my show to say his piece."

"The man's a disgrace to the film profession if he doesn't pull his movie posthaste," said LeBeau.

Scattered boos in the audience erupted again.

"Where is Kudlow, anyway?" said Coogan.

"Hiding his ass. Pulling his movie is the last thing he wants to do. He and his coproducers stand to lose tons of money if he does. The longer he stays in hiding, the longer he doesn't have to make a decision on his movie."

"You sound like you hate the man."

"I hate what he stands for—corporate greed in Hollywood."

"And yet he has the reputation of being one of the best directors in the business, a true auteur. How does that square with corporate greed?"

"His reputation is undeserved. He's a hack, pure and simple. He cranks out movies for money," said LeBeau, acid dripping from his lips. "In the end his movies are grindhouse schlock."

A chorus of boos swept through the audience.

"There are many who disagree with your assessment," said Coogan, picking up on the audience's reaction.

"They don't know him like I do. I'm talking about the real man, not the carefully crafted PR image. *I'm* an authentic auteur, not a phony one like Kudlow."

Chapter 64

Sitting in the VW Bug passenger seat, Grant answered his cell phone.

"Where are you?" said Sherry. "I'm at your apartment and you're not answering your door."

"I thought you were stranded in New York."

"I got attacked by a homeless person with a rusty can opener. He could have cut open one of my arteries. I was lucky I escaped. If I stayed there any longer, I would be risking my life."

"How could you afford a plane ticket?"

"I had to fly standby thanks to you. It was horrible. I sat in the middle seat between two fatsos. One of them kept groping my thigh."

"How could you afford standby?"

"Do you even care?" she said, raising her voice indignantly.

"Where were you really?"

"What's that supposed to mean?"

"It means, you're allergic to telling the truth."

"You should be happy I'm back in one piece. Instead you're insulting me," said Sherry, her voice cracking.

"Maybe you shouldn't be so mean to her," whispered Herb from the driver's seat. "She's your girlfriend. Is this how you treat your girlfriends?"

Grant covered his cell phone transmitter and spoke softly. "You don't know her like I do. She's a pathological liar. She'll say anything to get money out of me."

"She sounds like she had a rough time in New York."

"According to her, a train ran over her."

"How can you joke about her like that?"

"She's nothing more than a grifter. She swindled me out of my life savings. I should kill her."

Herb's eyes bugged out of his head. "What's got into you? You sound like a bloodthirsty thug."

"I'm not fooling around."

"Hello?" said Sherry. "Are you talking to someone? I can't hear you."

"I'm in the middle of something important," said Grant.

"And I'm not important to you?" said Sherry, her voice ringing with both disbelief and hurt feelings.

"I'm not lending you any more money. You wiped me out."

"I can't get into your apartment."

"There's nothing worth stealing in there."

"Shut up," she snapped. "How dare you?"

"I sold everything I had of value in order to lend you money for your probate lawyers for all that money you supposedly inherited."

"Why do you always blame me for your being broke all the time?"

"Because you're the reason I *am* broke. You're never gonna pay me back whether you inherit anything or not. Your supposed inheritance is another one of your lies."

"You're awful. How can you say such bitchy things to your girlfriend?"

"I bought your lies hook, line, and sinker," said Grant, filled with self-hatred thanks to his stupidity. "I really believed you were gonna pay me back with your inheritance because you said we were partners."

"How can you treat me like this?" said Sherry, weeping. "You said you would love me and support me forever."

"What?" said Grant.

He couldn't believe his ears. He had never said anything about supporting her forever.

"You're a monster," she said. "And *you're* the liar."

"You're a con artist, a fraudster—"

"I almost got run over by a train and assaulted because you left me to die."

She broke into tears again.

He hated hearing her cry, but he couldn't let her get away with her lies.

"You're the monster," he said. "You defrauded me out of hundreds of thousands of dollars, everything I had."

She continued crying. "You left me to die."

Grant terminated the call. If he listened any longer to her crying, he might max out his only credit card with a five-hundred-dollar credit line and lend her the money. She knew she could manipulate him with her tears.

He pocketed his cell.

"Don't you think you're being too hard on her?" said Herb.

"We don't have time for this. Let's check out that warehouse and see if Kudlow's inside."

"You're gonna lose her if you keep treating her like a rabid dog."

"A rabid dog? Listen to me. She's *worse* than a rabid dog. She's a professional scammer," said Grant, jackknifing out of the VW, eager to drop the subject, Sherry's voice still rattling around in his head like a pinball running amok. He scoped out the rusted chain-link fence. "It looks like we're gonna have to climb over the fence."

Herb slid out of the driver's seat and locked his door. He eyed the length of the fence.

"There must be a gate somewhere," he said.

"The kidnapers might have posted a guard to watch the gate, wherever it is. It must be around back. Let's climb the fence here. I don't see anybody watching. This looks like a pretty deserted neighborhood."

A stray mutt roamed the street, spotted them, and barked a couple times, his heart not in it.

"Shh," said Herb.

The mutt lost interest and wandered away.

"Not a watchdog," said Grant. "Are you sure this is where Kudlow is?"

Herb checked his cell phone tracking app. "That's what my app says."

"Let's go, then." Grant inspected the ten-foot-high fence. "I don't see any barbed wire or razor wire on top."

"Are you sure this is a good idea?"

"We have to save Kudlow. Come on."

Grant scaled the chain-link fence, which rattled and bellied as he clawed his way to the top. It wasn't as easy as it looked in the movies. When he reached the pipe on the top, he pulled himself up then pushed himself up until his torso cleared the pipe. He swung

243

his right leg to position his sneaker on top of the pipe, followed by his left leg, and leapt onto the asphalt parking lot beyond the fence. He landed on his feet and crouched into a ball to absorb the shock of hitting the asphalt.

"A good way to break your leg," said Herb, watching him.

"I dare you to do it."

Herb pocketed his cell phone, gripped the fence, and copied Grant's example.

"Ow," he said on landing.

"What's wrong?" said Grant.

"My foot hit wrong."

"Is it broken?"

Herb limped around. "I don't think so. I can walk. It just feels sore."

"All right. Let's get going before they see us."

They bucketed to the warehouse. Grant noticed Herb wincing in pain behind him.

Chapter 65

Jacquie Artois, the chairwoman of the Committee for Public Safety, entered Mayor Coombs's office. Fiftysomething with her white hair in a perm, Artois, a slight woman, stood five six. She was wearing a yellow power dress. She had a small mole an inch under her right eye, which her friends considered a beauty mark. Her enemies, and she had more than a few, called it by another name—a witch's mark.

Coombs sat behind her desk, watching Artois approach, expecting the worst. Artois had all the subtlety of a Death Star, wearing her acerbic personality on her dour visage.

"The Committee for Public Safety wants to know what you intend to do about the current wave of violence racking our city because of the horror movie *Necromaniac*, Madam Mayor."

"Have a seat, Madam Chairwoman."

"Thank you," said Artois, and sat down in front of Coombs's desk with an air of disgust.

"I'm waiting for a response from Norman Kudlow, the director of the movie."

"What kind of response?"

"I have asked him to pull his movie from theaters."

"Why do you feel you need to ask him to do your job?" said Artois, her lips curling into a sneer.

"I am the mayor, not a censor."

"With all due respect, you as mayor have the power to withdraw a dangerous movie from circulation. You have the power to remove any movie that is a threat to public safety."

"Where does it say that in my job duties?"

"You have formed our Committee for Public Safety and must abide by our decisions."

"I can't abide by them until I know them."

"Our committee has come to the decision that *Necromaniac* must be pulled forthwith from theaters as a threat to public safety."

"How do I do that without violating the First Amendment?"

245

"Free speech that incites violence must be censored."

"Which law are you citing?"

"We, the committee, have declared it so. Our job is to protect public safety. The depraved horror movie directed by the purveyor of filth Norman Kudlow must be removed from theaters before it incites more violence."

"The best way to handle this is to persuade Kudlow to pull his movie from theaters. Otherwise, there will be numerous protests, where scores of people may be injured."

"We just had a riot here. You need to act quickly before more riots sweep across the city and raze it."

"Banning the movie could foment just as many riots if not more."

"We at the committee disagree with your assessment."

"The only way the government can legally ban a movie is if it's considered obscene."

"Fine. Then ban it as obscene. It has a depraved sex scene in it between a human and a demon."

"I know which scene you're talking about. It's no worse than the one depicted in *The Exorcist* with the possessed child."

"Sex between a demon and a human is obscene."

"The scene does not show consummated sex between them. In other words, they don't have sex," said Coombs, feeling the urge to point out the obvious to Artois and humiliate her by belittling her intelligence. "So how can it be obscene?"

"It doesn't matter," said Artois, not perceiving the slight and tiring of the argument. "What matters is that the movie is inciting violence. If the only way we can censor it is by calling it obscene, by all means let's call it obscene."

She prepared to get up and leave as if that was the end of the argument.

"The sex scene does not incite violence," said Coombs.

"Admittedly, it's just a pretext to get the movie out of the theaters. What's wrong with that? As long as nobody is allowed to see the movie, that's what counts. No more cursed movie, no more movie murders."

"The producers could sue our asses off because of all the money they'll lose if their movie gets censored for an invalid reason like obscenity."

246

"I consider a movie obscene if it brainwashes viewers into committing murder."

"*Obscenity* refers to pornographic sex in terms of the law. It doesn't refer to violence per se. Most every movie made these days is riddled with violence, and, I repeat, there was no pornographic sex in this movie. Have you even seen the movie?"

"I have no interest in watching a depraved movie."

"If you haven't seen it, how can you call it obscene?"

"Let them argue it in the courts. The point is we'll get the movie out of the theaters if we censor it. By the time the case gets to the supreme court everybody will have forgotten about the movie, and nobody will want to see it."

"And the producers will sue us."

"They won't get *our* money. They'll get the taxpayers' money."

Coombs's face became stern. "We're here to make good use of taxpayers' money, not to throw it away on frivolous lawsuits."

"It's not frivolous when we're talking about human lives being lost on account of this decadent horror movie. There must be something seriously wrong with the director for him to make such a sleazy and evil movie."

Coombs found herself liking Artois less and less, picturing her as a vulture preying on carrion.

"Whether you like it or not, these types of movies make a lot of money," said Coombs. "That's why Hollywood keeps churning them out. We don't want to make enemies in the movie business. They rake in a lot of revenue in this town, enriching government coffers when we collect taxes."

Animated, Artois thrust to her feet. "We're not talking about money. We're talking about human lives. The life of every moviegoer should be our most pressing concern. Our committee has voted for you to censor the movie without further ado."

Artois slewed around and stalked out, her heels stabbing the floor like knives.

Coombs fumed. She wasn't taking orders from Artois or from anyone else. She didn't want to become known as the first mayor to censor a movie. On the other hand, she didn't want any more murders committed in LA movie theaters. And she didn't want any more riots, for that matter.

Kudlow was her only ticket out of this mess. She needed him to volunteer to pull his movie. Why the hell did he have to do a bunk?

She couldn't postpone making a decision about the movie much longer. If the cops didn't find him soon, she would be forced to put her reputation at stake, to go out on a limb, and to censor his movie. She felt in her bones that being known as the mayor who censored movies would torpedo her career in politics, especially in LA, the movie capital of the world. Donations from rich Hollywood hotshots would dry up in the blink of an eye.

She got on her phone and called her secretary.

"Sheila, I want to hold a news conference where I'm gonna make an announcement for Norman Kudlow to contact me ASAP," she said.

If only the Hollywood Psycho wouldn't strike again until Kudlow got in touch with her. She knew hope wasn't a strategy, but patience could be. She told her rapid heartbeat to take a siesta.

She withdrew her battery-powered sphygmomanometer from her desk drawer, attached the Velcro cuff to her upper arm, and took her blood pressure.

She gasped when she read the results. With these kinds of numbers she was in jeopardy of a coronary.

She knew a charge of obscenity would never stick. The movie had no sex in it, just words referring to sex. The same words appeared in thousands of movies.

Censoring the movie for violence would be a tough sell too because of the prevalence of violence in all movies.

The only option left to her was to ban the movie for *inciting* violence, which had never been done before as far as she knew. Movie fans would be up in arms. They would be on her case for the rest of her term. They might even demand her resignation.

She had to shift the blame to Kudlow. He was the one who had brought this misery to her beautiful city. He was the bringer of murders and riots. She saw blaming him as the only way to retain her job. She would do everything in her power to compel Kudlow to pull his movie from distribution—if she could ever find the bastard.

Chapter 66

"We need to find an entrance," said Grant as he and Herb worked their way around the warehouse.

Grant spotted the mutt staring at them fifty feet away.

"Isn't that the same mutt we saw before?" he said.

"Looks like it."

"We can't have him tagging along after us. Make him go away."

"How? At least he's not barking anymore."

"But he could start any minute." Grant faced the dog and waved his arms. "Go away," he stage-whispered with an angry expression on his face.

The mutt stared at him.

"We can't have him following us," he said. "He might start barking."

"I don't know anything about dogs."

"Say something to it."

Herb shrugged. "You look like a cat," he whispered to the dog.

The mutt scampered away.

"They don't like being insulted," explained Herb.

He watched the mutt as it turned back to look at him with sad eyes.

"I'm sorry," said Herb.

Grant grabbed Herb's arm. "Don't apologize to him or he'll come back."

Herb broke eye contact with the mutt.

"Now all we have to do is find the entrance," said Grant.

"It must be on the other side of the building," said Herb, hobbling slightly.

"How's your foot?"

"I don't think it's broken. It's sore. Walking on it should help it get better like basketball players do."

"Yeah. Walk it off."

They turned the corner of the warehouse.

Grant halted so abruptly that Herb bumped into him.

"What's wrong?" said Herb, staying behind Grant.

"An unmarked black Dodge Charger just pulled into the parking lot. Cops."

"How do you know it's a cop car?"

"That fancy antenna on its trunk. And the car's a Charger. Cops drive Chargers. Must be a plainclothes detective at the wheel."

Grant backed up behind the corner of the building to get out of sight of the car. He peeked around the corner to see who exited the Charger.

"Well, I'll be . . . ," he said.

"What?" said Herb, who couldn't see past Grant.

Herb tried to maneuver around Grant, but Grant pushed him back.

"Don't let them see you," said Grant.

"Who is it?"

"Those two cops who interviewed me at my apartment. Rivera and what's-his-name. Beasley. No, Kesey."

"What are *they* doing here?" said Herb, baffled.

"Dunno—unless they were able to track Kudlow's cell like we did."

Grant spotted a silver SUV and a grimy white van already parked in the lot, which meant people were inside the warehouse. One of them could be Kudlow, according to the signal his cell phone was sending.

"Maybe we should beat it and let the cops take care of this," said Herb. "If Kudlow was kidnaped like you say, it's the job of the cops to save him. We might as well get out of here. The cops might bust us for being members of the kidnaping gang."

Grant watched Kesey and Rivera pile out of their unmarked car and make for the warehouse door.

"They don't look like they're sneaking toward the warehouse," said Grant. "And they don't have their guns drawn."

"What's the big deal? They can draw their guns when they're in the warehouse."

"Look at the way they're strolling toward the door."

Herb peeked around Grant to watch the cops. "What am I looking at?"

250

"They're so complacent. It doesn't look like they're about to free a kidnap victim."

"Maybe they're cool under pressure."

Grant gave him a look.

"What?" said Herb.

"This looks suspicious as hell."

"Cops freeing a kidnap victim? Yeah, that's suspicious, all right."

"I'm serious. Something's hinky here."

The two plainclothes cops disappeared inside the warehouse and shut the door behind them.

"Why did they do that?" said Grant.

"Do what?"

"Close the door behind them."

"Maybe they don't want to be disturbed."

"But they must've called for backup like cops always do when they confront criminals, which means they should leave the door open."

"You think too much."

"I'm telling you it's hinky."

"I say we bug out and let these guys do their job," said Herb. "Their backup should be here any minute."

"You're a PI. Can't you sense things aren't right?"

"Cops freeing a kidnaping victim? What's wrong with that scenario? That's what cops do."

"A SWAT team yeah. Plainclothes cops?" said Grant, pulling a face.

Herb thought about it. "Maybe they're infiltrating the gang of kidnapers."

"The kidnapers would know that unmarked car they're driving is a cop car, just like I knew."

"Maybe everybody isn't as smart as you."

"I came here to find Kudlow. I'm not leaving until I do."

"If we interrupt a bust, we could be in deep shit."

"I'm convinced Kudlow's life is in danger."

"Think about what you're doing. If something's hinky like you say, you could get us both shot inside the warehouse."

"Your client's in there. Don't you want to make sure he's OK?"

251

"I—I—uh . . . I never liked being a PI."

"It's unprofessional to let down your client."

"The thing is I get scared doing this job. So many things can go wrong. I'm not the hero type."

"Everybody gets scared."

"But not as bad as me. Sometimes I'm so scared I can't even get out of bed in the morning. I think of all the things that can go wrong. Then all I want to do is shoot up."

Grant stared at the warehouse door.

"I'm going in," he said. "I can't shake the feeling something's wrong."

He produced his SIG, ejected the magazine, and checked it once again to make sure it was loaded. He jammed the loaded magazine back into the well in the SIG butt.

He stole toward the warehouse door the cops had used to enter the warehouse.

Herb watched him with displeasure. Herb didn't like the idea of his brother entering the warehouse alone even if he was armed with a SIG.

"Maybe the cops need backup," muttered Herb, withdrew his SIG P226 from his ankle holster, and hustled after Grant.

Chapter 67

On the concrete floor inside the abandoned warehouse, Kudlow, Towers, and DeShondra sat bound in three wooden chairs facing three figures wearing nun's masks and black robes. One of the nuns was standing behind a movie camera on a tripod and aiming it at the three captives. Kudlow was wearing a black T-shirt with Movie Whore stenciled on its chest in silver this time instead of white.

"Who are you people?" demanded Kudlow, his hands bound to his chair arms, his legs to his chair legs.

He tried to sound authoritative even though he had no authority here. His insides were churning with fear. Whatever was going to happen was going to be bad.

He could see that Towers and DeShondra were bound like him.

"We're members of the Committee for Decent Movies," said the man in the nun getup behind the movie camera.

"Are you the guys that blew up the theater in the Marina?" asked Towers.

"You're smarter than the average flack."

"What's your name?"

"You can call me Freddie," said the man behind the camera.

"You sound like you're proud you killed a bunch of innocent people in that explosion."

"Not enough people, I guess. *Necromaniac* is still being shown in theaters. We're fighters for common decency in movies. Indecent, degenerate movies like yours appall us."

"What gives you the right to blow up people?" said DeShondra, struggling to free herself from her bindings.

"Stop trying to break free."

DeShondra paid no attention to him.

Freddie strode over to her and slapped her face.

"Ow," she cried, her face smarting.

"I told you to stop it."

253

"Slapping a tied-up woman," said Towers. "What kind of a man are you?"

Freddie stepped toward Towers, who was sitting between Kudlow and DeShondra, and clobbered him in the face with his right fist.

Towers's head rocked back and forth from the impact of the blow.

"Asshole," he spat.

Freddie punched him again. "Shut up."

Towers's mouth fell to bleeding. He spat blood on the floor.

"I think you broke my jaw," he said, grimacing in pain.

"I don't want to mess up your face too bad. I want people to be able to recognize you when I shoot my horror movie." Freddie stepped toward Kudlow. "I especially want them to recognize you, the famous director of indecent dreck. Our movie's gonna be a lot scarier than your movie."

"I thought you call yourselves the Committee for Decent Movies," said Kudlow, eying the three nuns.

"You three are gonna be scared shitless when I shoot it. I'm gonna show you how to shoot a real scary movie, not that execrable mess you shot. Viewers aren't gonna want to commit violence after they see it. The violence will turn them off, not incite them like in your disgrace of a movie."

"What are you babbling about? Do you think it's easy to create a work of art?"

"It's easy to create a scarier movie than yours. Blood will flow."

"What's that supposed to mean? I used Kensington gore in my movies, not human blood. I'm not a barbarian. Where's your Kensington gore?" said Kudlow, casting around the warehouse and not seeing any.

"My movie's gonna be scarier than yours, because it's gonna be real. We're using human blood. The real thing."

"You better not be talking about a snuff film," said Kudlow, his heart palpitating like crazy, his palms soaked in sweat.

"What if I am? What are you gonna do about it?"

"How can you call yourself the Committee for Decent Movies if you shoot a snuff film?"

"How can you call yourself a movie director after shooting *Necromaniac*?"

"Nobody died while shooting my movie."

"No, three people were murdered while watching it."

One of the other nuns, shorter than her companions, adjusted the Fresnel light the movie crew was using as a key light focused on the three kidnap victims. The third nun was placing a backlight behind the three victims. When she was finished, she adjusted the fill light.

"You should be wearing leather gloves when you handle those things," said Kudlow, watching the nun adjusting the key light. "You could burn your fingers off, handling them."

"Shut up," said Freddie. "I know what I'm doing. I went to the USC Film School."

"I guess you flunked out."

Freddie advanced on Kudlow as if he was going to land a haymaker on Kudlow's face. Wincing, Kudlow flinched at the prospect. Freddie pulled back his fist at the last moment.

"I don't want to mess up your face," explained Freddie. "I want to make sure everybody who sees our film will recognize you."

"Nobody's gonna watch your stupid movie," said Towers, his mouth still leaking blood.

Freddie ignored him. He turned to Kudlow. "Are you gonna pull your sick movie from theaters?"

"I believe in freedom of speech. I have the right to show any movie as long as it's not judged obscene."

"Your movie *is* obscene."

"There's no sex in it—"

"Do you agree to pull your movie from theaters?" cut in Freddie. "Yes or no?"

"No."

"Even if it's inciting people in the audience to commit murder?"

"Movies don't incite people to commit murder," Kudlow said vehemently.

"Are you sure about that?" Freddie emitted a creepy laugh. "*I* saw your movie."

255

Kudlow felt beads of sweat rolling down his face. Anybody who could blow up a theater and kill scores of bystanders was capable of committing any atrocity. These fanatics were making his blood run cold.

"What are those?" he said, watching one of the nuns carry two black leather containers toward them, one about a foot wide and a foot-and-a-half long, the other the size of a hatbox.

"You'll find out soon enough," said Freddie.

"What do you plan on doing to us?"

"I'm gonna make you movie stars."

"I don't like the looks of this," said Kudlow, sweat flowing freely now.

"Don't worry about it," said Freddie. "Pretty soon you'll be dead."

"Wait a minute—"

"Like in horror movie dead. I had you going, didn't I?" said Freddie, amused.

"This joke has gone on long enough. Release us this minute."

"What's the big rush? Are you shooting another horror movie? Hear me out. *My* horror movie is gonna rock. I'm gonna teach you how to make a scary horror movie. Have you ever even seen a horror movie?"

"Of course I have. I've seen the best of them. *Psycho, The Birds, Halloween, The Thing from Another Planet, Invasion of the Body Snatchers*, the original and the remake with Donald Sutherland. You name it, I've seen it."

"Robert Aldrich's *Whatever Happened to Baby Jane?*"

"A nice piece of slick horror," said Kudlow, trying to act calm as his pulse rate ticked upward. "Aldrich generally isn't known for horror movies, but *Whatever Happened to Baby Jane?* is top-notch. And it starred the inestimable Bette Davis. She was also in the creepy film *The Nanny*."

"Did you ever see Mario Bava's *Blood and Black Lace?*"

"A classic. Bava's use of lighting is nonpareil."

"Then you'll appreciate the scenes in the movie I'm about to shoot."

Kudlow didn't know what Freddie was talking about and didn't want to find out, because Freddie was making his skin crawl. Kudlow wondered if screaming for help would do any good.

256

He doubted it. The warehouse was deserted, and the neighborhood he had seen before he entered the warehouse looked like a ghost town.

He picked up on a man and a woman entering the warehouse. He couldn't make out their faces as they approached through shadows. The only part of the building that was well lit was the so-called movie set.

"Help," DeShondra cried at the newcomers. "They're holding us hostage."

Chapter 68

Freddie turned to see who DeShondra was yelling at.

Kesey and Rivera approached him, lurking in the shadows so Kudlow, Towers, and DeShondra couldn't see their faces.

"Watch out," cried DeShondra. "They're kidnapers."

"How's it going?" Kesey asked Freddie.

"We're about ready to shoot," answered Freddie.

"Don't tell me you're part of this committee of wackos," said Kudlow, dumbstruck.

"I belong to the Committee for Decent Movies if that's what you mean," said Kesey. "Which doesn't include your sick movie, Kudlow."

"And you're OK with this nutbag shooting a snuff movie?" Freddie laughed.

"Whatever it takes to get your horror movie and other sick horror movies pulled from theaters," said Kesey.

"Who's to say what's sick?" said Kudlow.

"*We* are."

"It's a matter of opinion."

"Horror movies are sick because they're saturated with blood and gore. Viewers become inured to these movies' mayhem. The next step is for viewers to commit violence like the Hollywood Psycho stalking our city, because they have no feelings for their victims. Their feelings have been deadened by your trashy horror movies."

"Movies don't incite violence," said Kudlow. "Nobody has ever proved they do, because they don't."

"You're wrong," said Freddie. "We're gonna make a horror movie more depraved than yours and send it to the media so they'll demand the mayor pull your movie from theaters."

"Why should she?"

"Because she'll see that your movie is prompting filmmakers to make copycat movies, in other words, snuff films. If she doesn't censor your movie, more copycat snuff films will flood her office."

"My movie is not a perverted snuff film," said Kudlow, stiffening in his chair. "It's a work of art."

"It's degenerate crap."

"How dare you set yourselves up as judges of art. If you really are the Committee for Decent Movies, how can you shoot snuff films? You call snuff films decent?" said Kudlow, his voice brimming with outrage.

"They're a means to an end. They're meant to shock, and they will shock. And you, the director of the abominable *Necromaniac*, will suffer a horrible fate."

Kudlow felt his throat becoming dry. Nothing was worse than fanatics. These fanatics were willing to go to any length to make their point. The two newcomers weren't going to lift a finger to help him and the other hostages. The newcomers must belong to the committee.

"What's the holdup?" Kesey asked Freddie.

"Nothing. We're all set to go," answered Freddie, taking his place behind the camera.

One of the nuns held a boom mic over the set and signaled him that she was ready.

"Quiet on the set," said Freddie. "Action."

Chapter 69

His pulse pounding, Kudlow watched the third nun open one of the black leather cases, withdraw a meat cleaver from it, and approach DeShondra. As the nun held up the meat cleaver, its blade gleamed in the key light.

Transfixed by the meat cleaver, DeShondra widened her eyes with horror.

"Stop this insanity," said Kudlow.

"Shut the fuck up," said Freddie. "Quiet on the set."

Kudlow ground his teeth, anticipating the worst.

"Cue the music," said Freddie.

The boom mic operator switched on a tape recorder, which started playing Tchaikovsky's "Dance of the Sugar Plum Fairy."

The nun did a little dance to the music.

"What the fuck?" said DeShondra, horror contorting her face.

The nun danced a little longer then stepped toward DeShondra and raised the meat cleaver above her head.

"No," DeShondra screamed.

Watching with abject horror Kudlow struggled to break free from his bonds.

The nun swung the meat cleaver down on DeShondra's arm and severed it below the elbow. Arterial blood spurted out of her stump past the freshly sliced bright white ulna and radius. The forearm fell on the floor with a thud.

The sound operator lowered the boom mic toward DeShondra's head but not low enough to enter the frame. DeShondra's scream rent the air.

"She's lopsided," said Freddie with a giggle. "Chop off her other arm. I want symmetry in the frame."

"No," shrieked DeShondra.

The nun hacked off DeShondra's other arm.

DeShondra let loose a bloodcurdling scream.

"You sick fucks," cried Towers, appalled by the brutal attack on DeShondra.

"Call an ambulance," cried DeShondra, waving her blood-spewing stumps. "I'm gonna die."

"Do you recognize the scene, Kudlow?" said Freddie behind the movie camera.

"That's not a scene," said Kudlaw, his face leached of blood. "It's a felony."

"Name the movie," said Freddie, his patience wearing thin. "I thought you called yourself a horror film director."

"Call an ambulance before she dies."

"Name the movie, first."

"This isn't a game. Someone's life is at stake."

"If you don't name the movie, it's your fault she will die."

"Help," cried DeShondra, her voice becoming feeble as she lost blood.

"It could be any number of movies," said Kudlow, thinking fast. "Tarantino's *Reservoir Dogs* because of that little dance before the murder."

"That's not a horror movie."

"Call an ambulance."

"She doesn't have much time left," said Freddie in a smirking voice. "Two of her arteries are severed."

"Tell him," wailed DeShondra, grimacing in agony.

"*Hatchet for the Honeymoon*."

"Wrong," said Freddie. "We used a meat cleaver, not a hatchet. Time's running out."

Kudlow turned over horror movies in his head, playing scenes with meat cleavers in his mind. He remembered Freddie mentioning Aldrich's films. Kudlow couldn't remember if it was an ax or a meat cleaver in the scene he was thinking of.

"I'm gonna pass out," said DeShondra in a voice so low Kudlow could barely hear her.

"*Hush, Hush, Sweet Charlotte*," said Kudlow, remembering the shocking scene where a murderer lops off Bruce Dern's hand with a meat cleaver and proceeds to chop him to bits.

"Very good," said Freddie, "but very slow."

"Call an ambulance for Chrissake. You said you would."

"You took too long. Anyway, the scene isn't done yet. Don't you remember the rest of it?"

"Don't," cried Kudlow.

Freddie turned to the nun who gripped the meat cleaver. "Finish the scene."

The nun proceeded to chop DeShondra into pieces, blood splattering all over her nun mask, white cowl, and black robe. DeShondra screamed one last time before the nun decapitated her head, which unleashed a gout of carotid blood that thrust her head from her shoulders and catapulted it onto the concrete floor. Her head rolled a few times, leaving a trail of blood in its wake, before coming to a halt.

"Now that's a scary scene," said Freddie, filming the atrocity.

Kudlow threw up on his chest.

"What a time to get carsick," pooh-poohed Freddie.

"You monster," cried Towers, shutting his eyes so he wouldn't have to look at his blood-soaked, mutilated chauffeur.

DeShondra's blood pooled near Towers's feet. He squinted to see what was touching his shoe, then closed his eyes in consternation.

"That scene alone is scarier than your entire movie," said Freddie, gloating.

Overwhelmed by Freddie's depravity, Kudlow said nothing, fearing what would ensue.

"Poor DeShondra," said Towers.

"What about the three victims who died because of your sick movie?" said Freddie. "You probably don't even know their names. I'll clue you in. Nicholas Briscoe, Cindi Pataki, and Valentine Martinelli."

"What are you trying to prove?" said Kudlow, his nerves frayed by Freddie's brutal murder of DeShondra.

"You sound tired. I'm just beginning."

"You'll rot in jail for the rest of your life, asshole," said Towers.

"At least I'll be alive," said Freddie.

Towers stared at Freddie. "What's that supposed to mean?"

"Didn't you see what happened to your chauffeur?"

"No way. You wouldn't dare do that to me," said Towers with a quavering voice.

"Don't worry. We're not gonna use a meat cleaver on you."

"You better not," said Towers, letting out a deep breath.

"Is this really necessary?" said Rivera from the shadows, her shoes scuffing the floor as she walked out of sight.

"It's the only way we can get the mayor to pull Kudlow's movie from theaters," said Freddie.

"I don't want to have to watch this. You're committing murder on film."

"Exactly what Kudlow did in his movie."

"Bullshit," said Kudlow. "Nobody was harmed in my movie. Ask anybody who was involved in making it."

"Your movie brainwashed a moviegoer, or moviegoers, into murdering three people—so far," said Freddie. "There could be more murders on the horizon."

"That doesn't give us the right to kill people," said Rivera.

"Do you want to get *Necromaniac* censored or not?"

"Of course, I do. I wouldn't have joined this committee if I didn't want trashy horror movies banned from theaters."

"Then let me finish my movie."

"But you're committing murder."

"What is a couple murders compared to three or perhaps scores by the Hollywood Psycho creeping around in theaters?"

Rivera said nothing.

"You see my point," said Freddie.

"I hope you're done."

"We're only beginning."

"How many murders do you have to commit to make your point?"

"Three for three."

"God, no," gasped Rivera.

Freddie's answer sent a frisson down Kudlow's spine.

Freddie motioned to the nun who had beheaded DeShondra to retrieve the leather case shaped like a hatbox. She did so.

"You see, we got a nice hat for you," Freddie told Towers, chuckling.

"I got a battalion of lawyers, buddy," said Towers. "You touch me, and they'll bleed you white. You won't have two pennies to rub together when they're done with you."

"Lawyers aren't gonna be able to help you here, I'm afraid."

The nun carried the hatbox toward Towers.

263

"Get away from me, murderer," said Towers, cringing in his bonds. "What loony bin did they get you out of?"

The nun said nothing and opened the hatbox for Towers to see its contents.

Towers hung his mouth open, aghast, unsure what was going to happen next.

Chapter 70

Kudlow trembled as he watched the nun remove an iron from the hatbox. She plugged the iron's cord into an outlet on a power strip near the foot of the camera. For sure she wasn't going to start ironing clothes, because this was supposed to be a horror movie.

"That's right," said Freddie. "Let it heat up before you use it."

The nun approached Towers and stood with the corded iron in her hand.

"Where's the ironing board?" said Towers.

"We won't be needing one."

"Name the movie, Kudlow," said Freddie.

"What movie?" said Kudlow.

"I've already dropped numerous hints. This should be easy for the best horror film director in the business."

Kudlow tried to remember horror movies with irons in them. He had seen hundreds of horror movies, perhaps more. How was he supposed to remember one with an iron in it? Freddie had said he had given out hints.

Kudlow remembered one of the *Omen* movies had an iron in it used to commit murder. The one with Sam Neill in it. What was the name of it?

"*The Final Conflict*," burst Kudlow.

"Wrong," said Freddie.

"Let me think. I'll get it."

"The iron should be hot now," said Freddie. "Go ahead."

The nun reached toward Towers with the iron.

Towers eyes popped out of his head. "Tell him the movie for Chrissake."

Kudlow's brain whirred. Something by Fulci? No. Bava. This was easy. If he wasn't so scared because of what would come next, he would have told Freddie the answer right off the bat. It was one of the most famous scenes in horror movie history, as famous as the scene of Janet Leigh taking a shower in Hitchcock's *Psycho* and not living to tell about it.

265

"Your friend will be scarred for life if you don't give me the right answer," said Freddie.

"*Blood and Black Lace*," rasped Kudlow through a dry throat, his nerves frayed.

The scene of the villain burning the beautiful model's face with an iron and killing her was an iconic scene well-known by every horror movie director.

"Go ahead," Freddie told the nun.

The nun reached toward Towers's face with the burning iron.

"Stop her," screamed Towers.

"I gave you the right answer," said Kudlow, the tendons straining in his neck.

"That was an easy one," said Freddie. "Every film school student knows that one. I would have been very disappointed in you if you didn't know the answer."

Kudlow heard shuffling in the shadows where the two newcomers stood. *Scuff, scuff.* He figured the newcomers were sickened by the mayhem and were turning away from Freddie's despicable snuff film. If only they would come out of the shadows and stop this madness.

The nun applied the hot steel surface of the iron to the side of Towers's face. Towers screamed in agony, the flesh on his face sizzling and reeking.

"Stop it," cried Kudlow. "Enough is enough."

Smoke unfurled from Towers's face as he continued to wail.

"I want to recreate this scene so bad I can taste it," said Freddie. "And it's gonna be better than Mario Bava's, because it's real. It wasn't faked like his in *Blood and Black Lace*."

"What's wrong with you?" said Kudlow, struggling to break free. "Can't you see you're killing him?"

"That's the point."

"What?" said Kudlow, nonplussed.

"Like the Hollywood Psycho, the homicidal maniac you spawned with your obscene movie. He killed three people. Why aren't you as appalled by *his* murders as you are by the ones in my movie?"

"Of course, I am."

"Then pull your movie from theaters."

"My movie isn't inciting the psycho to kill."

266

Towers kept screaming as the piping hot iron burned through his face and eyeball.

Kudlow couldn't watch. He turned away and wished he could plug his ears to block out Towers's nerve-grating shrieks of agony.

"He's not moving," said the nun who was pressing the iron against Towers's face and coughing on the stench of burning flesh.

"Keep the iron to his face," said Freddie. "He could be faking passing out."

The flesh on Towers's left side of his face had burned away, leaving nothing but his skull exposed. His left eye had turned into sizzling jelly under the searing heat of the iron.

"I don't think he's faking it," said the nun in a woman's voice. She kept applying the iron to Towers's face. "There's no way he wouldn't react to the pain. It would wake him up if he was unconscious."

"Check his pulse."

The nun felt for the pulse in Towers's wrist. She shook her head.

"He didn't last very long," said Freddie, disappointed.

"I doubt the heat killed him. He must've died of shock."

"Shit happens."

Kudlow started breathing again. He didn't even know he was holding his breath. Towers's unspeakable death had unnerved him. Kudlow had been close to passing out.

Freddie's next words froze Kudlow's blood.

"You're my piece de resistance," said Freddie.

"Haven't you tortured and killed enough people?"

The thought of the iron burning his face appalled Kudlow. He could still smell the nauseating stench of Towers's burning flesh and could hear Towers's screams of anguish echoing in his mind.

"The Hollywood Psycho hasn't finished yet," said Freddie. "Why should I?"

"How do you know he hasn't finished yet?"

"Because your exploitation horror movie is still being shown in theaters. Everybody knows it's not a matter of *if* he strikes again but *when*."

"How can I argue with somebody as wrongheaded as you?"

"The problem is your eyes don't see what's really happening. I'm gonna fix that."

267

"The problem is you believe your own lies."

"Let him who has eyes see."

"You're insane."

"Get the knife," Freddie told the nun who was standing near Towers, iron in hand.

Kudlow felt his heart do a somersault. He was the only one left alive of the three hostages. It didn't take much imagination to figure he was the next victim for the snuff film. If he had any sweat left, it would be pouring out right about now. His shirt was already soaked. He was dying of thirst. He refused to beg the sadist Freddie for a glass of water.

Chapter 71

Expecting the worst, Kudlow watched the nun unplug the iron and place it on the concrete floor.

Whipping a black obsidian knife with a bone handle out of her rippling robe, she approached Kudlow.

"Are you familiar with an obsidian knife?" said Freddie.

"Not really," said Kudlow, disconcerted by the wicked black blade.

"It's the sharpest knife in the world."

The nun flaunted the obsidian blade three inches from his eyes, which bulged.

"That's good," said Freddie. "Quiet on the set."

"How many people do you have to kill to make your point?" said Kudlow, his eye twitching.

"You're the star attraction of my movie. It's not over until we shoot your scene."

As fast as it was already pumping, Kudlow's heartbeat accelerated. The nun closed in on him, holding her knife toward his face. It looked like she was going for his eyeballs.

"You can't do this," cried Kudlow through a hoarse throat.

"Name the movie," said Freddie, chuckling.

Kudlow tried to think of a horror movie where the villain gouged out someone's eyeballs. Roger Corman's *X: The Man with the X-ray Eyes* came to mind, but in that movie Ray Milland gouged out his own eyeballs. It was a gruesome act of self-mutilation. In Freddie's scene the nun was going to gouge out his.

Kudlow thought of the Shakespeare play *King Lear*, where Gloucester's eyes were gouged out with a burning poker. But that was a play, not a movie, even though it had been made into a movie starring Anthony Hopkins. *Lear* wasn't known as a horror movie, though. Freddie was talking about horror movies.

"The clock is ticking," said Freddie.

"Is it a horror movie?" said Kudlow, stalling for time.

"Of course, it is. You're the self-proclaimed Master of the Macabre. How can you not know the answer?"

"I'm thinking," said Kudlow, gnashing his teeth.

"Do you want me to hum the *Jeopardy!* theme song."

There was an eyeball mutilation in the low-budget *Would You Rather* with Jeffrey Combs. But it wasn't a famous movie. Kudlow figured the horror movie had to be famous for Freddie to want to mimic it.

"I don't have all day," said Freddie. "Make a guess."

"*X: The Man with the X-ray Eyes.*"

"Good movie, but wrong. Guess again."

Kudlow remembered a scene in Fulci's *Zombi 2* where an eye is impaled with a knife.

"*Zombi 2* by Lucio Fulci."

"Wrong."

"*An Andalusian Dog* by Bunuel."

"That was a razor blade that sliced the woman's eyeball open, not a knife."

"*Clockwork Orange*," said Kudlow, remembering the disturbing scene where Malcolm McDowell has his eyes clamped open to force him to watch movies that sicken him.

"Close but wrong again. That's not the scene we're gonna imitate. As you know, imitation is the sincerest form of flattery."

"There are a lot of movies with eye trauma. It could be any one of them."

"If you were a true master of horror films, you would know the answer."

"I'll get it," said Kudlow, seeing scenes from movies flash through his mind.

He couldn't remember any movie that had an eyeball impaled with an obsidian knife.

"Cut him," said Freddie.

"Hold your head still or you're gonna lose an eye," the nun told Kudlow as she held the knife close to his left eye.

"Cut him," Freddie told the nun, who was hovering over Kudlow, fixing to set to work.

Petrified, Kudlow couldn't move if he wanted to. Maybe she wasn't going to gouge out his eye. She had said she didn't want him to lose an eye.

270

The nun tugged on the eyelashes of Kudlow's left eyelid, stretching out the eyelid. She sliced off the eyelid and tossed it on the concrete floor. Blood poured into Kudlow's left eye.

Seeing red, Kudlow cried out in pain.

With her empty left hand the nun held Kudlow's eyelashes over his right eye and stretched out the eyelid so she could follow the same procedure she had used on his left. She flung the severed eyelid onto the floor next to its fellow. The severed eyelids looked like a pair of bloody butterflies that had crash-landed.

Blood gushed into Kudlow's right eye as he howled in agony.

"Oh, come on," said Freddie. "It doesn't hurt that bad compared to having your face burned off with a hot iron or getting decapitated. You're such a pussy. You wouldn't last long in one of your own torture porn movies. Of course, we're not done yet."

"What's next?" said the nun, her fingers dripping with Kudlow's fresh blood.

"Stanch the wounds. I want him to be able to see what happens next."

The nun used a handkerchief to stanch the two bleeding wounds over Kudlow's eyeballs and wiped off any blood remaining on his face.

Kudlow stared at Freddie, what he could see of him in the darkness behind the camera.

"Have you guessed the movie yet?" said Freddie.

Racked with pain, Kudlow tried but couldn't remember a movie where the victim's eyelids were sliced off.

"I improved the scene," boasted Freddie. "It's not exactly like it was in the movie."

How was he supposed to figure out the name of the movie if Freddie had changed the scene? In any case, Kudlow gave it his best shot, but the name of the film eluded him.

"Maybe the next part of the scene will cue you in," said Freddie. He turned to the nun working the boom mic. "Get her now."

The nun set down the mic and disappeared.

Kudlow didn't know what was going on. It was difficult for him to concentrate thanks to the pain emanating from his wounded eyes. He had to keep thinking of more horror movies that contained eye trauma.

271

Or Freddie was going to kill him.

Chapter 72

Kudlow's heart stopped beating when he saw the boom-mic nun return, frog-marching his wife Moira out of the shadows onto the set toward him, her wrists zip-tied behind her.

An expression of sheer terror on her face, Moira gazed at Kudlow. Wearing jeans and a loose boat-neck blouse, she was tall at five ten and wore her brunette hair in a pageboy cut. She had an almost luminescent white complexion.

"Norman," she shrieked, seeing Kudlow's disfigured face.

"Have you two met before?" said Freddie, gloating.

"Let my wife go," said Kudlow, seething. "She has nothing to do with any of my movies."

"But she has everything to do with *my* movie."

"They told me they knew where you were and would take me to you," said Moira.

"They're kidnapers," said Kudlow.

"They're hurting me."

"This has gone on long enough," Kudlow told Freddie. "Let her go."

"Not until I finish shooting my final scene." He turned to the nun who had mutilated Kudlow. "Stand behind Kudlow."

The nun followed Freddie's instructions.

"Hold his head so he's looking at his wife," said Freddie.

Again the nun complied.

"What are you doing?" said Kudlow, flabbergasted.

Freddie turned to the nun holding Moira captive. "Strangle her."

"No," cried Kudlow, his heart in his mouth.

The nun fell to throttling Moira.

Kudlow stared at the scene in horror.

Moira tried to scream but couldn't because of the nun's grip on her throat.

"Tell me the name of the horror movie this scene is from," said Freddie.

"You monster," said Kudlow, his blood boiling as the nun forced him to watch his wife's murder.

"Wrong movie. And it's *I Monster* starring Christopher Lee. You can't even get the title right."

Kudlow tried to recall scenes from horror movies, but he was so infuriated and terrified by the sight of his wife being murdered in front of his very eyes that he couldn't concentrate.

"You're killing her," he said, nauseated by the sight.

But he couldn't look away. The nun behind him held his head in place, and he couldn't shut his eyes without his severed eyelids.

"That's the general idea," said Freddie. "Now name the horror movie, Master of the Macabre."

Kudlow watched his wife's face turn blue as the nun continued throttling her not more than six feet away from him. Kudlow struggled in futility to break free from his bonds.

"Stop it," he cried, widening his eyes in horror at the sight of his wife in extremis.

"I'm disappointed in you. The great horror director and you can't name the horror movie this scene is from. Your reputation is a sham."

Kudlow kept thinking of horror movies even though he was consternated by what was happening a mere couple of yards from his eyes.

"Dario Argento," he shouted, seeing Moira slump in a lifeless heap in the nun's gnarly hands.

"What movie?"

"*Opera*. The scene where the psycho killer tapes needles under the victim's eyes so she can't close them and is forced to watch as the killer proceeds to murder her boyfriend in front of her."

"Bravo. It took you long enough." Freddie paused. "Too long, it seems."

The strangler laid Moira's lifeless body on the floor.

"Bastard," hissed Kudlow. "I'm gonna kill you with my bare hands."

"I hope that's not a critical assessment of my movie."

"It's a snuff film that should never see the light of day."

"Like your horror movie."

274

"Nobody was harmed in the shooting of my movie. There's no comparison," said Kudlow, heartbroken as he gazed with moist eyes at his wife's corpse.

"You still don't see how sick and depraved your movie is?" said Freddie in bewilderment.

"I see a homicidal maniac with a camera in front of me. You're like the main character in *Peeping Tom*."

"I'm teaching you a lesson," screeched Freddie. "I'm on the Committee for Decent Movies. How dare you speak to me like that."

The nun standing behind Kudlow let go of his head and retreated to the boom mic stand.

Kudlow sat limply in his chair, gazing with dolorous eyes at his wife's body.

"Do you know what I'm gonna call my movie?" said Freddie.

Kudlow said nothing. He kept staring at his wife, his eyes filling with tears.

"*Banned*," said Freddie. "Because that's what your movie should be: Banned. Am I getting through to you?"

"How do you not go to jail for these murders?"

"Filmmakers are artists. Artists don't go to jail. You proved it with your movie that incites filmgoers to kill and yet the cops haven't jailed you."

"What's going on here?" said Grant, entering the warehouse and approaching the set, gun in hand.

Herb wasn't far behind, his pistol drawn.

Chapter 73

Grant didn't know what to make of what he was seeing. It looked like a movie set with two corpses sitting in chairs, one of them headless. Another corpse sprawled on the concrete floor in front of Kudlow. It was Kudlow's wife, Grant realized with a start. Kudlow sat in the third chair. There was something about Kudlow's eyes that looked off. At first Grant couldn't tell what was wrong with them. Then he noticed Kudlow wasn't blinking, because the guy had wounds above his eyes where his eyelids had been shorn off.

"I suggest you put the guns down," said Kesey, emerging from the shadows with Rivera. "We're the LAPD. We have everything under control."

"Under control? People have been killed here," said Grant, devastated by DeShondra's dismembered body and Towers's disfigured face.

"It's just a movie. Nobody was murdered."

Grant recognized Towers's body. Grant knew Towers was Kudlow's flack.

"That's Bill Towers's body in that chair," said Grant.

"He's an actor. Put down your guns. Do you have permits for those things?"

"Why didn't you stop the killings?" said Grant, confused. "You're a cop."

"I'm not gonna tell you again. Throw down your guns."

Herb saw Kesey reach for his pistol in his arm rig. Herb shot him three times in the chest.

Rivera whipped out her FN 509 and trained it on Herb.

Grant double-tapped her in the head.

"Maybe we shouldn't have shot cops," said Herb, eying with horror the two corpses sprawled on the floor.

"They're corrupt cops," said Grant. "They were standing here watching innocent people being murdered. What kind of decent cops would do that?"

"They belonged to the Committee for Decent Movies," said Kudlow, roused out of his funk by the multiple gunshots.

"Isn't that the terrorist outfit that blew up the theater in Marina del Rey?" said Grant.

"Right. They kidnaped me and my entourage then tortured and killed DeShondra and Bill."

"We were making a movie," said Freddie from the shadows behind the camera.

"They also murdered my wife Moira," said Kudlow, his voice catching as he gazed at her crumpled body on the floor.

"Cops gone bad," said Grant, leering at the sprawled corpses of Kesey and Rivera.

"Who are these two nuns?" said Herb.

"There are three of them when you include the psycho director," said Kudlow. "They all made the snuff movie."

"Watch your mouth," said Freddie.

"Only a psycho would make a snuff film."

"I told you I did it to get your garbage flick off the movie screens. This is the kind of exploitation crap you make to earn a fast buck."

"My film is art. Yours is dreck and should only be kept as evidence to prove your guilt in three murders."

"Says the great film director whose latest 'arthouse' flick incited three murders."

Kudlow turned to Grant. "Watch those two nuns. They're dangerous. They had guns when they kidnaped us."

Grant trained his SIG P365 on the nun standing near the boom mic stand. The nun whipped out a pistol from under her robe. When Grant realized what she was holding in her hand, he squeezed off two shots at her upper body mass. Struck by the two slugs, she reeled backward and collapsed on the floor.

Herb fired two bullets at the other nun's head. Her mask flipped off as her head jerked back. Her knees turned to rubber. She slumped in a heap.

Grant heard footsteps running away.

"Don't let the killer get away," cried Kudlow, riveting his eyes on Freddie, who was fleeing toward the warehouse exit.

Grant fired at Freddie, hitting him in the back and spinning him around. Groaning, Freddie reached for his wounded back. He fell on his back and squirmed in pain.

"Good shot," said Herb. "I didn't know you were a marksman."

"Dumb luck," said Grant.

Herb scampered to Kudlow and released him from the ropes that bound him.

"My PI," said Kudlow, grateful. "I made the right decision hiring you. How did you find me?"

"I tracked your cell phone here," said Herb.

"Who's your friend?"

"My brother Grant."

Nodding, Kudlow stood up, rubbing his wrists, trying to stimulate his circulation.

Herb made for the two dead nuns and removed the mask of the unidentified nun Grant had shot. Unlike the other nun, this one was a man.

"Do you recognize them?" he asked Kudlow.

Kudlow eyeballed them and shook his head no. "I don't know anything about members of the self-styled Committee for Decent Movies."

"I don't care what they call themselves," said Herb. "They're terrorists."

"They're homicidal maniacs."

Grant set out for the nun he had brought down. The nun was writhing on his back and trying to turn over on his stomach.

Kudlow knelt beside his wife and held her cold dead hand.

"Tell me you're not really dead, Moira," he said, staring at her motionless face.

She said nothing.

"You can't really be dead," said Kudlow, still holding her hand, trying to warm it back to life.

She said nothing.

"Moira," he beseeched her.

Distraught, he looked away from her.

"Nothing would have happened to Moira if she wasn't married to me," he said.

"You weren't the one who took her out," said Herb.

Kudlow rose to his feet and cast a baleful glance in the direction of Freddie.

"Who's their sick leader?" said Kudlow, bristling with rage.

Grant approached Freddie, who was still squirming in pain from his gunshot wound.

"Take off his mask," said Kudlow.

Grant leaned over and tore off the nun mask from Freddie's face.

Consumed with anger, Kudlow stalked toward Grant then stood rooted to the spot when he saw Freddie's face.

"Bob LeBeau," said Kudlow in shock. "Of all people. I knew he was insanely jealous of me, but I didn't think it would come to this. He *killed* people to prove he was a better director than me."

Gun in hand, Grant wheeled around at the sound of the door opening behind him.

Stunned, he watched a good-looking, blue-eyed, five-eight blonde in her thirties strut toward him. She had a pouty face, just right for a selfish woman who thought about nobody but herself.

"What are you doing here, Sherry? There's no money here."

"Is this how you treat your girlfriend?" she said, put out.

"Ex-girlfriend," said Herb, approaching them, his gun at the ready.

"How did you know I was here?" Grant asked Sherry.

"Herb told me."

Herb stood beside her and snaked his arm around her waist. They kissed.

"You're not good enough for her, Grant," said Herb.

Grant couldn't believe his eyes. His own brother in cahoots with Sherry. Grant needed time to process this revelation. He didn't have time. He saw Herb training his piece on him.

"You treat your girlfriends like crap," said Herb. "No wonder you don't have one."

Grant managed to regain his composure.

"You two together were spending all those loans she scammed out of me?" he said, struggling to come to grips with the realization.

"We needed money and we knew you had some," said Sherry. "All I had to do was tell you I'd pay you back and you always paid

279

me," she added with a glint of triumph in her eye, proud of her skills in deceit.

Grant was barely able to bridle his fury. He couldn't believe his own brother would connive against him with his grifter girlfriend.

"She kept asking for another loan because we knew you had more money," said Herb. "It wasn't until I came out here and met you that I realized you had loaned everything you had to her, making you useless to us as a piggybank. Drop the piece, brother."

Grant figured he wouldn't have enough time to train his SIG P365's muzzle on Herb before Herb could squeeze his SIG P226's trigger and take him out.

"Why?" said Grant. "Are you afraid I'll shoot you? It wasn't long ago you begged me to waste you."

"Would somebody tell me what's going on?" said Kudlow, bewildered.

"I love your horror movies, especially the current one, but this is personal," said Grant.

"I think we can stop with all the killing at this point. Somebody should call the cops and let them handle this."

"What's the point of shooting me, Herb?" said Grant.

"Because—"

Grant whirled around when he heard a noise behind him.

Chapter 74

He saw Mandy drive into the warehouse on her chugging motorcycle, followed by a skinhead who weighed over three hundred pounds straddling his Harley. They were both dressed in black leather. Grant figured the guy was Mandy's Mongol boyfriend. The Mongol had a raft of silver studs and zippers on his black leather motorcycle jacket that boasted on its left breast pocket the Mongols California insignia which pictured Genghis Khan in shades riding a chopper.

Grant could make out sea green tattoos of spiders and their webs lacing the boyfriend's thick, corded neck.

The two bikers drove their grumbling hogs toward Grant and the others.

"How did you know I was here?" said Grant, bemused.

"I told her," said Herb.

"Why?" said Grant with disbelief.

"It was a trade for information," said Mandy, halting her motorcycle near Grant, killing the engine, and continuing to straddle the bike. "He wanted to know what I had on you, and I wanted to know where you were, so we traded info."

"Why did you want to know where I am?"

"Because you owe me money and you better pony up or I'm gonna tell the cops about you-know-what. Guess who I brought with me," said Mandy, gesturing toward her companion. "Meet Bruno."

The skinhead unleashed a mirthless grin at Grant. One of the gorilla's front teeth was missing. Maybe it wasn't a grin. Maybe it was a grimace.

Wincing, Grant pointed at his ear thanks to the deafening roar of the Harley in an enclosed space.

Bruno killed his Harley engine, remaining on his bike.

"Where's the money?" said Mandy.

"You're wasting your time," said Grant. "Nothing's changed. I'm still broke."

"I think you should reconsider," said Mandy. "Bruno doesn't like your answer. He can change your mind easy. You'd be surprised how fast he can do it."

"No matter how fast he is, he can't change the facts. Anyway, aren't you forgetting something?"

"What am I forgetting?"

Grant held up his SIG P365. "I'm the one with the gun."

"So am I, big brother," said Herb. "Be careful with that thing or I'll be forced to shoot."

Still smoldering at Herb's multiple betrayals, Grant turned to Herb. "What kind of a brother are you? I should never have given you that piece."

"I had to find out what she had on you. And I'm glad I did. Her info was invaluable. It led me straight to the identity of the Hollywood Psycho."

The warehouse became quiet. It was so quiet Grant could hear himself breathing.

"Thank God," said Kudlow. "Now I don't have to pull my movie from theaters. Do you know where this guy is?"

"I do," said Herb.

"Tell the cops so they can bust him before he has a chance to get away."

"I already figure I know who it is," said Mandy, "but I want my money first."

"Am I the only one who doesn't know who it is?" said Kudlow.

"Grant is the Hollywood Psycho," said Herb.

"Are you nuts?" said Grant, screwing up his face.

"You were at the Hammond Theater when the third murder was committed. Your ticket stub proved you were there at the time of the murder."

"So were hundreds of other people."

"That's where Mandy comes in. She says she saw you at the scene of the first murder. You were in the theater and you were sitting near the victim. What are the chances that you would be at both theaters when the murders occurred? Slim and none."

"She's mistaken. That's why I never paid her. I have nothing to fear if she goes to the cops. I wasn't at that theater. She must have seen someone else that looked like me."

"That's the biggest bunch of bullshit I ever heard," said Mandy. "You were there and you know it."

"Why would I kill three people I never met?"

"There was something you said about the Hammond Theater murder that stuck in my mind," said Herb. "You said a *woman* was killed there. How would you know the victim was a woman if you weren't there?"

"I must've heard it on the news."

"The cops hadn't released any information on the victim at that point because they hadn't notified the next of kin."

"You're mistaken. I heard it on the news."

"I have more evidence."

"So far you have zilch."

"Remember what you told me," said Herb. "You said ever since you had writer's block you've wanted to kill people."

"Wanting and doing are two different animals. Look at me. I'm a writer, not a killer. I write about serial killers and murderers. That doesn't make me one. I kill people only in my books, not in real life."

"I found out from cop hearsay that a knife was the murder weapon in the three murders. You always carry a knife strapped to your ankle."

"This is crazy."

"You said the demon in the movie was incredibly real. Maybe you believed you were possessed by it when you killed those people."

"I'll quote Kudlow. Movies don't incite people to kill."

"Your world is collapsing around you, Grant. You're losing it. You declared bankruptcy and you broke up with Sherry, not to mention you can't write. You're alone in the world and you can't make a living anymore."

Grant shrugged. "I'm not denying my life is hard. If the world isn't kicking you in the teeth every day and knocking you flat on your ass, there's something wrong with you. It's all about getting up and continuing to fight."

"You have writer's block. Writer's block is psychological. Your head's messed up. You can't write, because you'd rather commit murder. You used to be a writer. Now you're a serial killer."

"This is all speculation. You can't prove any of it." Grant stared hard at Herb. "You want me out of the way so you can have Sherry to yourself."

"You treat your girlfriends like crap," said Sherry.

"I could never create a character in my horror novels as despicable as you. All you do is scam and lie to feed your greed. You care about nobody but yourself. You're a sociopathic scammer."

"*You're* the one who cares about nobody but yourself."

"I told you I was going broke, and you kept spending more of my money."

"That's your fault if you can't make a living. Don't put it on me."

"You're the worst person I ever met in my entire life."

Sherry gave him the finger. "And you're a loser. I should have known you were also a serial killer."

"I'm taking you to the cops, big brother," said Herb.

"You need proof to go to the cops," said Grant. "You got squat."

"I have the ticket stub you bought that puts you in the Hammond Theater at the time of the third movie murder."

Grant had wondered what had happened to the ticket stub. Now he knew. Good old Herb.

"My name's not on it," said Grant. "What good is it? It could belong to anyone. It could belong to you, since you have it."

"What about when the cops examine your knife you always carry to see if it matches the wounds in the murder victims?"

Grant's mouth felt dry. "A lot of knives have the same size blade."

"Maybe they'll find the blood of one of your victims on it."

"No way."

Herb took a step toward Grant.

"You're not limping anymore," said Grant.

"I needed an excuse to stay behind you so I could keep my eyes on you. I didn't want you to bug out without my knowing it."

"Why would I bug out? I came here to free Kudlow. I wasn't going anywhere till I freed him."

"You really love his movie, don't you?"

"What of it?"

284

"I knew he was the murderer," said Mandy. "The first day I met him he acted like he had something to hide. But I want him to pay me before you take him to jail."

"Let's call the cops and get this over with," said Kudlow.

"Whatever you do don't pull your movie from theaters," said Grant. "It's the work of a brilliant creative artist. Everybody should have the right to see it."

"He's everything you wanted to be in life but aren't and never can be," said Sherry.

Grant laughed. "What do *you* know about art? Nothing. The only thing you know about is how to scam people with your looks."

"Drop your gun," said Herb, taking umbrage at Grant's treatment of Sherry.

"How long have you been cheating with him behind my back?" Grant asked Sherry.

"You're a cheapskate loser. I shouldn't have to borrow money from you. You should just give it to me. What kind of a boyfriend are you?"

"Herb's a junkie. He's an improvement?"

"He cares about me. All you care about is—I dunno—what *do* you care about? You don't give a damn about me. You let me get assaulted in New York. I could have died there thanks to you."

"It's time for you guys to quit blabbing," said Mandy. "Gimme five grand, and I'm outa here."

Grant was tired of arguing. He would hand over his SIG to Herb. After all, he had nothing to fear from the cops. There was no smoking gun that could be used to convict him. The idea that he was a murderer was comical. He was a writer. A writer with bad track, but a writer all the same.

He turned his SIG horizontal and made to hand it to Herb.

Herb shot him twice.

Grant felt two thumps in his chest as the slugs ripped through it. His knees buckled. He felt warm blood pouring down his chest. He landed on his knees then fell on his face.

Chapter 75

Kudlow knelt beside his wife again.

"You're not really dead, are you, Moira?" he said. "You can't be." He held her cold hand and gazed into her blank eyes. "You don't have to play dead anymore. The danger is over. We're safe."

"What's with him?" said Mandy. "Another nut case?"

"You saw my brother," said Herb, agitated. "You all saw him. He was getting ready to shoot me. He's a serial killer. I had to kill him."

"You blew away my golden goose. I'm out five grand because of you."

Bruno glowered at Herb.

"Don't look at me," said Herb. "I don't have it."

"We saw you take out that guy," said Mandy.

"It was self-defense."

"It looked to me like he was surrendering."

"His gun was aimed at me."

"He was handing it to you."

"He was pointing it at me and he was getting ready to pull the trigger," said Herb, sweat bubbling onto his face.

"If you don't give me five thousand bucks, I'm gonna tell the cops I saw you shoot your defenseless brother when he tried to surrender."

"That's a lie. He wasn't defenseless. He had a gun in his hand."

"Gimme five grand, and you'll never see me again."

Kudlow stood up, forlorn, still staring at Moira's lifeless body. At last he turned toward Mandy, a haggard expression on his face.

"I'll give you five thousand bucks if you promise to forget about this and never contact me again," he said.

"No problem," said Mandy.

"Make it fifty grand," said Bruno, pulling a Ruger EC9 pistol on Kudlow. "You're that rich movie director with an infinity pool in Holmby Hills, aren't you? You can spare fifty grand easy. Probably a lot more, but we're not greedy."

Herb shot Bruno in the head, which split down the middle like a hatchet blade had hit it. Bruno collapsed, firing a wayward shot that hit no one. He dropped his piece on the floor. As he fell, his Harley fell with him and crushed his leg. He felt no pain. He was beyond feeling.

Herb looked stunned. He had never seen a single bullet split a man's head in half before. Maybe Bruno had suffered a previous fracture in his skull.

"Bastard," Mandy screamed at Herb, her eyes fiery with rage.

Her face flushing, she kicked down her hog's kickstand and dismounted. She leaned over, scoffed up Bruno's Ruger from the floor, and wheeled around to fire it at Herb. Herb double-tapped her in the chest with Grant's SIG P226.

She moaned, stumbled, and fell on her side, her head canted.

"Jesus," said Kudlow, surveying the corpses strewn in the warehouse. "We got more corpses than the final scene of *Hamlet*. How are we gonna explain this massacre to the cops?"

"What happened to your eyes?" said Sherry, wincing in disgust at them.

Kudlow whipped out his shades from his trouser pocket and put them on.

"Nothing," he said. "Where were we?"

"We were talking—," said Herb.

"Wait a minute," cut in Kudlow. "Who are that man and woman over there?"

He pointed at Kesey and Rivera.

"They're cops," said Herb.

"Are you sure? Why would cops take part in a snuff movie?"

"I'm positive. I met them at Grant's apartment."

"Holy shit. We got dead cops here?"

"They were cops gone bad. They were part of the terrorist Committee for Decent Movies that blew up the Marina theater."

"The cops aren't gonna like seeing two of their own lying dead here whether they're dirty or not. They're gonna make damn sure their comrades in blue end up smelling like roses after this is done."

287

"We tell them the truth," said Herb. "These terrorists kidnaped you and your entourage and wasted everyone but you. We took out the three terrorists and the two dirty cops who were working with them and saved you."

"Eh, I dunno. Maybe you better revise that."

"This isn't a script undergoing rewrites."

"I'm telling you the cops aren't gonna believe your story the way you told it. Lemme think." Kudlow paused in thought. "Say the three terrorists shot the two cops when the cops tried to bust them. Then you killed the terrorists."

"But that's not true."

"If you tell the cops the truth, they're gonna do everything they can to poke holes in your story. Nothing pisses them off more than having one of their own accused of being dirty. They'll buy my version without suspecting you of lying."

Herb shrugged. "Fine. Whatever. You're the filmmaker. You guys know how to tell a convincing lie. As long as we all tell the same story. Got it, Sherry?"

"No problem," she said.

Kudlow glanced at LeBeau's lifeless body sprawled on the concrete. "I still can't believe LeBeau would do something as depraved as this. And yet, there's no denying Hollywood *is* a jungle where players will stoop to anything to get ahead—even commit murder, it seems."

"Anybody's capable of any crime the way I see it. My own brother was a homicidal maniac."

"He deserves to be dead," said Sherry. "He couldn't care less if I died in New York. Homeless people wanted to assault me with rusty can openers when I had no place to stay, and he wouldn't buy me a plane ticket home. A miser and a loser."

"What about the bikers?" said Kudlow.

Scratching his head Herb chewed it over. "They tried to rob fifty thousand bucks from you at gunpoint. I shot them to save you."

"And your brother?" said Kudlow, eyeballing Grant's motionless body.

"He's the Hollywood Psycho. I killed him in self-defense when he resisted a citizen's arrest."

Kudlow nodded. "It might work."

"Of course, it will. It's the truth."

Kudlow smiled at Herb. "You saved my bacon. I'm gonna give you a reward of a hundred grand."

"*All right*, Herbie," said Sherry, hugging Herb and kissing him on the lips.

"Did anybody call an ambulance yet?" said Kudlow.

"It's too late for an ambulance," said Herb, surveying the cadavers sprawled around him. "How about a meat wagon?"

"Some of these people may still be alive," said Kudlow.

He searched LeBeau's corpse, retrieved his confiscated cell phone, and punched out 911.

"Suit yourself," said Herb.

"What made your brother turn into a homicidal maniac? You knew him better than anyone else, since you grew up in the same family. Did he drown cats when he was a kid or something?"

Herb walked over to Grant's body and regarded him, deep in thought.

"Nothing like that," said Herb. "Grant wrote horror novels. None of them sold well. At some point he developed writer's block. When he couldn't write anymore, he started hating everybody. I'm no shrink, mind you, but maybe he got it into his head that everybody was somehow preventing him from writing. He became unbalanced. He went to your horror movie, and it struck a chord with him. He identified with the homicidal demon. Maybe he thought he had a demon inside him aching to get out. Once he let the genie out, he couldn't put it back in the bottle. It took over his life, and he had to keep killing."

"I thought you were gonna say writing horror novels turned him into a homicidal maniac," said Kudlow.

Herb shook his head no. "When he was writing the novels, he was OK. It was when he *wasn't* writing them that he became homicidal. When he was writing, he had an outlet for his murderous impulses. Without his writing, the only outlet he had was in the real world, which meant he had to kill real people, not fictional characters in novels." He paused a beat. "Listen to me—a dime-store shrink," he added, amused at the idea.

"Do you think my movie turned him into a killer?"

289

Herb thought about it, knitting his brows. "He was already messed up psychologically. He would have started killing sooner or later whether he saw your movie or not."

"That's a relief to hear."

"Take my opinion with a large grain of salt. I'm just a layman without an MD after my name."

"Nevertheless, I believe you're right. This guy was a ticking timebomb ready to be set off by anything. My movie didn't make him a killer. He was already a killer lying in wait. Anything can trigger a psycho. If it wasn't my movie, it would've been something else. You can't blame things for turning people into homicidal maniacs. Put the blame where it belongs—on the killer."

"He was always mean," said Sherry, striding up to Herb and hooking her arm around his. "It doesn't surprise me he was a serial killer."

She leered down in disgust at Grant then kicked him in the slats.

"Take that, you rotten creep," she said.

Chapter 76

Grant wasn't dead yet. He didn't make a sound even though the impact of the toecap on Sherry's shoe had hurt him. He was facing away from the others. He gritted his teeth and said nothing. He didn't want them to know he was alive. He had heard the snakes talking about him. He wanted to kill all of them except Kudlow. Kudlow was an artist who deserved to live. Sherry was a scammer and a two-timer, and Herb was a double-crossing junkie. Grant had trusted both of them with his life, especially Sherry. And see where it had got him.

Grant wished he was back in a movie theater watching *Necromaniac*. Although it was a scary horror movie, it was nowhere near as dreadful as his life. He felt like such a dolt for trusting his scheming girlfriend and his duplicitous brother. How could he have been so stupid? Well, Herb could have her. The two grifters were made for each other. He wouldn't be a bit surprised if Sherry swindled Herb out of the hundred-grand reward and skipped out on him.

Grant didn't want to think about those two pieces of work anymore.

His life savings were gone thanks to them, leaving him with nothing.

It wasn't so bad to lose everything now that he had nothing to lose. His life had been locked in a doom loop for some time. Play the hand you were dealt. Nothing begat nothing. He had no future.

He pictured himself sitting in a theater, watching Kudlow's film. If he had to die, he would like to die watching *Necromaniac*. The movie hadn't made him into a killer. It was the demon in the movie. Kudlow and Herb didn't understand that the demon was a living thing inside a fictional movie. The film was a work of art, but the demon had somehow gotten into it and was able to get out of it and possess spectators of the film. The demon had possessed him, controlled him, and ordered him to commit murder in the movie theaters.

291

His eyes shut, Grant ran the movie in his head. He would see the demon in his mind's eye any minute. He smiled as his life ebbed away.

ABOUT THE AUTHOR

Multi-award-winning author Bryan Cassiday writes horror fiction and thrillers. His postapocalyptic horror thriller *Horde (Zombie Apocalypse: The Chad Halverson Series Book 6)* won both the Independent Press Award for Best Horror Novel 2022 and the American Fiction Award for Best Horror Novel 2021. His Scott Brody thriller *Threads* won the Independent Press Award for Best Thriller Novel 2023 and the American Fiction Award for Best Hard-Boiled Crime Novel 2022. He lives in Southern California.